ONE REMAINED SEATED

Maria Black, M.A., Principal of Roseway College for Young Ladies, is faced with murder in the cinema when a stranger seated in Number 11 on Row A is found to be dead. Assuming her role of detective, she becomes Black Maria — the crime solutionist. Working with Inspector Morgan, the local police chief, they go behind the scenes of a cinema, into the homes of those workers who'd maintained the entertainment industry — and into the recesses of a killer's mind . . .

JOHN RUSSELL FEARN

ONE REMAINED SEATED

Complete and Unabridged

LINFORD
Leicester

First published in Great Britain

First Linford Edition
published 2008

British Library CIP Data

Fearn, John Russell, *1908 – 1960*
    One remained seated.—Large print ed.—
    Linford mystery library
    1. Women school principals—Fiction
    2. Murder—Investigation—Fiction
    3. Detective and mystery stories
    4. Large type books
    I. Title
    823.9'12 [F]

    ISBN 978–1–84782–333–5

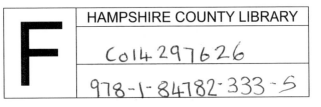
T. J. International Ltd., Padstow, Cornwall

This book is printed on acid-free paper

1

The man in the ill-fitting grey overcoat and with a slouch hat pulled well down over his eyes might have been alone in the railway compartment for all the attention he paid to his fellow-travellers.

He was preoccupied with his own thoughts, tracing backwards through fifteen years. His body was freed at last from implacable walls and iron-hard routine, but not his mind. It insisted on lingering in the circumscribed area of a prison cell. Even now, speeding away from it on this rickety, noisy train, he could still feel the cold walls that had hemmed him for so long.

With a squeak and a rattling of doors the train stopped, shattering the country-side with a volcanic outburst from its safety valve. The man in grey lurched to his feet, took down a cheap suitcase from the rack, and then opened the door. He stepped out into a cold, bracing wind, wavering station lights, and the clangour of milk cans. Far away a voice was mournfully wailing 'Lang'orn! Hall change for Lex'am!'

Feeling for his ticket, the stranger walked towards the exit barrier. He was revealed now as tall and heavy-shouldered. His face was powerful, with a strong, ugly mouth, long, pointed nose, and bushy eyebrows. Handing in his ticket to an inspector at the barrier, he asked:

'Where's a good place to stop for a day or two?'

'Might try the 'Golden Saddle', sir. Not bad. Straight up the 'igh Street there.'

'Thanks,' the other said briefly; then with a sudden squaring of his shoulders, like a man who has much to do, he turned to face the fitful lights which bobbed along the vista outside the station entrance.

Langhorn was an agglomeration of ill-assorted frontages, of shops that were unashamedly converted houses, of higgledy-piggledy roofs and badly planned forecourts jutting out on to the pavement to snare the unwary.

Here and there, however, modernism had arrived. It showed itself in a closed snack bar sandwiched between two old buildings; it was revealed again in the façade of a cinema. The stranger noticed that the hotel he sought was anything but modern even though it had a clean, inviting aspect. His attention swung back to the cinema directly facing it across the narrow street.

The cinema's entrance way was marked by two rotund pillars of white tiling supporting a red canopy. The place called itself LANGHORN CINEMA in red stone cubist letters over the entrance. Post-war fuel regulations forbade neon outside, but beyond the glass doorway in the foyer lilac tubes flickered in and out attractively and spasmodically illuminated the placarded features of Hedy Lamarr.

As yet it was only half-past six and the cinema was not open to the public. It possessed no sign of life at all except for the ginger head of a girl just visible through the grille of the advance-booking office. It was cunningly imbedded in one the huge side pillars and so was set beyond the doors and almost on the street itself.

The stranger hesitated. For some reason the place had an uncommon fascination for him, so much so he walked up the four pseudo-marble steps and looked into the foyer intently through the glass barrier.

Looking out onto the chilly night from the warmth of her cashier's box Mary Saunders saw the stranger's dogged, putty-grey face in profile, illuminated ever and anon by the neon. He looked forbidding, and she decided he looked as though he had walked out of the thriller serial that the cinema screened every Saturday afternoon.

The stranger stood peering, gripping his cheap suitcase. Though the foyer was empty he seemed to be looking longingly for somebody or something.

At last Mary Saunders could stand no longer. She raised the glass slide before the grille bars and peered out into the draughty street.

'Anything I can do for you, sir?' she asked politely.

The man descended two of the steps and stooped to look to look at her through the gold-painted filigree. 'What time do you open, miss?'

'Half-past seven, sir — and the performance starts at quarter to eight, finishing at ten o'clock . . . '

'It doesn't matter when it's over . . . Look, that poster on the foyer there — next to the picture of Hedy Lamarr. It is advertising Lydia Fane in 'Love on the Highway'. Is that on now?'

Mary pointed up through the bars of her cage to the underside of the canopy. 'It's advertised up there, sir, on the streamer . . . '

The stranger looked above him at a lengthy oblong board painted green along its borders and suspended by chains. It swung to and fro in the cold wind and a long paper sheet within it advertised Lydia Fane in gigantic letters with 'Love on the Highway' in a small scroll beneath it. As yet, with the canopy lights off, it was not immediately visible from below.

'Starting tonight, sir,' Mary explained. 'Runs tonight, Tuesday and Wednesday.'

'Can I book?'

'Certainly, sir — Circle only, though. We block-book the Stalls for regular patrons . . . ' Her slim arm went up to the charts out of the stranger's view.

'Circle will do,' he decided. 'I want the best seat in the front row for tonight, tomorrow and Wednesday night . . . '

Mary Saunders blinked. Then she drove the point of her blue crayon through seat A-11 on the charts for that night, the next, and Wednesday. Skilfully she thumbed the ticket-blocks and then handed three tickets under the goldwork.

'Seven-and-six, sir, please.'

Without a word the stranger planked down three half-crowns. 'Do you have matinées?' he asked, as he took up the tickets and prepared to go.

'Every day except Monday, sir.'

'Thank you, miss.'

He picked up his case, looked once more at the streamer under the canopy, then began to walk across the road towards the 'Golden Saddle'.

That same evening, still in his grey coat but with his hat resting on the plush balustrade in front of him, he watched the programme through with that immovable fixity which seemed to be a habit with him . . .

And the following evening at precisely the same time he was once more in A-11 in the centre of the row. This time the usherette in charge of the Circle remembered him from the previous night and wondered to herself what anybody could wish to see twice in such an indifferent programme.

★ ★ ★

Frederick Allerton always left home for duty at the Langhorn Cinema with a profound sense of the responsibility ahead of him. Maybe his comparative youth — he was twenty-one — caused him to magnify his position out of all normalcy, but it did at least make him extremely conscientious. As the chief projectionist of the cinema he took pride in the fact that everything depended on him, that the smiles or curses of the patrons would in the main be the outcome of his control. And in his five years of employment, creeping up from lowly rewind-boy to chief, he had shown himself ambitious, a clever electrical engineer, and at times an excellent showman. His key-job and low medical grade had kept him at his post, a diligent controller of the whirring, hot machines that plough through miles of celluloid, different and indifferent.

At six-forty-five precisely on this Wednesday evening he took his usual farewell of his parents, buttoned up his overcoat, and went out through the kitchen into the back garden. Cold wind under icy December stars smarted his cheeks as he tugged his bicycle from the outside shed. He threw one long leg over the saddle and rested his foot on the pedal. With the other foot he pushed himself along until free of the pathway up the side of the house — then he went sailing illegally down the pavement to his favourite dip in the kerb and so out into the road.

With a whirr his homemade dynamo came into being and cast a fan of radiance on the asphalt of the quiet suburban road ahead of him. To his rear the red companion light glowed in baleful warning. He was rather proud of his dynamo, as he was of all his electrical handiwork, but it troubled him that the damned thing had developed an obstinate flicker. Now and again it would go out and leave him pressing against searing wind and darkness — then back the light would come with exasperating brilliance. Still, he knew the way blindfolded: the only worry was the possibility of the police happening on him at the wrong moment.

To reach the centre of Langhorn he had two miles to cover, and he usually reckoned to do it in exactly ten minutes — longer if the wind was against him. Tonight it was against him all the way and he pedalled with his head down against it, cursing under his breath.

Eleven minutes after leaving home he reached Langhorn High Street, but beyond a brief glance ahead he did not bother to survey it thoroughly. It was dark now, anyway, as far as the shops were concerned. The only light came from the lamps edging the kerb at needlessly wide intervals and the canopy globes of his destination.

Stubbornly he pedalled onwards, preparing for a sharp right turn when he neared the cinema . . . Then the dynamo went off again. He threatened it savagely, reached down with one hand to bang the dynamo against his front wheel — then all of a sudden he was knocked off his saddle and landed somehow with the bicycle round his legs. Near him somebody was floundering in the road and cursing him fiercely.

'You — you damned idiot! Why didn't you have a light on . . . ? God! My leg.'

Aided by his youth and long thin body, Fred Allerton was quickly on his feet, vaguely aware of a tingling knee as he helped to raise a heavily-built man in a grey overcoat and slouch hat.

'Idiot!' the man repeated, rubbing his leg. 'You might have broken it.'

'Evidently I didn't, though,' Allerton

said cheerfully. 'You see, my dynamo doesn't always work as it should. I never even saw you . . . '

'It comes to something when a man can't step off the pavement without a blasted cyclist knocking him flying. No light — no bell. I've a good mind to tell the police about this.'

'All right, if you want to get awkward about it!' Allerton could be very short-tempered sometimes. 'You can find me at the Langhorn Cinema. I'm the chief projectionist.'

The man in the grey overcoat looked at him for a moment; then without another word to signify his intentions, he walked off towards the pavement, heading in the direction of the 'Golden Saddle' hotel. Allerton watched him, then after a guilty look about him he trundled his somewhat lopsided machine towards the cinema, raising the cycle on his shoulder as he walked up the steps.

'Who were you rowing with?' asked Bradshaw.

Bradshaw was the doorman, though there had been occasions when the more select patrons had called him a commissionaire. It was left to the insensitive cinema staff to tell him what he really was. To the public he was merely a big, six-foot man with shoulders widened by the epaulettes on his bottle-green uniform. His face, red by nature, had an almost fiery tint through constant exposure to the winds that chose the High Street as their sporting ground. Blue eyes, inflamed round the edges with grit, gazed with disconcerting fixity from under the gleaming peak of his cap.

'I was rowing with an idiot,' Allerton answered briefly, pushing through the little assembly of people awaiting the cinema's opening. 'Anyway, how did you know?'

'I 'eard you shouting, of course. Wind's that way tonight.'

Allerton grunted, eased the bicycle from his shoulder, then entered the foyer. Mary Saunders looked round the door of her cage and called a greeting. But Allerton ignored her. He was in a bad temper and his knee hurt. And that nosy-parker doorman *would* have to be outside four minutes before his usual time . . .

Allerton dumped his bicycle in the disused sweet-stall near the stairway leading to the Circle and closed the imitation bronze door upon it. He tugged off his overcoat and hat, releasing an untidy mop of brown hair that had become wiry through the influence of static electricity — then he headed for the manager's office. But the manager had not yet arrived. The door marked PRIVATE was firmly locked.

With a shrug Allerton turned back to the Circle staircase with its soft, luxurious carpet — then he paused as Nancy Crane came hurrying down with her black silk frock billowing a little from her shapely legs. Allerton admired them silently as she came down to his level.

'Where's the boss, Nan?' he asked her.

'How should I know if he isn't there?' Nancy Crane had the oddest way of mixing her words, but she did it so disarmingly that nobody objected. She was small, dainty, with blonde hair and delicately reddened lips. Her very blue eyes made Allerton's young heart skip a beat every time she looked at him.

'I only asked,' he said defensively.

Nancy felt the golden curls at the back of her head with a slender hand. 'Anyhow, is *that* any way to greet your fiancée?'

'Sorry, Nan ... I'm having a bad evening.'

Nancy's blue eyes regarded him. He certainly looked morose, more so by reason of his rather high cheekbones, sombre dark eyes, and drooping corners to a large mouth.

'Oh? What's caused it?' she asked.

'I knocked a man down with my bike. If he reports it the police will summon me or something. You know how the boss is about things like that. Smears the reputation of the cinema. I might get fired!'

'With labour so short it isn't plentiful? Not a bit of it! You didn't give your name to the man you knocked down, did you?'

'No. But I told him my job and where to find me.'

'The things you worry over!' Nancy murmured, inspecting herself in the bevelled mirror embedded in the wall by the staircase. 'I wouldn't!'

Nancy Crane had no need to expect trouble anywhere. She was pretty enough to get whatever she wanted from almost any young man — and what was more, she knew it. But she had plenty of sense as well as above average looks, which was one reason why she looked forward to becoming Allerton's wife. Better than anybody, except his parents, she knew his worth.

'Tell the boss I was going to ask him about tomorrow's programme,' Allerton said, starting up the stairs. 'It's Wednesday night, remember, and if the film transport doesn't come within the next hour he'll have to ring the renters.'

'Okay, I'll tell him,' Nancy promised, and devoted herself to getting her hair to her liking . . .

★   ★   ★

Within the disciplined quiet of Roseway College for Young Ladies Miss Maria Black, M.A., the Principal, sat studying

15

the evening paper. Her pupils, had they been able to look over her shoulder, would have been surprised to find the *Langhorn Times* open at the amusement section.

' 'Love on the Highway' . . . Hmmm!'

Maria Black put the paper down and fingered the slender gold watch-chain gleaming against the black satin of her dress. Her strongly cut, expressive face was pensive — yet somehow irritated.

'Just where *are* all the gangster films these days?' she mused presently. 'I could have sworn that 'Death Strikes Tomorrow' was showing at the Langhorn. Maybe I confused it with another cinema. 'Love on the Highway' indeed! Lydia Fane? Never heard of her . . . Yet one must do something for a change and no other cinema seems to have anything appealing.'

She rose and began to pace the warm study slowly. To Maria Black the problem of finding the right picture to visit was just as intricate a business as solving a mystery; and at both she could claim distinction. It annoyed her, though, to find that her love for a crime picture was unrequited this Wednesday night.

Coming to a decision she pressed the bell-push. By the time the bloodless housemistress, Eunice Tanby, had come into the study Maria Black was dressed in a severe but smart hat, a heavy camelhair coat, and was putting her umbrella on her arm.

'Ah, Miss Tanby! You will be good enough to take over for a couple of hours. I have decided that I shall relax at the Langhorn Cinema. It's my last opportunity to see 'Love on the Highway'.'

'Yes, Miss Black,' Tanby assented colourlessly.

'Say it,' Maria invited dryly. 'What do I want to see such a picture for? Frankly, I don't — but one must have a change. And you know my private passion . . .'

'Yes, Miss Black. Crime — crime films — or just films.'

'A very apt summing up,' Maria approved; then she swept out of her study and up the corridor to the outdoors. In five minutes she boarded the Langhorn bus that rattled its way between Roseway

College and Langhorn Square.

The bitter wind was gusting as she descended in the town's main square. Pushing against it and half closing her eyes against whirling dust she made her way slowly up the High Street, keeping well within the shelter of the closed shops for protection. She was wondering why she had chosen such a vile night to visit a very mediocre picture . . . Then the sound of voices made her glance up. She paused, puzzled for a moment by a dim, unexpected vision in the roadway ahead under a street lamp.

' . . . I've a good mind to tell the police about this!'

'All right, if you want to get awkward about it. You can find me at the Langhorn Cinema. I'm the chief projectionist.'

Maria began walking on again, watching as the distant tangle sorted itself out into two men facing each other — the one big and burly in a light-coloured hat and coat, the other the tall, spare figure of Fred Allerton. Maria knew him well enough by sight and smiled to herself.

'Frederick getting himself into trouble

again, apparently,' she murmured. 'A good man at his work from what I hear, but just a trifle too impetuous . . . '

By the time she had moved another five yards the two men had separated — the big man towards the 'Golden Saddle' hotel and Fred Allerton into the entrance-way of the cinema. As Maria walked up the cinema steps and waited by the glass doors for them to be opened she saw Allerton in the distance of the foyer beyond talking to Nancy Crane.

'Nasty night, Miss Black,' observed the doorman.

'Decidedly cold,' Maria agreed. 'One expects little else in December, however. I notice, my man, that Lydia Fane is billed as the star of this picture tonight. I am a fairly keen — hmm! — film fan, but I do not recall ever having heard of her!'

'Nor me, mum, but the boss says she's a star and he's fixed the publicity that way, so there it is. What I've seen of the film — nippin' in between times, as you might say — it's rank.'

'That's his polite way of putting it, Miss Black,' Mary Saunders remarked, peering out into the night through her prison bars. 'I'd suggest you to go back to the school.'

'Such bad salesmanship!' Maria reproved, smiling. 'Never turn patrons away, Mary!'

'But you're more than a patron, Miss Black: you're pretty nearly an honoured guest. It'd be a shame to take the money.'

Mary sat down again behind the grille and only her ginger hair was visible. Other people were collecting rapidly now, forming a small queue down the steps. At last Bradshaw received the signal from inside the foyer and threw the doors open wide.

Winter and Maria swept into the foyer together. She stopped at the ordinary booking office with its big sign over the top — STALLS ADMISSION BY BLOCK BOOKING ONLY. Behind the gilded grille sat plump Molly Ibbetson, ponderous but thorough, her shining black hair a curious mixture of waves and curls.

''Evening, Miss Black,' she said pleasantly, her full-moon face with its rouge-and-powder effects breaking into a smile. 'Your usual Circle ticket?'

'Thank you, Molly — if you please.'

Maria took it and then proceeded majestically on her way through the foyer. Just as she neared the Circle staircase the manager came out of his office at the base of the stairs and closed the door behind him decisively.

Gerald Lincross was not just the manager of the Langhorn Cinema; he was the owner as well. A man in his late forties, he was to his patrons merely the medium-sized smiling man with the half-bald head who welcomed them in — and out — in his faultless dress suit and crackling white shirt front and collar. His remaining hair was black and curly while his features were somewhat pointed and the mouth flat, seeming more so because of false dentures which fitted too far back. Always he was smiling, always deferential, with concern for the welfare of his patrons — regular and casual — always peeping out of his round and somewhat childlike blue eyes.

'Good evening, Mr. Lincross,' Maria greeted him, pausing.

'Why, Miss Black . . . ' He came and

shook hands with her. 'How are you? Chilly weather, eh? To be expected, near to Christmas.'

'Yes,' Maria agreed, then she changed the unoriginal conversation. 'Frankly, Mr. Lincross, I am not intrigued by your choice of a film for the first half of this week. 'Love on the Highway' sounds like a filler to me. I could have sworn I saw an advertisement for 'Death Strikes Tomorrow'.'

'You did,' Lincross acknowledged, smiling. 'It should have been here for Monday, yesterday, and tonight, but at the last moment the renters changed it. Just one of the trials of the business, you know. I'm making do with 'Love on the Highway' and I expect I shall hear about it from my patrons — if they are as observant as you, that is.'

The patrons were now coming in steadily. As they streamed past to Stalls and Circle Lincross inclined his shoulders back and forth like a mechanical doll and wore a permanent smile.

'Well, Mr. Lincross, I will leave you to your duties,' Maria remarked.

He did not answer. His attention had apparently been caught by a big man in a grey overcoat and soft hat coming in through the main doorway with a little swarm of people in front of him. He was tall enough to be visible over the heads of the people preceding him.

Suddenly Lincross turned and noticed that Maria had raised one eyebrow at him questioningly. 'Forgive me, Miss Black,' he murmured. 'Just a thought that occurred to me . . . I must see Miss Thompson immediately.'

He bowed briefly to her then hurried to the doorway leading into the Stalls. Maria shrugged to herself and started the long climb of the Circle stairway. Halfway up, where the stairs took a sharp left-hand turn, was a polished door marked STAFF ROOM ONLY — PRIVATE. Maria went past it to the left where yet another private door leading to the projection-room was sunken into the wall. So she continued up the last flight of stairs into the Circle.

'Good evening, Nancy,' she greeted, as the pretty blonde girl tore the admission ticket in half. 'Still on the treadmill, I notice.'

'A girl must live,' Nancy observed, with uncommon philosophy, then reached for the ticket of the man following Maria.

She went across to her usual seat in the third row from the front, left block, and settled herself with her umbrella standing up beside her, her right hand clamped firmly on its handle. As usual her attention was centred on the incoming people.

A friendly buzz of conversation, unintelligible but distinct, made itself apparent over the Sousa march thumping from behind the green-and-gold curtains covering the screen. Floodlights of amber and mauve flickered across those curtains, worked most dispassionately — had the audience but known it — by a spotty youth in overalls in the projection room.

Smoke rose in increasing density to the ventilator grille stretching across the gently arching ceiling. It was a very wide ventilator, painted yellow to imitate gold and the filigree designed in diamond shape. It stretched from wall to wall like a gilded chasm in the roof. Farther away, over the area occupied below by the Stalls, were two smaller ventilators, circular, and perhaps two feet in diameter. Behind them fans whirred to suck out foul air . . .

Maria lowered her eyes from an absent survey of the ventilators to a big man in a grey overcoat and soft hat. He walked slowly down the white-edged steps to the front of the Circle, took his half-ticket from Nancy Crane, and then lumbered along to the seat in the exact centre of the row — A-11. With a clatter the risen people on the row sat down again and the big man took off his hat and laid it carefully on the plush-topped rail in front of him.

Beyond noting that he had thinning grey hair and a face, in profile, of uncommon strength, Maria paid no more attention to him, though back of her mind she remembered that she had seen him coming in at the foyer doorway. Not that it signified, only . . . well, he was different, somehow, possessed such an air of power and sombre purpose.

2

When Fred Allerton entered the winding-room at the top of the stone steps leading to the projection-room itself he was still on edge. He came into the wide, stonewalled room filled with its electrical equipment and transit cases with the corners of his mouth dragged down.

He glanced about him to satisfy himself that the electricity rectifier for the arc lamps was working normally, and that the switch controlling the big fan in the auditorium ceiling was in the 'On' position. Then he looked to the far end of the room where, under a bright lamp, Dick Alcot was winding film from spool to spool with the tired air habitual to him.

'Everything okay, Dick?' Allerton asked; then he frowned as he looked at the work-bench. 'Say, where's that old house telephone I had lying about here? Seen it?'

'Not for some time . . . ' Dick Alcot turned and clamped lean hands down on

26

each of the spools to stop them rotating. The film tightened between them and lay like a band of glass under the light.

'Funny,' Allerton mused. 'Maybe I put it in the cupboard or somewhere . . . '

Alcot wiped his hands on a rag and then lounged forward. He was a fellow of average height, twenty years old, prided himself that he was devoid of emotion and admitted his regret that he had married at nineteen. In appearance he was nondescript, with lank black hair which insisted on dropping a forelock over his left ear, rather prominent grey eyes, and a face deathly pale either from constant indoor work or incipient anaemia. As the second projectionist most of the work fell on him, but believing it was a sign of a weak mind to show annoyance he never complained. Anyway, he and Fred Allerton were the best of friends.

'You don't look too happy, Fred,' he commented. 'That telephone will be knocking around somewhere . . . '

''Tisn't that,' Fred interrupted. 'I'm afraid of some trouble that may bring in the police . . . '

'Hell! The police? Why? I thought our fire regulations had been approved.'

'Not that,' Allerton growled. 'Something else.'

Without explaining further he left the winding-room and slowly mounted the four stone steps into the projection-room itself. As usual it was gleaming cheerily, the concrete floor stained deep red and highly polished. It had a friendliness all its own. Valves glowed brightly on the sound-reproducing equipment, meter needles quivered on their graded scales. On the wall were two notices — one ordering NO SMOKING, and the other exhorting operators to save their carbon stub-sheathing for salvage.

Allerton looked about him absently, mechanically checked the silent projectors ready threaded for the evening performance; then he walked the five-yard distance to the separate steel-lined enclosure where lay the record cabinets, slide-lantern, and floodlight controls.

In here sat Peter Canfield, his fingers playing over a small switchboard. At each movement the lights on the curtains in the auditorium changed colour. Peter Canfield had done this job for a year now, and being a youth of sixteen without any real ambition whatever would probably go on doing it until the crack of doom . . . Big for his age, his fresh-complexioned face covered in adolescent spots, he sat now controlling the floods with one hand and the reproduction equipment with the other. As the record of Sousa's *Il Capitan* came to an end he swung round the tuner to the twin turntable and faded in to the *Blue Danube* when he caught sight of Allerton looking at him.

'Hello, chief,' he said briefly.

Allerton nodded but did not speak. He was looking beyond Peter into the Circle, through the wide porthole. Down the white-edged steps a big man in a grey overcoat was descending. Presently he took his ticket from Nancy Crane and sat down in A-11.

'Same man!' Allerton whistled.

'Who?' Peter Canfield looked through the window. 'Say, Nan Crane looks like a million tonight! If she wasn't twenty years old I could fall for her myself.'

'Shut up,' Allerton ordered, then he peered at the hall clock. 'Half-past seven,' he murmured. 'I might just be able to manage it ... You look after these records, Peter. I'll be back in a minute or two.'

Allerton hurried across the projection-room, slapped open the swing door and fled down the flight of steps to the bottom. He stepped through the private doorway on to the Circle staircase angle halfway up to the Circle itself. People were flowing past him from below, toiling up the steps.

He went down the stairs until he came within view of the main foyer. Gerald Lincross was there in his usual place by his office door, his head and shoulders moving back and forth in perpetual greeting.

This was all Allerton wanted to see. Turning, he followed the people up the stairs and so into the Circle. When he got to the head of the stairs he stepped aside and touched Nancy Crane on the arm.

'You're on strange ground, Fred,' she murmured, taking tickets mechanically.

'Better not let the boss see you here!'

'Do me a favour, Nan! You see that fellow over there in the front row? One with the grey overcoat? Ask him to come here a moment. It's very important I see him. If I don't it may cost me my job . . . Be a sweetheart and help me out. I'll take the tickets while you go.'

Nancy looked at his uncommonly earnest face, then she hurried down the steps to the front row. Allerton could not hear what she said, but at last the big man got up, snatched up his hat, and wormed his way out of the row while the remaining tenants of Row A stood at indifferent attention to let him pass.

Allerton took tickets mechanically as he watched the big man climb the steps with Nancy bobbing urgently behind him.

'This — this gentleman wants to see you,' Nancy explained hastily, nodding to Allerton.

He handed the ticket-string back to the girl and looked at the big man a little uncertainly. 'Sorry to bother you, sir — but I'd like a word with you. If you'd come this way . . . '

'I came here to see a picture, not you,' the man growled.

'I know — but this won't take a moment. There's time.' Insistently Allerton caught hold of the big fellow's arm and led him down the steps until they came to the private door at the base of the projection-room staircase. Allerton opened it and motioned the stranger inside — then he closed the door again. Between the cool stonewalls under the single electric light they stood facing each other.

'I'm the man who knocked you down tonight in the High Street,' Allerton said abruptly. 'I'm — '

'I know who you are — the chief projectionist here. You told me that. What do you want?'

'I want to appeal to your sense of decency. Don't report me to the police.'

The big man looked surprised. 'And you have raked me out of my seat just to ask me that?'

'I'm scared of losing this job. You see, I've got a boss who at the mere mention of police goes off in a tantrum. He always

32

avoids them even when they call about the fire regulations, and leaves it all to me. If he found I'd been mixed up with them, even for such a trifling offence as a bad bicycle lamp, he'd fire me on the spot. So, if you'll promise me . . . '

A faint smile twitched the corners of the stranger's powerful mouth. 'All right,' he said finally. 'I'll not say anything. I was furious at the time, I admit — but I really never had any intention of reporting it.'

'Thanks!' Allerton breathed in relief. 'Thanks indeed!'

He opened the door, and the stranger walked out towards the staircase — just as Gerald Lincross came up from the foyer. For a moment he paused and stared fixedly at the stranger. The stranger too paused and looked back at him — just as if he were measuring him — then with a slight shrug of his big shoulders he went on up the stairs.

'What's the idea, Fred?' Lincross's voice was acid. 'Since when have you taken to inviting outsiders into the projection department?'

'I haven't, sir,' Allerton answered

quickly. 'I just asked him in here, at the bottom of the stairs, so I could say a few words to him.'

'What sort of words? What the devil are you talking about?'

'It's — it's private, Mr. Lincross.'

'We'll discuss it later,' Lincross snapped, looking at his wristwatch. 'Better get back on your job. Time's nearly up.'

Fred Allerton watched Lincross's black-suited figure hurry up the stairs into the Circle, then he turned back again into his own department and closed the door and locked it according to regulations. His emotions exploded in one word.

'Damn!'

⋆　⋆　⋆

True to tradition Gerald Lincross stood just at the top of the Circle steps as the lights in the auditorium began to dim gently. He always did so at this time, with Nancy Crane standing very quietly beside him. She presumed he made his survey to assess takings for the performance and to be sure that everybody was comfortable

— but she could not help but notice that this time he did not look around as much as usual. Instead seemed to be looking straight in front of him to where the big man in the grey overcoat was just settling in his seat once more . . .

Then on the screen the news flashed into being, transforming Lincross's white shirt front into a dully gleaming shield. The audience was picked out in dim silhouette and the red lights in the ceiling sprang into being together with the clock-light . . . That first tension had gone. The performance was on its way.

Lincross turned away and went down the steps from the Circle. Nancy Crane relaxed on to the little stool fitted to the wall and waited for latecomers.

Over in A-11 the man in grey sat watching the screen, but with some boredom. Obviously he waited only for the feature picture. Three rows behind him on the left Maria Black still held her umbrella and watched the parade of daily events . . .

Up in the projection-room Fred Allerton was checking his power meters and looking more depressed than ever. Dick Alcot stood on No. 1 projector, half leaning on it, his pallid face illumined by bright purple light as the glare of the arc light passed through the mauve inspection shield in the lamphouse. The projector whirred steadily, its intermittent sprocket keeping up an incessant staccato. From the monitor speaker in the concrete ceiling came the voice of the commentator recounting the news of the day.

'Something biting you, Fred?' Peter Canfield came out of the record room and looked at Allerton's troubled face.

'Nothing you can help,' Fred responded. 'Get below and fix up those trailers for tomorrow . . .'

Peter nodded and went out whistling. Allerton stood thinking, then as Alcot glanced at the decreasing film in his top spoolbox Allerton took up his position beside the second machine and switched on the arc. As the news came to an end he opened up and 'Love on the Highway' flashed on to the screen.

'One thing I don't understand about this film,' he said, as Alcot methodically threaded up his own now motionless machine. 'This Lydia Fane. She doesn't do half as much as that other girl in it — Betty Joyce — and yet she's billed as the star on our posters. Seems cock-eyed.'

'Whole darned film is cock-eyed if you ask me,' Alcot summed up, and snapped the sound-gate shut with an air of finality.

'Seems to me — ' Fred Allerton broke off as the service telephone buzzed beside his elbow. He picked it up and pressed the button. 'Yes?'

The voice, presumably speaking from the back of the stalls below, was indistinct. This was usual with a service telephone, and the noise in the projection-room from the monitor speaker together with the clicking machinery made Fred Allerton shout twice for a repetition.

' . . . hall speaker rattling. You'd better fix it.'

'Okay,' Allerton responded, and hung up.

'Trouble?' Alcot inquired.

'Near as I can make out one of the hall speakers is rattling. I'd better hop down and see to it. Take over for me, will you?

Oh — don't forget to step the sound up three faders when she fires that revolver. There are three shots, remember. We might as well wake 'em up outside.'

Alcot nodded and walked over to the twin machine. Allerton hurried downstairs, passed Peter Canfield cementing trailers together in the winding-room amidst an overpowering odour of amyl-acetate, and so finally let himself out on to the Circle staircase.

Soon he was in the foyer. Nobody was in sight, not even the doorman or manager. He hurried to the door of the Stalls, swung it open and passed into the smoky warmth and red-lit gloom beyond.

'Who rang?' he asked one of the two usherettes standing at the back of the Stalls.

'Rang what?' Violet Thompson asked, her face dimly visible.

'Somebody rang and said the speakers were rattling.' Allerton kept his voice low, 'Who was . . . ' He broke off and looked towards the screen where Lydia Fane had just appeared in the dressing room scene. Her voice as she screamed out a sentence quivered unbearably.

'It *does* rattle!' Allerton breathed. 'I'll settle it!'

He went hurrying off down the blank abyss of gangway and the two usherettes saw a dim rectangle of light become visible low down on the right-hand side of the screen as Allerton switched on the back-stage light. Then as he closed the door the light blanked out.

He was absent five minutes — then ten, but gradually the rattle in the voices of the players began to disappear. Then presently the half-somnolent audience was jerked into momentary life by the resounding triple bang of Lydia Fane's revolver. The oily-looking gentleman who had been trying to foul her reputation collapsed most realistically.

Another seven minutes went by, then Allerton came hurrying like a ghost from the remoteness of the theatre.

'That fixed it!' he whispered, as he went past Violet Thompson. She had not the vaguest idea what he was talking about for her unaccustomed ear was not attuned to variations in decibels or purity of reproduction — so she just gazed blankly as Allerton hurried out into the foyer and across to the manager's office.

He tapped, and peered in. Lincross was there, looking unusually flushed and not in the best of tempers.

'Well?' he asked curtly.

'I fixed that rattle, sir,' Fred explained.

Lincross looked at him as though he wondered what he was talking about.

'The hall speakers were rattling. One of the chains had worked loose and the vibration from the voices made it rattle against the metal hornwork.'

'All right. And don't forget I want a word with you before you go home.'

Allerton nodded dubiously, took a final look at those childlike and yet threatening blue eyes, then he closed the office door behind him. Troubled, he went up the stairs to resume his duties in the projection-room . . . As he passed the stair room door at the staircase angle it opened suddenly and Molly Ibbetson came out. Plump and easy-going, she did not often look worried — but she did now.

'Anything wrong?' Allerton paused and looked at her creased brow.

'No . . . ' The dark eyes glanced away from him. 'No, Fred, there's nothing wrong. I'm just a bit puzzled, that's all.'

Without elaborating, she closed the staff-room door and went off slowly down the stairs into the foyer. As Allerton looked after her, he had the oddest feeling that Molly Ibbetson had been up to something . . .

★   ★   ★

When the National Anthem was played and the lights began to glimmer back into being in the auditorium Nancy Crane relaxed happily. Standing to one side of the main flow of people leaving the Circle she nodded to them cheerfully as they wished her a good night. Towards the close of the exodus came Maria Black, umbrella in hand, her face wearing an expression both of boredom and annoyance.

'Did you enjoy it, Miss Black?' Nancy murmured.

'No, young lady, I did not! If I can find

Mr. Lincross in the foyer I shall tell him exactly what I think of 'Love on the Highway'! A glaring case of taking money under false pretences . . . '

Nancy laughed and watched Maria go purposefully down the stairs; then she followed her, branching off into the staff room to sweep up an armful of neatly folded dustsheets. Humming to herself she hurried up into the Circle again, to commence the job of covering the seats for the night — then she paused and glanced in surprise at the front row. The big-shouldered man in the grey coat to whom she had spoken earlier in the evening on Fred Allerton's behalf was still in his seat, head drooping forward, his hat on the plush balustrade in front of him.

Nancy Crane sighed and put down her dustsheets. She knew the picture had been pretty boring, but it didn't warrant a patron sleeping on beyond the end of the performance, surely? She sped nimbly down the steps and hurried along the row, shook the man by the shoulder.

'Sorry, sir, but it's time to go . . . '

The man in A-11 still sat on, chin on

chest, hands in the pockets of his coat. Nancy felt a vague thrill go down her spine. She shook him again, more forcibly.

'The show's over, sir!' she shouted.

Still there was still no response, so she took the risk of stooping and peering into the man's face . . . Almost instantly she jerked her eyes away, her heart thumping furiously. The man's eyes were partly open and staring fixedly at the base of the barrier in front of him — but in the centre of his forehead, just above the dent made by his undivided eyebrows, was a small neatly drilled hole and the merest trickle of blood.

'Oh!' Nancy's eyes widened; then the full shock of her discovery dawned on her. '*Oh — God!*' she gasped hoarsely.

Twisting round, she blundered out of the row, half fell up the white-edged steps, and then went racing for the Circle exit.

'Mr. Lincross!' She shouted the manager's name as she ran. 'Where are you, sir?'

As she tumbled down the last steps into the foyer she saw Lincross in his gleaming shirt front standing talking to Maria Black. Except for them and Molly Ibbetson in her pay-box preparing for departure there was nobody else in view.

'What's the matter, Miss Crane?' Lincross asked, as the girl came hurrying to him with a pink face and startled eyes.

'Upstairs, sir — in the Circle. A man's still there — I think he's dead!'

'Dead?' Lincross gave a start then glanced at Maria Black in wonder. 'Dead?' he repeated, looking at Nancy again. 'What in the world are you talking about, miss?'

'He's in A-11 . . . ' Nancy Crane fought hard to control herself. 'I thought he was asleep, but when I looked at him closely I saw that he wasn't. There's a little hole in his forehead and — and some blood!'

Maria reached forward and grasped the girl firmly by the arm as she stood shuddering with reaction. 'Try and be calm, Nancy,' she murmured. 'It must have been a shock — but don't get hysterical. I'll stay beside you.'

'Th-thanks.' Nancy flushed redly. 'It's true, though!' She glanced at Lincross.

44

'Go and look for yourself, sir . . . '

'It would be as well,' Maria agreed, and still holding Nancy by the arm, led the way up the Circle stairs.

As they came into the Circle Nancy detached herself and pointed to the front row where the man in grey sat. Lincross, coming up behind, looked too. His flat mouth set tightly.

'Come,' Maria murmured, and went forward slowly, then when she reached Row A she stood aside as Lincross went along past the seats, put a hand under the man's jaw and tilted his face upwards. There was no longer any room for doubt: Nancy Crane had not exaggerated.

'Definitely dead,' Maria commented, from the row behind, and she released the man's pulse. 'Apparently shot in the head from a distance, which at least excludes his neighbours in the audience.'

'Why . . . a distance?' Lincross asked, complete bewilderment at the situation registered on his face.

'No powder marks, no tattooing, no scorching. So evidently this is not a suicide, Mr. Lincross, nor a murder by a neighbour close at hand . . . However, my theories don't signify. You must send for the police and leave this man exactly as he is.'

Lincross nodded, his childlike blue eyes still reflecting amazement that such a thing had happened in his cinema; then he forced himself to deal with the situation and headed towards the Circle exit. Maria Black looked back at the dead man thoughtfully, glanced about and above her, then she too climbed steadily up to the exit. Nancy Crane was standing there, moving uncertainly from one dainty foot to the other.

'What — what am I supposed to do, sir?' she asked Lincross, as he came past. 'Shall I cover the seats or . . . '

'Certainly not! Have a bit of sense, girl! Find those usherettes still in the cinema and tell them to come into the foyer. And the cashiers. The police will be here shortly.'

'If I'm home not so early I'm likely to get into trouble,' Nancy objected.

'Can't be helped.' Lincross continued down the stairs. Just as he passed the projection-room's main doorway, Fred Allerton opened it and came into view with a transit case on his shoulder. Within it 'Love on the Highway' was packed in its humidor tins ready for the collection by the film transport at midnight.

Behind Allerton came Alcot, then Peter Canfield.

'Just a minute, you three . . . ' Lincross turned to them. 'You can't leave yet. A man has been shot dead. We found him in the Circle. I'm sending for the police. It's the man you spoke to, Fred.'

There was a grim silence for a moment and every spark of colour went out of Allerton's cheeks. Lincross nodded towards the foyer and went on his way.

'And a dead man queers my supper,' growled Alcot.

'Not just dead, Dick — murdered,' Allerton said pointedly.

'Either way it has nothing to do with us,' Alcot insisted.

'But we stay just the same — because the boss says so,' Peter Canfield observed, locking the projection-room door and handing Allerton the key. They went down the stairs into the foyer. Behind them, her face pensive, came Maria Black. Then Nancy Crane came down to her side.

'I suppose, Miss Black, this is right up your street? Everybody round here knows you're a detective — not official though. You got a lot of publicity when you solved how that girl who came to your school was hanged. Remember?'

'You'd better find the usherettes,' Maria murmured. 'Join me afterwards.'

Nancy nodded and hurried ahead. Once in the foyer Maria picked a plush armchair for herself and settled in it calmly. Presently Nancy came back, her work of rounding-up completed.

She settled in the chair close to Maria and looked at her earnestly. 'It must be exciting to be a detective, Miss Black!'

'It has its moments, Nancy,' Maria admitted. 'However, don't forget that I am a Headmistress. Criminology is merely a hobby. In any case I cannot upset police procedure ... Yet,' she finished, smiling inscrutably, 'here am I sitting here, when I could be on my way home if I chose. As a member of the audience and seated behind the dead man I am not at all suspect. It is a fact that a criminal puzzle draws me irresistibly, Nancy.'

The girl nodded and looked about her as the staff began to assemble in the foyer. Fred Allerton, Alcot, and Peter Canfield kept in a tight little group by the pay-box. Violet Thompson and Sheila Brant, the two Stalls usherettes, fully dressed in overcoats and with scarves wrapped over their heads, hesitated by the exit doorway. Bradshaw the doorman was upstairs as yet, changing into his ordinary clothes . . . Mary Saunders was touching up her auburn hair before the mirror near the Circle stairway. Molly Ibbetson was seated on a distant chair, swinging her short chubby legs and adjusting the bandeau round her ebon hair.

From her position at the far end of the foyer Maria Black could study each one of them under the bright lights — and she did, quite impartially, as though surveying a class of girls at Roseway . . . then she glanced round as Lincross came hurrying out of his office, beads of perspiration on top of his bald head.

From the centre of the foyer he looked round on the assembly.

'I've 'phoned Inspector Morgan,' he announced. 'He'll be here soon — and until then I'm afraid you will have to stay. Except you, Miss Black. There is no reason why . . . '

'I am here from choice, Mr. Lincross,' Maria smiled. 'I know Inspector Morgan very well — a most worthy representative of the local constabulary. I'll be quite interested to see what he does.'

Lincross shrugged, then he glanced towards the stairs as Bradshaw came down them in mackintosh and cap. 'Afraid you can't leave, Bradshaw,' Lincross said.

'I know,' Bradshaw grunted. 'And this means I'll be late for my goodnight drink . . . Rotten do, I call it.'

He sat down in a chair and lighted a cigarette. Sensing he was conspicuous standing in the centre of the assembly Lincross too found a seat. The uneasy silence that enfolds employer and employee when circumstances bring them into close proximity dropped . . .

At ten-fifteen by the foyer clock, ten minutes after Lincross's phone call, there came the noise of a car stopping near the outside entrance. A few seconds later the glass doors swung apart to admit the persevering Inspector Morgan and Sergeant Claythorne of the local constabulary.

Morgan was of medium height but packed as solidly as a West Highland bull; and he was very nearly as pugnacious. His eyebrows were the most obvious thing about him — black, astonishingly bushy, overhanging eyes of sapphire blue. A short nose and a prominent chin completed a face that typified dogged persistency rather than actual keenness. From under the edges of his official cap hair peeped in close-cropped bristles.

Sergeant Claythorne was very different — tall and twenty-six, with the delicate complexion of a girl. His height and by no means dull intellect were the sole qualifications that had shoe-horned him into the local force. Maria Black could still recall the day when he had been a highly sensitive schoolboy.

''Evening, sir . . . ' Morgan directed his attention to Lincross after his gaze had encompassed the assembly; then he glanced for the second time towards the figure in a distant corner and added with emphasis, 'And good evening, Miss Black!'

Maria nodded imperceptibly and Morgan cleared his throat.

'Sergeant, you'd better wait outside the front doors there.'

'Right, sir.'

The doors opened and shut behind Claythorne's lanky figure then Morgan tugged out a notebook from the breast pocket of his uniform and looked at Lincross.

'Man dead in the Circle, you said? Where is he?'

'Still in the Circle,' Maria remarked dryly, getting to her feet.

'I *meant*, has he been moved?' Morgan's voice was bitter.

'No, Inspector — he's just where he was,' Lincross answered.

Morgan nodded and cast a disapproving blue eye at Maria Black, then he followed Lincross up the staircase to the Circle then down to Row A. The Inspector came to a stop before the motionless man in seat 11 and looked at him critically. After a long scrutiny of the puncture in the man's forehead he gazed across the cinema towards the dusty, closed curtains covering the screen — then up above at the ceiling with its big ventilator arch and the fan-grids over the stalls.

'Interesting business, Inspector, isn't it?'

Morgan turned sharply as he saw Maria Black seated with her umbrella at the end of row B watching him. Morgan could have sworn that in an indirect way she was laughing at him.

'Yes,' he answered briefly, feeling that her forbidding presence upset his authority. Then he glanced at Lincross standing beside the balustrade. 'I've got fingerprint and photograph men on the way from Lexham. Be here any time — though I don't see a fingerprint man is much use with no weapon in sight. Dr. Roberts won't be long, either . . . For the moment

I think we'll go back into the foyer.'

The two men and Maria returned below to find the assembly talking among themselves impatiently.

'This won't take long,' Morgan told them, looking round. 'I just want a few questions answered, that's all. Who found the body?'

'I did.' Nancy Crane stood up nervously.

'*You* did. And you'll be — an usherette?'

'Miss Nancy Crane is my supervising usherette,' Lincross explained. 'She takes her instructions from me and sees to it that the other girls follow them out. That is excepting the cashiers.'

'I see.' Morgan made a note. 'And your address, Miss Crane?'

'26, Wellington Crescent. In Langhorn here, of course.'

'Well, young lady, just tell me exactly how you found him. What were you doing?'

'I was going to cover the seats up as I do at nights most times — then I saw that man, just sitting. I thought maybe he wasn't awake and so I tried to shake him up. When I saw that hole in his head I told Mr. Lincross.'

Morgan stared hard. 'Do you always talk in that back-to-front sort of way, Miss Crane?'

'Al-always,' she stammered. 'Ever since I was ill as a child . . . '

'What about the rest of the people in Row A,' Morgan asked. 'Was that row full?'

'Yes,' Nancy agreed, and Lincross nodded his semi-bald head in confirmation.

'Then how on earth did the row empty with that man seated dead in the centre of it?' Morgan asked blankly.

'I can answer that question,' Maria Black remarked, strolling forward. 'I was seated three rows back from Row A on the left, and I noticed that that row, in common with many others, practically emptied itself before the end of the performance. The film was decidedly mediocre. What few people there were left on Row A at the end of the show found it easier to leave by the ends instead of passing the man whom they assumed was asleep.'

'Ah-ha,' Morgan said, scribbling again. Then he looked once more at Nancy. 'All right, miss, that's all I need to know from you — except for one thing. Had you ever seen this man before?'

'Twice, sir. He came Monday night, and again last night.'

Morgan's eyebrows rose. 'He must have enjoyed the picture if nobody else seemed to . . . '

'Couldn't be that, Inspector,' remarked Mary Saunders from the far end of the foyer — and Mary was a girl who had her wits about her. 'You see, he booked for all three nights before he had even seen the picture. I know because I gave him the tickets.'

'Well, that's very interesting. All right, I'll come to you later. Thanks, Miss Crane, that's all — unless you have some information you would care to volunteer?'

Nancy hesitated slightly and glanced across towards Fred Allerton as he lounged beside Alcot and young Canfield. She caught an expression from him and then looked back to the Inspector.

'No, Inspector — there's nothing else.'

'All right,' Morgan said briefly. 'You can go home if you wish.'

Nancy turned towards the Circle staircase on her way to the staff room. Maria's cold blue eyes followed her shapely young figure out of sight, then they strayed across to Fred Allerton — and so finally back to Inspector Morgan as he went over to Mary Saunders,

'So, miss,' he remarked, after taking down her name and address, 'the man booked three seats without seeing the picture, did he? When was this?'

'About half-past six on Monday evening. I'd never seen him before. I noticed him looking through the glass doors into the foyer — we were closed then, of course. He seemed to be looking at the placards we have in here. When I asked him if he were looking for somebody he asked me a question instead.'

'Which was?' Morgan prompted.

'It was something about 'Love on the Highway'. He asked me if it was showing that night — Monday night. I told him it was. Then I showed him the streamer poster we have hanging under the canopy. He booked three tickets — all, for Monday, Tuesday, and tonight.'

'Did he ask for A-11 or did you give it to him?'

'He asked for the best seat in the front row, which we usually consider is A-11.'

'He didn't give his name?'

'No,' Mary said. 'But I think you might get it from the 'Golden Saddle' Hotel across the road. I think he was staying there. I can see across the road from my advance booking box, you know. I saw him come out of there once or twice.'

'Good!' Morgan seemed relieved at finding something tangible to seize. 'Thank you, Miss Saunders. You may get off home, too, any time you wish.'

Mary Saunders got up and headed for the swing doors with a brief 'Good night!' Moments later Nancy Crane came hurrying into sight, her trim overcoat neatly belted in to her waist and a woollen pixie-hood framing her pretty face.

'Good night,' she murmured, glancing round under her eyes, and then she followed Mary Saunders into the blustering wind outside.

Morgan was about to say something, when there was the sound of a car at the front entrance. In a moment or so two men entered, one of them carrying equipment and a mackintosh-covered collapsible tripod under his arm.

'Upstairs, boys — Circle,' Morgan ordered. 'See you later.'

The two nodded and went on their way through the foyer.

'Fingerprint and photograph men,' Morgan explained, looking round the group.

'Without me questioning each one of you individually, do any of you know anything about this dead man which might help me? We know he has been here three times, presumably to see 'Love on the Highway', but is there anything else? You . . . ' The doorman found himself under scrutiny. 'Did he speak to you at all?'

'Not a word,' Bradshaw said. 'I saw 'im come in each time, though.'

'Did he look as though he *wanted* to see the picture?' Morgan asked. 'Did he — look *eager*?'

'Like 'ell he did!' Bradshaw was candid. ' 'E looked as though he wanted to shoot somebody! Big, 'eavy face with tight lips. Grim-like.'

'He was not a regular patron?'

'Never seen him before,' Lincross remarked.

'All right,' Morgan decided. 'That's as far as we can move now. Those of you who wish to go can do so — and give your names and addresses to Sergeant Claythorne as you leave . . . I'd like a few words with you, though, Mr. Lincross.'

'With pleasure,' Lincross assented, then he waited while Morgan opened the glass doors and called Claythorne inside to take the names and addresses. The youthful sergeant had just started on his task when the doors swung open to admit a small man in a big overcoat and bowler hat, carrying a medical bag. He was sallow, harassed-looking. Maria Black recognised him as Dr. Roberts from farther up the High Street, the Langhorn G.P. who acted

60

as police-surgeon in addition to his own practice.

'Came as soon as I could,' he said cryptically, nodding to the Inspector. 'Where's the body?'

'In the Circle — A-11.'

'Thanks. 'Evening, everybody. Cold night . . . ' Roberts went on his way towards the staircase, and the fingerprint and photograph men passed him on the way. They came to a halt beside Morgan.

'Waste of my time, Inspector,' the fingerprint man said, with a hint of reproof. 'Nothing for me to do — and only blurs on the chair arms. Find the weapon that killed him and then we've got something.'

'As if I didn't know,' Morgan growled. 'All right, thanks. And let me have those pictures first thing tomorrow morning.'

'Okay,' the photographer nodded, and headed for the doors with his companion.

Morgan stood watching as Sergeant Claythorne came to the end of his name and address collecting, then he studied each of the staff as they began to file out — until it came to Fred Allerton's turn.

As it happened he was the last on the list, but before he could leave Lincross spoke.

'I think if anybody can tell you about the dead man, Inspector, he can!' he said.

There was no vicious satisfaction in his tone, no veiled suggestion that he was making an accusation. It sounded just like a plain statement of fact. In any event Allerton paused and turned round, looking at the manager very directly.

'Oh?' Inspector Morgan brisked up suddenly. 'Well, what about it, Mr. — er — ?'

'Allerton,' Fred said quietly, walking slowly back into the foyer centre. 'I'm the chief projectionist.'

'And you knew that man in the Circle?'

'Only by sight — '

'Enough to take him into privacy behind the projection-room door and have a talk with him before the show,' Lincross pointed out. 'I saw that for myself. In fact, Inspector, I asked Fred here why he did it and he told me it was a private matter.'

'So it was!' Allerton snapped, on the defensive. 'I give you my word that I

62

don't know the man's name or anything at all about his murder.'

'Yet you went out of your way to talk to him?' Morgan insisted.

'Yes . . . ' Allerton could sense the cold suspicion in the Inspector's voice. For a reason he could hardly explain he found himself thinking about plump Molly Ibbetson, looking so surprised, creeping out of that staff-room door. Why did they have to pick on him? They had let the girl go with nothing more than a name and address —

'You went out of your way — to talk to him!' Morgan's emphatic voice came out of fast-running speculations.

'It was personal,' Fred Allerton said, forcing himself to be attentive.

'I see. Just personal.' Morgan nodded slowly. 'All right, Mr. Allerton, I'll not detain you now. Perhaps we'll have another little chat in the morning . . . You can go if you want.'

Allerton tightened his lips, wondering if he ought to go and get his bicycle from the disused sweet-stall, and decided against it. So with an almost inaudible good night he turned and left. Morgan looked after him thoughtfully, then at the sound of hurrying feet across the foyer he turned to find Dr. Roberts approaching.

'Death caused by a small slug,' he pronounced. 'I'll remove it in the morning. Apparently it has gone straight through into the brain and caused instant death. As to the direction of the slug — which I'm judging by the size of the entrance wound — the possible speed of entry, and so forth, I'll go to work on it tomorrow. No time now. Probably need the X-ray to trace it . . . Well, night, everybody.'

' 'Night, and thanks,' Morgan responded, as the doctor hurried out. Then, the turning to Lincross:

'I've nothing more to ask you — unless you've anything to add to your statement about that fellow Allerton which might help me?'

'Afraid I haven't, Inspector. I've said my little piece.'

'Altogether,' Maria remarked, in the momentary hush, 'a most intriguing business, Inspector.'

He looked at her doubtfully as she stood blandly smiling. 'Precious little to go on though except the fact that the dead man was apparently staying at the hotel across the road; I'll be over there to make inquiry first thing in the morning . . . ' Morgan paused at a sudden thought. 'Shot with a slug!' he whistled. 'That probably means either an air-rifle or an air-pistol — and it would be bound to make a noise in a quiet cinema even if a silencer were fitted . . . Miss Black, you were in the audience. Did you hear anything?'

'Nothing unusual,' Maria answered. 'As to that there is possibly one probable explanation — but of course it is not for me to interfere . . . There is, however, one thing very much in your favour, Inspector — and that is the time of death. If that film 'Love on the Highway' were to be run through again you would see exactly what I mean.'

'I would?' A sense of suspicion that he was being taught his own business welled up in Morgan's mind. 'I'll think about it,' he promised stiffly.

Maria smiled faintly. 'I shall hope to have the chance of seeing you again, Inspector. Good night — and to you, Mr. Lincross.'

'Good night, madam,' Lincross murmured, bowing from the waist in that automatic fashion he had — and Inspector Morgan noticed that he never took his eyes from Maria's heavy, retreating figure until she passed beyond the glass doors . . .

Then he seemed to relax. 'Rather — er — eccentric lady,' he commented, glancing at the Inspector.

'Oh, I wouldn't say eccentric. Eccentrics aren't given the job of ruling a girls' college, sir. She's deep as the sea — that's what it is. I'm wondering just how much she has dug out of this business already.'

'Oh?' Lincross affected surprise.

'She's a criminologist — on the q.t. Sort of hobby . . . '

66

3

Fred Allerton, his shoulders hunched against the freezing wind, walked swiftly down the street in the direction of home. He was glad now of his decision not to cycle for the road was glazing with frost. Then to his surprise a slender figure in a belted overcoat and pixie-hood emerged suddenly from the shelter of Atkinson's, the second-hand dealer.

'Why, Nan! I thought you'd gone home long ago!'

'I'll walk with you as far as the end of the street,' the girl said quietly. 'I want a word with you.'

Linking arms, Fred held on to her tightly as they negotiated the treacherous pavement. He was wondering what had prompted her to stand several minutes in freezing weather to wait for him.

'I'm trying to decide whether I ought to have told Inspector Morgan about it — or not,' Nancy said presently.

'About what?' he asked, in a flat, hard voice.

Nancy drew him to a standstill. 'You know you signalled me to keep quiet when the Inspector asked if I knew anything more about — about the man in A-11.'

'And rightly! You know how the boss hates the police, in spite of his good manners tonight . . . ' Allerton stopped his impetuous rush of words and looked down into the girl's troubled eyes.

'It wouldn't have mattered anyway,' he said finally. 'Lincross gave me away — said he'd seen me talking to that man at the foot of the projection-room stairs.'

'You mean the boss did see you?' Nancy gasped.

'Does it matter? It's all so innocent — just knocking the chap down with my bicycle. He was the one. I told you about it, remember? And you told me not to worry over it.'

'Things were different then.' The girl's gloved hand gripped his arm. 'Fred, you made a clean breast of what you wanted to see that man for, didn't you?'

'No. Didn't see why I should.'

'But, dearest, the man's dead! Murdered probably. The Inspector will think you did things that you didn't if you don't tell the truth . . . Fred, you must tell him! Next time you see him. If you don't, then I shall.'

'Well, perhaps you're right,' he sighed. 'You usually see farther than I do. But don't you see, I haven't done anything . . . ' He broke off, wrestling with the preposterous situation.

'But the man in A-11's dead,' Nancy insisted.

'Oh, come on!' Allerton slipped an arm round her waist. 'You're shivering! I'll see you home this time and then I'll be on my way. Of all the confounded cock-eyed evenings! One would think I was a murderer — or something!'

It was nearing midnight when Maria Black let herself into the college grounds through the private gate. She hurried across the quadrangle and through the side doorway into the staff quarters of the building. Her study smelled warm and comfortable as she came inside it and emerged thankfully from the depths of her coat.

She switched on the electric radiator, then filling the kettle she plugged it in to boil. While the water heated she paced in front of her desk, pulling gently at her gold watch chain.

'A slug which enters a man's forehead with such power that it penetrates the skullbone and kills him — A slug fired by a weapon which either makes no noise, or else it was timed to match the revolver shots in the film . . . Oh, yes, come in,' she broke off, as there was a knock on the door.

It was the Housemistress who entered, She cut rather an amazing figure in her dressing gown and flowered boudoir cap.

'Oh, then it *is* you, Miss Black . . . ' She gave a wan smile of relief. 'When you were so late arriving home I decided to wait up in my study for you. I heard you pass along the corridor a little while ago. At least, I assumed it was you.'

'Very considerate of you, Miss Tanby,' Maria approved. 'Sit down, please —

Share a pot of tea with me. I'm just about to make one.'

Tanby sat down wearily, took the cup of tea Maria presently held to her and then watched her superior stir her own tea pensively.

'I am late, Miss Tanby, because I had to walk through this freezing weather and over slippery roads — the 'bus service having ceased long ago — and because a murder investigation has just commenced at the Langhorn Cinema.'

'A murder? There?' Tanby set down her cup and widened her pale grey eyes.

'Murder occurs in the most unexpected places,' Maria remarked dryly. 'However, you need have no fear. I am not taking any part in the business. After all, it is no concern of mine.'

'No,' Tanby agreed, inwardly relieved that she would not have to take over the duties of deputy-Headmistress after all

'Except for one thing,' Maria sighed. 'I can see the good Inspector Morgan setting off up the wrong road and involving somebody whom I think is perfectly innocent in complicated circumstances. If that happens I shall feel it my bounden duty to say a few things — to Morgan if not to anybody else.'

'I see,' said Tanby vaguely, and obviously she did not.

'You will forgive me detaining you a moment or two,' Maria proceeded, sitting back in her big desk chair. 'But according to Sherlock Holmes in one of his cases, there is nothing clears up the mind so much as bouncing your ideas against somebody else. Now, as an outsider, knowing nothing of what has gone on, what would you say if a man went to see a film three times, booking in advance, mark you, with apparently nothing to guide him except the foyer posters? Speaking generally it proved to be a most indifferent picture. So why did our friend who met his death do it?'

'Well . . . I'd say, offhand, that he wanted to see something in the film very particularly. And, if you'll excuse me, Miss Black, how do you know that he had never seen it before? He might have, at another cinema. For my own part I have seen 'San Francisco' three times in Lexham, but I'd willingly see it three more times in Langhorn.'

'A point well taken,' Maria conceded. 'He *might* have seen it elsewhere and knew what he was getting. Thank you, Miss Tanby — that thought had not occurred to me.'

Tanby drank her tea slowly, then presently a faint gleam entered her eyes as she looked at her superior.

'You saw the picture, Miss Black. What was there in it that might have intrigued a man? Was there, for instance, any — er — sex appeal?' Tanby felt colour struggling unaccustomedly into her cheeks. 'I mean — some men will visit a film many times if it contains a — a bathing scene, or perhaps a fan dancer.'

Tanby's voice faded away like a singer's top note as Maria's icy blue eyes regarded her.

'No, Miss Tanby, there was nothing so indecorous! I grant, however, that there is truth in what you have said. No, this was a perfectly ordinary picture, a triangle drama with a shooting. I was impressed by the fact that the sound was much louder on the three revolver shots than on the rest of the picture, and for that reason I am inclined to suspect that the slug that hit our friend in A-11 was fired at exactly that moment.'

'Is that possible?' Tanby asked, feeling rather sleepy.

'Assuredly! Many writers aver that the assassinator of Abraham Lincoln, one John Wilkes Booth, timed his shot with the drum-roll of the orchestra to muffle the sound. The idea is not unique: this is merely a modern version of it . . . However, it is getting late, Miss Tanby.'

'I'll say good night then, Miss Black.' Tanby rose thankfully. 'And thank you for the tea.'

Maria nodded absently, lost in thought. At length she opened a drawer in her desk and took out a black leather book and laid it in front of her. She opened it at a clean sheet and began to write —

This may not develop into anything, but it is worth noting down. I was present tonight at the Langhorn Cinema when a patron was shot dead by a copper alloy slug in the skull.

I may take a hand in the investigation. Am not sure. If I do I will record my notes. The outstanding question just now is: was the shot fired synchronously with the revolver shots (three) in the film? If so, from where? And where is the weapon?

The time is 12.40 a.m.

⋆ ⋆ ⋆

The following morning Inspector Morgan was at the Langhorn Cinema by nine o' clock. Evidently Lincross had been expecting this for the staff found him already in his office when they came drifting in. Fortunately for them he had too much on his mind to question why they had failed to arrive on time.

Shown into the manager's office by the doorman, Morgan seemed in a genial mood. He usually was until things got too tough for him.

'What I want to know,' Lincross said, when the greetings were over and cigarettes were lighted, 'is how this affair is going to affect my cinema. Can I open as usual?'

'By all means! We've no need to interfere with normal business. We can find out all we want in the mornings.'

Lincross looked relieved. 'I'm glad to hear that . . . Now what can I do for you? How can I help?'

Morgan considered. 'Before I can make any definite advance I'm waiting for Dr. Roberts' full report. You saw us have the dead man's body removed late last night, of course, and you know the search we made — futilely, alas! — for a weapon. Well, Roberts is working on the dead man now. I've been over to the 'Golden Saddle', but all I can discover is that our friend registered there in the name of Douglas Farrington and took a room for a week. His few personal belongings failed to reveal a single clue of interest.'

'Which sort of limits things,' Lincross confessed. 'So what's next?'

Morgan rose decisively. 'I'm going to take a look at the Circle from where our friend sat, if you don't mind.'

Lincross followed the burly Inspector

from the office and up the Circle staircase. At the very top of the stairs Nancy Crane was dusting seat-backs busily, a red bandeau round her blonde head and an unbecoming green overall spoiling the slim lines of her figure.

''Morning, young lady,' Morgan greeted.

''Morning,' Nancy whispered back, and as she went on dusting she reviled herself for having been so timid last night. The Inspector had just got to be told the truth. But later on — Lincross had arrived too, and after all, the information was for Morgan alone.

So Nancy Crane went on dusting. She watched Morgan settle in A-11 and look about him. Lincross stood facing him, with his back to the balustrade.

'I don't know about these things, of course,' Lincross said, 'but it does seem odd to me that a man could have a slug driven into his head with such blinding force that it killed him, and yet he failed to attract the notice of the people immediately around him. Tell me, wouldn't he — jump?'

An odd expression crossed Morgan's

face, as though he had received a shock and an idea at the same time.

'Possibly he might have jumped,' he conceded, with caution. 'But I've sat beside people in cinemas and theatres and they have jumped quite a lot . . . ' Surprisingly he skated away from the subject. 'What puzzles me, Mr. Lincross, is how the shot was fired without anybody hearing it! And I'd like to know what happened to the weapon.'

Presently Morgan looked straight before him at the curtains over the screen, drab now without the play of coloured lights.

'To all intents and purposes,' he said, 'the shot came from somewhere there. How far is it to the screen? About forty feet?'

'My chief knows exactly,' Lincross replied. 'I'll call him.'

He turned and mounted the steps to the Circle exit. Nancy Crane, watching, tossed her duster aside and hurried down to where the Inspector was sitting gazing at the big ventilator arch in the ceiling over his head.

'Oh, Inspector . . . ' Nancy hesitated

78

nervously at the end of the row.

'You want to see me, miss?'

'Yes . . . ' Nancy edged in towards him. 'You see, I didn't give all the evidence I know of last night.'

'Evidence? Of last night?'

'Evidence about Fred Allerton, He's my fiancé, you know. He talked to that man . . . '

'I know that,' Morgan said briefly.

'But I know what they talked about! They talked about Fred's bike lamp!'

To Nancy's surprise, Morgan burst out laughing. 'A bike lamp! What was he trying to do? Sell it?'

'No — the lamp was out when he came up the main street. Fred ran into that man and knocked him down. He said he might tell the police, but he didn't because he was shot. To stop him doing what he might have done Fred had a private word with him when he saw he was in the audience.'

Morgan sorted it out ponderously, then said: 'And how do you know about this?'

'I went and asked the man to see Fred. Against rules, of course, but after all he is going to be my husband. Fred, I mean.'

Nancy looked up sharply as Lincross reappeared at the top of the steps with Allerton beside him. She made a sudden pretence of inspecting the ashtrays and so wormed her way gracefully from the danger area. She sensed that Lincross was watching suspiciously.

'You want the distance from here to the screen, Inspector?' Fred Allerton asked. 'It's forty-seven feet, rule measured when I needed a fresh projection lens recently.'

'Thanks.' Morgan made a note and then looked up at Fred Allerton's troubled face. 'What,' he asked, 'is behind the screen?'

'The hall horns — the speakers,' Fred answered. 'They're five feet across the mouth and fastened with girders and chains. Behind them are felt curtains acting as baffles. Except for fuse boxes and stage lights that's all there is behind there.'

Morgan got to his feet decisively. 'I think we'll take a good look behind there. Wasn't much time last night. Have the curtains drawn back, will you?'

Allerton hurried up the stairs, shouted an order to Peter Canfield in the winding-room, then waited for the Inspector and Lincross to catch him up. All three of them then went down into the Stalls and so along the right-hand gangway to the door at the foot of the stage. Reaching inside Fred Allerton switched on the back-stage lights.

'Pretty dirty,' he warned. 'Watch your clothes.'

Morgan glanced up at the screen, the curtains now having been drawn back, then he followed Allerton into a narrow passageway with two tiny fifteen-watt lamps casting a yellow glow on stone walls. There was just room for the three of them to advance in single file — then they climbed four stone steps to the level behind the screen itself.

'There you are, Inspector,' Allerton said.

Morgan bent his head back and stared up at the massive metal speakers above him. He felt the strong chains supporting them, and then the dusty felt hemming them in.

'Big enough,' he admitted, then he turned to inspect the screen. He gave an exclamation of surprise. 'Hello, then it isn't solid! I never noticed last night with the curtains drawn outside it!'

'No, Inspector — no cinema screen is solid these days. It is a sheet of stretched rubber, braced round the edges with lacing fastened on to a wooden framework so it can be tightened up. There are not far short of a quarter of a million holes in the screen, each hole the size of a pinpoint. They cover its entire area. The reason is, of course, to permit sound to pass through the screen to the audience.'

'Think of that!' Morgan sounded as happy as a schoolboy with a jar full of tadpoles. Inquisitively he peered through the misty transparency on to the dimly lighted auditorium outside.

'This means,' he said portentously, 'that anybody here could see the audience outside?'

'Certainly,' Allerton agreed. 'From here, when a film is being shown, the light through the projector lens looks like a distant star, and it doesn't dazzle you because it is so far away. But the audience is plainly visible because the light reflects from the screen on to the people.'

'Could one see . . . as far as the front row of the Circle?'

'Yes, one could,' Allerton admitted, 'but not with any distinctness.'

'But one could see to the front row?' Morgan persisted.

Allerton nodded in the dim light and Lincross's blue eyes went a trifle wider. Apparently Morgan was satisfied on this point, however, for he began to run his fingers over the stretched rubber of the screen's back, feeling the myriad hole indentations . . . Then suddenly he moved forward and looked at one particular area more closely.

'What's this?' he asked sharply. 'A hole?'

Allerton and Lincross both moved to his side and looked at a roughly circular opening perhaps a quarter of an inch in diameter.

'This been here long?' Morgan questioned.

'Never seen it before,' Allerton replied.

'This is a comparatively new screen, Inspector,' Lincross explained. 'That hole was certainly not there the last time I inspected here — about a fortnight ago.'

'It might have been caused by some of the lads at the Saturday matinée,' Allerton suggested. 'If they don't like a picture they throw things at the screen sometimes — ice-cream cartons, stones from cata-pults . . . '

'I doubt if a kid's catapult would have enough penetrating power to pierce this rubber with a stone,' Morgan remarked, an odd note in his voice. 'And even if it had, the edge of this hole would show the rubber fabric bent inwards — towards us. The edges on this are bent *outwards*, towards the audience.'

Fred Allerton looked at the hole again, then he felt himself go suddenly hot.

'You are quite sure, both of you, that you don't know how this hole got here?' Morgan asked.

Allerton licked his lips and felt dust upon them.

'I don't,' he said. 'And I'm sure Mr. Lincross doesn't.'

'No reason why I should,' Lincross added. 'I've no reason to come behind here except for routine check-up. You were in here last night, Inspector. Didn't you notice — then?'

'No. I was looking for the weapon. Anyway the screen doesn't show up clearly with the curtains drawn over in front of it.'

'Well — what about you, Fred?' Lincross asked. 'You were in here during last evening's performance to fix the speaker. So you told me afterwards, anyway.'

'You were in here — last night?' Morgan repeated deliberately.

Allerton looked embarrassed. 'Yes, I was. Somebody rang up the projection-room and said that the hall speakers were rattling, so I came in here and put things right. The chain had come loose and the vibration of the voices was making it jar against the metal side of one of the horns.'

Morgan looked up at the chains solidly bolted into place.

'Came loose?' He frowned. 'How could it?'

'I don't know . . . Just one of those things, I suppose.' Allerton pointed to the chain in question. 'There it is.'

'How long did it take you to fix the repair?'

'Oh — about twenty minutes maybe.'

'Difficult to think hemmed in here,' Morgan said. 'Let's get outside.'

Out in the theatre once more, Morgan knocked down three seats in the front row and motioned to Allerton and Lincross to sit on either side of him.

'No need to get windy, you know,' he smiled. 'I'm only putting things together — or else taking them apart. But I did think, Mr. Allerton, that you had told me everything last night.'

'I did!' Allerton insisted. 'In so far as I thought it mattered, that is. It never occurred to me to mention my exploit behind the screen.'

'Tell me something. Would that hole be visible to the audience while the picture was showing?'

'Might be, if there were any very light scenes. But there weren't — not in 'Love on the Highway'. I doubt if a hole like that would be noticed beyond, say, the first six rows in the stalls here. And I give you my word I didn't see it when I fixed the speaker.'

Morgan gazed hard at the screen from under his amazing eyebrows and asked another question.

'Who telephoned you about the defect in the speaker?'

'That I don't know, Inspector. It's hard to distinguish voices in the projection room when they come over the telephone. Too much noise.'

'But surely you could tell whether it was a man or a woman?'

'Must have been one of the usherettes,' Lincross put in. 'I didn't telephone, and the only other man would be Bradshaw. It couldn't have been him because I was searching for him about that time and couldn't find him.'

Morgan merely looked thoughtful, then he asked yet another question. 'Are the usherettes here?'

'All of them,' Lincross assented. 'They're working mornings as well while cleaning staff is short. Shall I get them together?'

'In the foyer, if you don't mind . . . '

Morgan followed Lincross up the gangway with Allerton trailing behind him.

'Look here, Inspector,' Allerton said worriedly. 'I hope you're not getting ideas about me killing that man by firing something or other from behind the screen?'

'I'm paid to deal in facts,' Morgan answered. 'You've seen the facts up to now — same as I have. We'll let it go at that for now.'

Allerton maintained morose silence while he stood in the foyer and the usherettes were gathered together, wearing their dust-caps and overalls and looking subduedly excited.

'The Inspector has a few questions to ask,' Lincross explained. 'All he wants is the truth — and no exaggerations.'

Morgan cleared his throat vigorously. 'Girls, something went wrong with one of the speakers behind the screen last night. Is that right?'

'That's right,' volunteered Violet Thompson, who looked after the left block of

Stalls. 'Fred here came down and put it right.'

'You rang up and told him it was wrong, then?' Morgan asked sharply.

'No, I didn't.' Violet looked surprised. 'In fact I had hardly noticed that there was anything wrong, anyway . . . Did *you* ring, Sheila?'

Sheila Brant, guardian of the Stalls' right block, shook her head. 'No, I didn't. Fred came down and asked who *had* rung, though — then he dashed back stage. As he came back Vi and I heard him say something about 'that's fixed it!' '

Allerton looked at both girls blankly. 'One of you girls must have telephoned!' he insisted. 'I answered. Just who was it?'

There was a silence, both of surprise and dismay. Allerton clenched his fists and looked at Morgan quickly.

'Look here, Inspector, *somebody* rang!'

'So you say,' Morgan agreed. 'But I am sure these young ladies have no reason to lie. What about you, Miss Crane?'

'Oh, I'm nowhere near the phone,' Nancy said quickly. 'I'm upstairs, a good way from down here.'

'I never saw anyone go near the phone,' Violet Thompson said. 'And it was within my range of vision all the time.'

'Is the phone connected to anywhere else in the building?' Morgan questioned.

'No,' Allerton said. 'Straight line from Stalls to projection-room.'

Morgan frowned at the impasse, then asked: 'When did the sound trouble start?'

'I noticed it right at the beginning of the show,' Nancy Crane said. 'But I couldn't tell Fred because if I'd left my post I shouldn't have been there and Mr. Lincross would have wondered why I wasn't.'

'Mmmm . . . Could your two companions in the projection-room hear the voice on the phone, Mr. Allerton?' Morgan asked presently.

'Impossible. I was the only one who heard it — and I know it makes things tough on me.'

'We'll see — don't get excited,' Morgan smiled. 'Maybe we've advanced more than you realise . . . Well gentlemen — I'll be seeing you again. Goodbye for now.'

Morgan ambled out of the foyer through the open doorway to his car outside. Little flakes of snow showed up against the dark blue of his uniform as he went.

'I'm sure he thinks I did it!' Fred muttered.

'He'll have to prove it, though,' Lincross said, with unexpected consideration. 'Sorry I had to tell him so much, but after all I daren't repress anything. I'm the owner of this place, you know.'

Allerton said nothing more. He wondered why he did not run after Morgan and tell him to question Molly Ibbetson. She had been looking very puzzled. Yet what could there be in a staff room to produce such an emotion?

4

Maria Black was writing in her study half an hour before lunchtime when the house-phone rang. She picked it up, continuing to write steadily with her other hand.

'Miss Black, there's a Miss Nancy Crane to see you,' came the voice of Mason, the college porter. 'She won't tell me her business: she simply says it's urgent.'

Maria glanced through the window. Through a fine blur of snowflakes across the quadrangle she could see a girlish figure standing by the gates.

'Very well, Mason. Show her up to my study, will you?

Maria put her work on one side and settled back in her chair, conscious of satisfaction at the girl's advent: it meant, perhaps, that the Langhorn Cinema tragedy was not going to pass her by after all.

Nancy Crane was shown into the study, her pretty young face healthily coloured by icy wind. In her woollen pixie hood and neat belted overcoat she looked just what she was — a still very young woman venturing into hallowed precincts.

'Well, Nancy, this is a pleasant surprise!' Maria rose and grasped the girl's cold hand cordially. 'Sit down, do — and loosen your coat a little or you will not feel the benefit when you leave.'

'Th-thanks, Miss Black.' Nancy tried not to appear awed by Maria's commanding majesty. She pulled off her pixie hat and released her fluffy blonde hair.

'Now, what is the trouble?'

'I dashed up here on my way home to dinner,' Nancy explained, as Maria resumed her desk seat. 'I want your advice. I'm so afraid for Fred, you see. He has as good as got himself arrested for murder . . . '

'Oh, come now!' Maria protested. 'I hardly think the cinema murder is so simple that Inspector Morgan has solved it already. He hasn't actually arrested Fred — Mr. Allerton — yet, has he?'

'Actually no — but he's verging. Fred keeps on condemning himself without seeing that he is doing so.'

'Suppose,' Maria suggested, 'you start at the beginning? Be absolutely accurate and don't exaggerate. That is a common failing with young people . . . Now, fire away!'

Nancy did just that, talking in her roundabout fashion for several minutes. When she had finished she looked at Maria with a mixture of hope and fear.

'So, Nancy,' she said finally, 'somebody telephoned Mr. Allerton and only he seems to know about it?'

'Yes. I know it's just circumstantial evidence . . . But you should have seen the look on the Inspector's face! If ever a man said 'You did it!' without saying it, he did!'

'A trifle confused in expression but I gather your meaning,' Maria murmured.

'You see how it adds up — to Inspector Morgan, I mean,' Nancy went on. 'He finds nobody apparently telephoned Fred; he knows Fred talked to that man: and he may know a lot of other things, too. He was behind the screen this morning with Fred and Mr. Lincross. I'm getting worried. Do — do you think I did right by telling the Inspector why Fred spoke to that man last night?'

'It is always as well to tell the truth as far as the law is concerned, Nancy. Innocent people have nothing to fear: the law is too thorough to make many false convictions. I don't think Mr. Allerton will be arrested — not without very strong new evidence, anyway.'

'Miss Black, would you try to prove that Fred didn't have anything to do with this murder? He's liable to get himself in a hole through not realising how serious things are.'

'To ask me to prove that Mr. Allerton is innocent, my dear, is only half the problem. He may be guilty.'

'No!' Nancy's hand went to her lips in shocked surprise. 'He can't be!'

'So might you — or Mr. Lincross, or the doorman, or anybody on the staff,' Maria went on calmly. 'If I interest myself in this business, it will not be to prove that Mr. Allerton is innocent, but to endeavour to find out whom is guilty. I don't think I can do anything, though. I cannot upset the police, you know.'

'But you can work with them. You did when that girl got hanged in your college here.'

'Of course,' Maria admitted, 'I did have the advantage of being a witness of events in the auditorium. I have information too which might help the police . . . '

She paused and checked the time on her watch.

'Twelve-thirty, Nancy,' she proclaimed, rising. 'I must be on my way to lunch, and so must you . . . I'll have a word with Inspector Morgan and see how things are going. Just you carry on as though nothing had happened.'

'I feel loads better for hearing you say that, Miss Black!' Nancy's blue eyes were shining happily again as she bundled her soft hair into her pixie-hood. 'Now I must fly!'

Nancy shook hands and then hurried out of the study, belting her coat about her as she ran.

Maria smiled faintly as she watched the

girl go speeding across the white film covering the quadrangle.

'Our ambitious young friend, Fred Allerton, has a very fine wife in store for him,' she murmured. 'I sincerely hope her devotion is not misplaced . . . '

★ ★ ★

Eunice Tanby's nebulous fear of the night before that she might have to take over the duties of deputy-Headmistress merged into reality after lunch when Maria Black left Roseway and took the 'bus to Langhorn Square. From there she walked to the modest headquarters at the far end of High Street where Inspector Morgan held sway.

The Inspector did not look too surprised as Sergeant Claythorne showed Maria into the private office. He greeted her cordially enough and waited with a certain ominousness as Maria put her umbrella on one side and shook melted snow from her coat revers.

'Something on your mind, Miss Black?' he asked presently.

'I have always something on my mind, Inspector . . . ' Maria finished shaking her coat, then: 'Having a few moments to spare I thought I would see how things are progressing at the Langhorn Cinema.'

'I'm getting along all right,' Morgan said, moving the papers on his desk with a pretence of industry.

''All right' is meaningless, Inspector. Who was the dead man? Do you know?'

'Not yet.' Morgan was obviously annoyed. 'Beyond being registered at the 'Golden Saddle' as Douglas Farrington, I've failed to find out a single thing about him. He had no wallet on his person, nothing that might act as a clue. It is just as though he thoroughly destroyed every trace of his identity before meeting his death.'

'Hmmm . . . ' Maria compressed her lips. 'Most inconsiderate of him.'

'I suppose,' Morgan hesitated, 'that I may ask your reason for being here? Apart from asking how things are progressing, I mean. You're not implicated in this business at all, you know.'

'I'll tell you exactly why I am here,

Inspector — because I am interested in the welfare of two very deserving young people. Nancy Crane, the supervising usherette at the Langhorn; and Frederick Allerton, the chief projectionist. They are engaged to be married, and I would not like to see the nuptials upset.'

'Who is likely to upset them?' Morgan asked heavily.

'I'm afraid you are, unless we can get some straight lead on this business.' Maria gave a sigh. 'Nancy Crane came to see me this morning, and — '

'Confound the girl! I had an idea she might do that.'

'Do you object?'

'Not exactly, but I like to do things in my own way.'

'I can quite understand that.' Maria gripped her umbrella handle firmly. 'Naturally I shall not try to impede you. But to interpret the law literally, Inspector, nothing can stop me working beside you. I can only be called to account if I obstruct the course of justice and of course I shan't . . . Now, with that little detail out of the way suppose we get down to business? For instance, have you had a report yet from Dr. Roberts?'

With the resigned expression of a man bowing to Fate, Morgan fished amidst the papers on his desk and produced a typewritten memorandum.

'This is the report,' he said. 'The man in A-11 died as the result of a copper slug fired through the front of his skull into the brain. It seems that the slug made a cleanly drilled hole in the front of his skull and was not deflected in its course. It was removed from the brain by dissection and then sent to ballistics for analysis . . . I'll read their findings in a moment.'

'Hmmm . . . Most intriguing.'

Morgan put the report down and took on an air of confident authority. 'You see, Miss Black, a projectile usually takes a straight course between entrance and exit wound, and it is this fact which gives the line of fire. Though the slug was stopped by brain tissue before passing right through the head there was enough of its track visible to make an estimate of direction possible. From the photographs of the dead man's position it appears that he was shot from a point near the cinema screen — probably from a point behind it.'

'Shot with what?' Maria questioned.

'Maybe a rifle — An air rifle perhaps. Some makes are very powerful. I've checked the distance from the screen to seat A-11 and it is forty-seven feet. A powerful air rifle might fire a slug that distance.'

'You mentioned a ballistics report on the slug; I would be glad to hear it.'

Morgan picked up the relevant sheet. 'It's interesting — and a bit unusual,' he said. 'The slug is not the conventional waisted type but apparently home-made. It bears marks of rifle-lands where it left the gun muzzle, but being copper — which is pretty malleable — they obviously impressed themselves in the metal when it was fired. Nothing else peculiar about the slug; no possible way of identifying the rifle from which it was fired. There is the point, though, that the slug is made of pure copper without a single adulterating alloy. Spectroscopic analysis has shown that. Pure copper is unusual in a slug. One usually finds a compensating element such as cupro-nickel. But here we have a home-made slug of pure copper.'

'Very interesting.' Maria leaned back in her chair. 'So our slug was fired from the direction of the screen, was it?'

'I've pretty well proved that,' Morgan answered, complacently. 'This morning I found a quarter inch hole in the screen, with the edges of the hole forced outwards towards the audience. In other words, just the kind of hole one would expect to find if a slug had been fired from back-screen. Naturally the hole would be somewhat larger than the slug.'

'You have included the sudden resistance to the slug's propulsion by it hitting the screen?' Maria questioned.

'Well . . . yes.' Morgan did not sound as though he had. Quickly he steered the conversation and went into all the details of his cinema discoveries. Maria listened attentively, her forehead puckered, then when she had all the facts she regarded the desk in front of her.

'You are assuming then that against the light — having only dim reflected light from the screen, which illumination would rapidly decrease with the square of the distance, of course — our unknown killer fired an air rifle over forty-seven feet of distance right in the dead centre of a man's skull?'

'That,' Morgan said guardedly, 'is how it looks — at present.'

'Then I trust it will undergo revision, for it strikes me as frankly impossible, especially with the initial check to the slug when it struck the rubber of the screen . . . However, I am glad to know what you did back-screen. Nancy Crane told me you had been behind there.'

'That girl is too inquisitive!' Morgan decided. 'Incidentally, I'm still worried over another point. Can you conceive of a man getting a slug in his skull and yet not jumping sufficiently to attract the attention of those seated next to him? Lincross asked me that this morning, and because it caught me off guard I sidetracked him.'

'The man *would* jump,' Maria said. 'He would jump from violent reflex action if nothing else — but to me it is perfectly clear why he did not attract attention. You see, Inspector, everybody else jumped too — at that identical moment! Myself included.'

'I don't quite follow.'

'From which I gather that you haven't taken my advice and had the picture run through again. Had you done so you would have found that at one point three revolver shots are fired after a long period of relative quiet. Since the picture was boring many people were half asleep. At the revolver shots the sound was raised several degrees and the sudden reports from the screen made many people jump. I assume that our friend in A-11 got the slug at that moment. Those beside him might quite easily have thought that he jumped at the revolver shots.'

'Now I get it!' Morgan breathed.

'I'm glad,' Maria conceded dryly. 'The shot was not fired at any other time in the evening or it would have been heard: it was timed exactly with the screen shots which came in rapid succession. I suggest that the timing was with the *second* shot.

It would allow the killer to know the moment had arrived to fire his own weapon — the firing of the first shot being his signal — and also since the shots followed rapidly on top of each other he would be safe enough to cause his victim to jump on shot two as he would on shot one. Nobody, in that brief confusion, would notice the split timing . . . Had he fired simultaneously on the third shot it might have been too late.'

'Yes, indeed!' Morgan said, nodding.

'Now,' Maria proceeded, 'a film takes an exact time to run through a projector — though I understand that certain houses have a variable control. I hardly think there will be one in a small country cinema like the Langhorn. The point is this: the normal speed of a film is ninety feet a minute. So by running it through again and comparing times we can get the exact minute the shot was fired. Our task then is to find out where everybody was at that time. By 'everybody' I mean the staff of the cinema. The audience hardly enters into it — unless some extraordinary new evidence comes along.'

'We'll do just that,' Morgan agreed, grateful for this blast of fresh air down the more fog-ridden corridors of his brain. 'Then I — '

'And at the same time,' Maria went on slowly, 'we might be able to judge what there is about this picture which so enthralled our friend . . . Incidentally have you a good photograph of him?'

'Surely.' Puzzled, Morgan handed across a double photographic print — one profile and one full face — of the dead man as the photographer had taken it the previous night. Maria studied it intently for a moment or two and then she gave a nod.

'I think it might be as well, Inspector, to bring this along when we run the film. Just a guess on my part but it may be justified. And now . . . ' Maria got to her feet decisively and buttoned up her coat collar. 'I think we should go along and see if Mr. Lincross can arrange a private show for us.'

Morgan got up from his chair. 'Why does it have to be run at the Langhorn Cinema?'

'Naturally it could be run at a private

projection theatre, but there might be slight differences in timing due to mechanical aberrations. I insist that to establish the exact time the film should be run in the self-same theatre under the self-same conditions. Besides, seated in the front row of the Circle we might get new ideas on the problem.'

5

The matinée was in progress at the Langhorn Cinema when Morgan drew his car up outside the entranceway. At the top of the four pseudo-marble steps Bradshaw stood muffled in his bottle-green greatcoat, peering through the snowflakes. A faint surprise registered on his beefy red face as Maria and Morgan emerged from the car and came up the steps towards him.

'’Afternoon, Miss Black — Inspector. Turned out bad like.'

'Very,' Morgan agreed shortly. 'Mr. Lincross in?'

'Aye — in his office.'

Bradshaw pushed open the swing doors and Maria led the way into the cosy foyer. From her position behind the ordinary pay-box grille Mary Ibbetson watched the proceedings with lambent dark eyes. Things had never been so interesting since she had taken over the job of cashier.

Lincross was not surprised to see the Inspector, but his eyes widened at the vision of Maria, ample and commanding, shaking her coat lapels impatiently, She took the chair he proffered and sat down beside the desk. On top of it an electric fan was whirling gently. The draught was welcome. The little room was intolerably stuffy.

Morgan elected to stand by the big sash window of frosted glass. 'I've decided to have that film 'Love on the Highway' run through again,' he said, answering Lincross's inquiring look. 'I'll have to leave to you the details of getting it back.'

'It won't be easy to get 'Love on the Highway' back, Inspector,' he said.

'Why not?'

'Shortage of copies. It was picked up last night by the film transport, of course, and was taken back to the London renters. It would then be sent out — probably this morning — to whoever has booked the film after us. There are probably no more than half a dozen copies in these days of raw stock shortage and all of them will be scattered across the country. So, with no spare copy and with other copies in use at various cinemas I don't see how . . . '

'In circumstances like these the law can demand the film,' Morgan pointed out. 'And, sir, it is going to! I don't want *any* copy, either: I want the self-same copy. Maybe you'd ring up the renters and see what you can do?'

Lincross shrugged and turned to the telephone. In a few minutes he was speaking to London. Maria and Morgan listened to the one-sided conversation and gathered from it that while the self-same copy was still available it was transport that presented the problem.

'I'll call you back,' Lincross said finally. 'Well, Inspector, there it is. They can't spare a special transport to get the film here, and the railway is uncertain to a quiet spot like this — especially so if this snow gets very thick.'

Morgan scowled. 'I suppose I could go and get it myself, but it would take up a lot of my time — '

'I think,' Maria interrupted him, 'I have

a suggestion! I have a friend staying in London at the moment — a Mr. Martin. He would bring it if I were to ask him.'

'You mean that American roughneck who helps you now and again?' Morgan asked doubtfully.

'The same,' Maria agreed, unabashed. She snapped open her handbag, took out a notebook and ran her fingers down a list of addresses. 'Yes, I was right. His last address *is* in London. And I can reach him on the telephone — If you would allow me, Mr. Lincross?'

Presently she had the number she wanted and a Cockney voice answered her. There was another brief pause then the voice was replaced by pronounced American.

'Yeah? Who wants what?'

'Mr. Martin? This is Black Maria speaking.'

Morgan glanced at Lincross and the manager shrugged helplessly.

'Maria, huh? Well, this is sure one prize smack across the kisser! Hiya, Maria! You started playin' games again?'

'I never play games, Mr. Martin,

though there are times when I apply my modest powers to a crime problem. Are you at liberty to lend a little hand?'

'Sure I am — right on the button. Lucky you got me squattin' down in this joint 'cos I might ha' been with the boys, else at Boiler-house Bessie's. Well, what's the dope?'

'I want you to call at the Sunrise Film Corporation in Back Wardour Street and go to the dispatch department. You will make yourself known as Mr. Martin — I'll arrange the details — and you will bring away a film transit case containing a picture called 'Love on the Highway'. Have you got that?'

'You betcha. Then what?'

'You will take the train from London to Langhorn here — you know the way from your last visit — and will deliver the film at the Langhorn Cinema in the High Street. Then you will telephone me from this cinema to the college to say that you have arrived. I in turn will advise the police.'

'Okay. Look, Maria, you workin' on

that cinema bumpin' off? I read something in the morning paper about the police wantin' any relations of the dead man to show their pusses. Don't the flatfoots know who he is?'

'I will go into that when I see you, Mr. Martin,' Maria answered. 'Tell me, how are you fixed for money? Should I wire some to you?'

'No need! A guy like me ain't without a spot o' nickel in his pocket . . . I'll be seein' you, with 'Love on the Highway' — else I'll bust me belt.'

'Hmm! I trust no such embarrassment will occur. Thank you again, Mr. Martin, and goodbye.' Maria rang off.

'Can we trust him?' Morgan asked dubiously.

'Implicitly, Inspector. Flamboyant, even vulgar, but a man of sterling worth.'

'Unorthodox, anyway,' Lincross commented, taking the chair Maria vacated and reaching for the phone. 'I'd better tell the renters they'll have a visitor.'

After making matters clear to them, he hung up and glanced at Morgan. 'Anything else, Inspector?'

'Yes, I'd like another word with your chief projectionist.'

Lincross got up and left the office. Through the open doorway Morgan and Maria watched him enter the Stalls' entrance, presumably on his way to the service-telephone. Then the doors swung shut behind him.

On the desk top the fan whirred monotonously, rustling its paper streamers and setting the electric light swinging gently on its flex. Though it was only mid-afternoon the snowy December day was rapidly closing in.

After a while Lincross reappeared and resumed his seat at the desk. Only a moment after him Fred Allerton came in.

'Something wrong, sir?' His voice was more or less steady — until he caught sight of Maria and Inspector Morgan.

'Only a question, Mr. Allerton,' Morgan said. 'I believe that during the run of the film 'Love on the Highway' you put up the sound of the revolver shots. Why was that?'

'Simply a matter of editing,' Allerton shrugged, his hand on the doorknob as though poised for quick departure. 'It is left to the chief projectionist's discretion to edit a film if he wishes. If he thinks he can get a better result by raising or lowering sound during certain sequences in the picture, he does just that. I always put the sound up two or three faders during songs, exclamations of amazement, revolver shots, slaps in the face, and, so on. It heightens the realism. Anyway, this film was pretty dull until the revolver shots, so I thought I'd awaken anybody who might be dozing.'

Allerton's weak smile faded away as Morgan remained coldly unresponsive. Then Lincross cleared his throat.

'Fred is quite right, Inspector, This 'editing' business is done all the time in most cinemas.'

'I see . . . I was just thinking that in this case it was most convenient . . . Did you do this editing yourself, Mr. Allerton?'

'No — I was back-stage repairing that faulty speaker. I left instructions with my second, Dick Alcot, to step the sound up on the revolver shots.'

A faint gleam came and went in

Morgan's eyes; 'All right, Mr. Allerton — thanks. That's all I wanted to know.'

Allerton seemed as though he were about to say something more — then evidently reconsidering he gave a nod and went out, closing the door behind him.

'I suppose,' Lincross said, 'that you are thinking that the stepped-up revolver shots in the film synchronised with the actual shooting of the weapon which killed the man in A-11?'

'I am,' Morgan agreed; 'but that doesn't *prove* anything even though it is significant. One of the biggest stumbling blocks is to decide where went the rifle that fired the slug. You can't put a weapon that size in your pocket . . . I've a few other details to attend to so I'll leave you for now, sir, and see you again when this American fellow brings the film.'

'You wish him to phone you when he gets here, Miss Black?' Lincross asked.

'I think it would be best — if the Inspector is agreeable? I am afraid Mr. Martin will not — er — have any 'truck with a flatfoot', as he puts it.'

'All right,' Morgan growled. 'It's as

broad as long, anyway. 'Afternoon, Mr. Lincross.'

As they left the cinema Maria and Morgan found that the snow was fast transforming the High Street and pavement into a deepening valley of cotton wool. It came down in silent, scurrying whirlpools as they climbed into the car.

'I'll run on to Roseway,' he said briefly. 'Too bad for walking . . . '

'Most generous of you, Inspector.'

In about ten minutes Morgan drew up outside the college gates. 'You'll come to the midnight matinée, of course?' he asked, as Maria climbed out.

'Naturally, Inspector. And you will bring that double photograph?'

He patted his breast pocket reassuringly.

'One last thought, Inspector . . . ' Maria peered in at him with snowflakes clinging to her hair and nose. 'What *was* Allerton's motive? Is there any man alive who would kill a man because of his fear of the police over such a trifle as an unlighted bicycle lamp? And, secondly, since the incident only happened on the same night whence came the rifle so conveniently?'

The car door closed sharply and Morgan was left watching that heavy figure in the camelhair coat moving through the drifts in the school gateway . . .

Maria discovered that it was twenty to four when she re-entered the warmth of her study, and upon the blotting pad were various papers awaiting her attention. She put the electric kettle on to boil and then settled herself to deal with essentials before freeing her mind for exploration of the problem absorbing her.

At four-thirty she relaxed and pushed the finished reports on one side, and brought out her black book and began writing:-

Glad to say that I am involved in the puzzling Langhorn Cinema murder case. The identity of the dead man is still not known, but I derive interest from the fact that he had apparently destroyed every scrap of evidence about himself. Why?

Had he expected to be murdered he would have left clues as to his identity in order to bring his killer to justice. True, he is registered in the name of Douglas Farrington but because of the lack of any clue regarding his occupation or intentions, it seems possible the name is purely fictitious.

Fred Allerton, the chief projectionist, is much involved in this. But there are certain irreconcilable facts ... If he only met the man yesterday evening (the evening of the murder) through the medium of a bicycle mishap — which I saw myself from a distance — how was Allerton able to provide the necessary reason for attending to a hall speaker? How did he get an air rifle so conveniently? How would he get one into the building without being seen? Had he hidden it down the leg of his trousers, then he could not have cycled.

Since he was on his way to work when he collided with the stranger he had no chance whatever to decide on a sudden scheme of murder. And the motive of his fear of losing his job through police proceedings — since I understand the manager dismisses anybody who becomes involved with the law — is decidedly weak.

I incline to the belief that Allerton is the victim of circumstances, unless possibly he was acquainted with the stranger before last night's mishap and actually had had time to plan everything. However, in the words of Sherlock Holmes — 'it is dangerous to state the facts of an accusation before one has all the data.'

Nor is Allerton the only one under suspicion. I also have my eye on Gerald Lincross, the manager-owner; Bradshaw, the doorman . . . Yes, even Nancy Crane, the supervising usherette. A girl who is outwardly somewhat scatterbrained and extremely pretty, and yet evidently has enough intelligence to direct the other usherettes in their duties. This girl is something of an anomaly. On the other hand I may be doing her a grave injustice . . .

Shall determine matters more clearly

when 'Love on the Highway' is run privately late this evening . . .

The time is 5.02 p.m.

* * *

Towards six o'clock the snow ceased, but it had left a white blanket over Langhorn to a depth of two inches. The broad-shouldered man in the hideous check overcoat and green pork-pie hat blew out his cheeks expressively as he descended from the London train on to Langhorn Station platform.

He carried a big square steel transit case on his shoulder. His solitary travelling companion handed out a suitcase — then placing his yellow brogued feet carefully in the snow he padded towards the station exit.

'Say, feller, where's a good place for a guy to park himself round here?'

The ticket collector looked up at the red face and inquiring blue eyes. 'Matter o' fact, I'm a bit windy of telling you. A man asked me that last Monday and then I find in the papers that he got murdered.

Same fellow: I recognised the description. It sorts of makes one — uneasy.'

'I don't kill quick,' Pulp Martin grinned. 'Tell me.'

'Best place is the 'Golden Saddle'. But I'm not taking any responsibility for saying it . . . Straight up High Street, left-hand side, nearly opposite Lang'orn Cinema.'

'A natural!' Pulp murmured under his breath. 'Right opposite the old murder joint. Okay, pal — thanks a lot.'

With the freshly fallen snow the town looked even more back-to-front than normally, the only lights coming from the scarce street lamps, the 'Golden Saddles'' entranceway, and the bulbs under the canopy of the Langhorn Cinema.

Pulp crunched through the snow past the closed shops, glanced momentarily into dark windows and saw confectionery offerings in the streetlamp glow — went past an ironmonger's, a second-hand stores, a dry cleaner's, and a newsagents. Then he came to the synthetic steps of the cinema and mounted them to find the doors locked. Putting down the transit case he thumped the glass.

'What's the idea?' demanded a girl's voice.

Pulp turned and saw that what seemed to be a bellying pillar at the side of the steps had opened into a lighted rectangle. A ginger-haired girl was looking out at him, her sharply intelligent face lined by a golden grille.

Pulp came back down the steps, stooped and grinned at her. 'So *you're* the bird in the gilded cage! Hiya, sugar!'

'What — do you want?' Mary Saunders asked deliberately.

'I'm looking for a big shot named Lincross. I've got a film here making a dent in my shoulder. Open up the joint . . . '

'Oh, you'll be Mr. Martin! Mr. Lincross said you might arrive while everybody was at tea — except me. That's why he had the canopy lights left on to guide you. I'll let you in.' Mary slammed the shield back over the pay-box window.

Pulp waited, the case back on his shoulder, and presently Mary's slender figure appeared through the glass. She snapped back bolts and stood aside as Pulp came in, towering head and shoulders above her in his revolting overcoat, dropping little hummocks of snow from his shoes.

'Where do I dump this darned case?' he demanded.

Mary looked about her and finally pointed to an alcove. 'Drop it there. I'll tell the manager when he comes back.'

'Okay.' Pulp lowered the case. Then he pushed up his hat on his carroty hair. 'Where do I grab a phone, sister? I've Black Maria to contact.'

Mary looked up at him blankly. 'Who?'

'Black Maria, the detective, who runs Roseway College for Nice Pieces.'

'Good Lord! Miss Black — ! I see. You can phone from my pay box there.'

Pulp nodded and squeezed into the little area with some difficulty.

'Maria?' he asked finally. 'Yeah — this is Pulp . . . I got it here, just like you said. What . . . ? Tell Lincross to phone you when you can start the show? Oke! Me — ? I'll park myself at the 'Golden Saddle' across the road . . . Huh?'

Mary observed Pulp leaning forward attentively.

'Yeah, I'll try, Maria. So the guy stopped there, did he? Ticket collector told me that too — an' I read it in the noospaper . . . Find out about him? Okay. You'll ring me when to join you here? Oke! Be seein' you.'

Pulp rang off and wriggled himself to his feet. 'That's that, Sugar. When this guy Lincross blows in tell him to phone Maria and say when he can fix a show for that film I've dumped. Get it? I'm goin' over to that joint across the road.'

'I'll tell him,' Mary promised.

Pulp nodded, his bright blue eyes going up and down the girl's attractive lines.

'You an' me should have rung doorbells long ago,' he said ambiguously, then he turned and went out. In three minutes he was ringing for attention at the reception desk of the 'Golden Saddle', his travelling-case beside him.

An immense woman in black silk appeared presently.

'Can a guy park here, lady?' Pulp asked her briefly.

'Do you mean a car, sir — or yourself?' Mrs. Janet Ainsworth was accustomed to peculiar visitors.

'Meself. I want to grab a site to lie on for a few nights. What've you got?'

'I have only one room, sir, I'm afraid. Vacated rather tragically, I'm sorry to say.'

Pulp grinned. 'You mean that the guy who had it got bumped off in the movie house across the street, huh? That don't worry me: I'll take it.'

While he congratulated himself on his stroke of luck he signed his name in the register — then he looked at the name above with the same room number. A red ink line was through it.

'Douglas Farrington, eh? That the guy?'

'Yes, Mr. — er — Martin.' Mrs. Ainsworth peered sideways at the register. 'The room is quite at liberty now, though. Here is the key. The police have removed all Mr. Farrington's belongings . . . I wouldn't have mentioned it at all, you know, only you seem to know all about it.'

'You betcha,' Pulp assented, and gave nothing away. 'When do we eat?'

'Dinner will be at seven, in the dining-room across there,' Mrs. Ainsworth nodded to mahogany doors. 'You'll just have time.'

'Look, lady . . . ' Pulp turned back to the desk confidentially. 'What sort of a guy was this Douglas Farrington? I've only read the papers and they don't tell much. I'm sort of interested, on account of havin' the same room.'

'I knew very little about him. He went out a great deal. In fact I believe he only asked two questions while he stayed here. One was to inquire the whereabouts of Millington Terrace — which is about half-a-mile from here — and the other was the whereabouts of Greystone Avenue. That's about ten minutes' walk away.'

'Heck!' Pulp picked up his travelling case. 'Maybe he was going to print a street guide . . . Okay, lady, I'll be seeing you around . . . '

★ ★ ★

At ten-thirty that same evening Inspector Morgan called for Maria in his car and drove to the Langhorn Cinema through powdery frozen snow. Entering the foyer together, they found Lincross lounging by the ordinary pay-box and Pulp Martin smoking an atrociously strong cigarette, prowling up and down in his outsize overcoat.

'Hiya, Maria!' he greeted her, as she came through the doorway. 'How's tricks?'

'Splendid, Mr. Martin, thank you. I see you have already made yourself known to Mr. Lincross — This is Inspector Morgan of the Langhorn Police Force. Inspector, my assistant — Mr. Martin.'

'I don't reckon to have no deals with the dicks,' Pulp said dubiously, shaking hands nevertheless. 'But since Maria thinks you're on the level it's okay by me.'

'Thanks . . . ' Morgan gave a grave smile. 'Your choice in assistants surprises me, Miss Black,' he murmured.

'Then it needn't!' Pulp declared flatly. 'Maria and me met up in New York together, see — when she figured out a murder — an' we've sort of stayed together on problems ever since. I helped her figger that mystery when that dame got bumped off in her school. An' I'll help her again, see!'

Maria gave a little cough and loosened her heavy coat. 'Now, about this film — '

'There it is, Miss Black,' Lincross pointed to it. 'I'm having Fred Allerton and Dick Alcot come back after they have had some supper to run it for you. They'll be here shortly.'

'Splendid! Then, we can adjourn to the Circle and take our seats in readiness. And incidentally, Mr. Martin, do not forget to remind me about your expenses . . . '

Lincross led the way up the Circle staircase. 'I take it,' he turned to Maria as they came to the summit of the stairs, 'that you wish to occupy the same seat as our — unfortunate patron?'

'That is our intention, Inspector, is it not?'

'Be as well,' Morgan agreed heavily, as though he were anxious to avoid argument.

So they filed into Row A, Maria herself taking the fatal seat. There was a warm tobacco-laden haze brooding in the hall, a mephitic hangover from the evening performance. The place had a drab, uninteresting appearance with all the main ceiling lights off and only a single three-hundred-watt bulb giving illumination. Down below the red safety lights were out too.

Maria's eyes moved gradually to the ornate ventilator spanning the width of the ceiling over her head. Pulp, seated next to her, craned his head back and gazed also.

'Figgering somethin'?' he murmured.

'Yes.' Maria kept her voice low. 'I was just thinking how much easier it would be to kill a man by firing from above, through that grating, than it would be to hit him from the screen.'

'You mean to say a guy shot from as far away as the screen and hit the guy in A-11 here? Just like that?'

'It sounds impossible, Mr. Martin, but that is the position as it appears at the moment. But had anybody shot from above the slug would have entered the top of the man's skull and not his forehead. However, I am bearing in mind possible amendments to the obvious. As Smith and Glaister remark in their *Recent Advances in Forensic Medicine* — 'there are a considerable number of variables to be taken into consideration when dealing with wounds caused by projectiles'.'

'Yeah, I reckon that's right. But don't the sawbones who examined the body know the difference in speed between a slug from that screen and one from above?'

'Assuredly — and that is where the 'variables' come into it. A slug, or any projectile, can be misleading when it is impeded in its path upon entering the body — as it was here by the skull-bone. Sometimes it is not easy to compute distance from velocity. Anyhow, we'll deal with that later. Tell me, you are fixed up satisfactorily at the 'Golden Saddle'?'

'In the dead guy's very room.'

'Excellent! And have you found anything?'

Pulp shrugged. 'Not yet — but I haven't given it the real cold prowl yet. I will later.' Pulp crushed out his strong-smelling cigarette in the ashtray in front of him. Then there were sounds at the top of the Circle steps and Fred Allerton came hurrying down them.

'We'll be starting in five minutes, sir,' he said to Lincross. 'We're spooling the film up now.'

'Right,' Lincross assented.

'And remember,' Morgan added, 'to start on the exact minute to help timing. Put your sound up on the revolver shots . . . Do everything just as you did it last night.'

As Allerton hurried away again, Maria found Pulp whispering in her right ear. 'Of course, there's one thing I found out, only I don't see that it matters much.' He tugged out a notebook and consulted it. 'The dame who runs that hotel said that A-11 had asked two questions while he was there — the quickest way to get to Millington Terrace and Greystone Avenue.'

Maria frowned. 'That is most interesting even though it does not present any profound significance at the moment — '

The light went off suddenly, uncontrolled by the usual slow dimming resistance. There came the soft whine of the electric motor drawing back the curtains in front of the screen, then 'Love on the Highway' boomed forth.

Pulp Martin glanced down at his luminous wristwatch: it read exactly ten to eleven.

Gradually, the story struggled to unfold itself. Apparently it was the history of a local girl making good, Betty Joyce as the local girl essaying a gallant effort with impossible material. In fact she did her best to make good for exactly thirty-five minutes of the film's running time — then in came the glamorous, streamlined Lydia Fane, amazingly blonde, as the unwelcome lady in the case. At exactly eleven-thirty she shot the hero — with three shots that rang sharply through the theatre as the sound was raised on the projection-room fader.

'So,' Maria said from the gloom, 'the man in this seat was shot at exactly eight twenty-five, since — '

'No,' Lincross interrupted. 'You are forgetting that we ran the news and trailers first. They took up twelve minutes.'

133

'Of course!' Maria sounded quite annoyed with herself.

'Then he was shot at eight thirty-seven,' Morgan said deliberately. 'That's all we need to know. We don't have to suffer this ham acting any more, do we?'

'I think we should . . . ' Maria was watching the picture intently as a close-up of Lydia Fane came into view. 'At least until Lydia has finished her little performance. She does not appear again after concluding this scene.'

'For a star,' Morgan commented, 'it is a pretty meagre part. I'll stake my boots that Lydia Fane was billed outside as the star — and inside, too, for that matter.'

'Quite correct, Inspector,' Lincross agreed. 'Due to a mix-up in publicity I got her name as top star instead of Betty Joyce. It does happen sometimes. As a matter of fact this film was sent in a hurry, anyway, so it's no wonder something went wrong.'

The scene faded out and opened into a dance-hall shot. Maria stirred: 'If you have had enough, Inspector — ?'

'I had enough long ago! Have them

finish it, Mr. Lincross.'

Lincross ascended the Circle steps. In a few moments the film suddenly stopped and a solitary light blazed back into being in the ceiling. The curtains returned to their position across the screen.

'Well, we have at least established the time,' Morgan said. 'But precious little else!'

'But we did!' Maria protested. 'Did you not notice something interesting about Lydia Fane?' She got to her feet as Lincross came down the steps again.

'Mr. Lincross, do you happen to have any publicity stills from this film?'

'Sorry, no,' he apologised. 'I returned them this morning — as I always do after a film has finished its run.'

'Then we must examine the film itself — that close-up of Lydia Fane in particular. You see, Inspector, I have now seen this picture twice, and so I have perhaps noted more about it. I think there is a distinct resemblance in the girl's features to those of the man who died . . . You have the photographs of the man with you?'

'So that's what you wanted them for!'

'Correct. I recalled a similarity of features. And there is something about the right ear . . . '

'I'll show you to the winding-room,' Lincross offered, and led the way up the projection-room stairs to where Dick Alcot was just about to run the picture's most recent reel on to the stripping plate.

'A moment!' Morgan restrained him. 'Is this the reel we told you to stop showing? The last one?'

'It is,' Alcot said evenly, and stood aside.

Morgan took the slack up between the wound and unwound portions and held it to the light. Gradually he began to wind until he came to the close-up frames of Lydia Fane. Maria watched him keenly, then searched in her handbag for a strong lens. In silence Lincross and Pulp Martin looked on, then in a few moments Fred Allerton came down from the projection-room and joined the party. His features seemed to tense a little as he saw the examination in progress.

'Here!' Morgan exclaimed suddenly.

'Here's a shot showing her right ear and part of her face . . . '

He felt in his pocket hurriedly and brought out the dual print of the dead man, one of the photographs taken from almost the same angle . . . Maria screwed a watchmaker's lens into her eye and looked at the film.

Slowly she and Morgan looked first at the film, then at the print, until gradually it became forced on them that there were remarkably similar features in both faces. The noses had the same unusual length and high bridge, the lips the same strength of purpose.

'You notice the right ear, Inspector?' Maria breathed. 'The long, narrow lobe and very clear sulcus curve?'

'Right enough.' Morgan lowered the film back to the bench. 'It does look as though this girl is some relation of the dead man's.'

'Of course,' Maria observed, 'no two people in the world, not even twins, have identical ears, any more than fingerprints — but certain oddities do reproduce themselves now and again, usually in similar noses, colour of eyes, or similar ears. Here the ear and nose in each case might even belong to the same person, making allowance for smaller size on the part of the woman.'

'Which proves what?' asked Lincross.

'According to Mendel, the biologist,' Maria said, 'the characteristics of a father are more often handed down to a daughter than to a son — and, conversely, the same with mother and male offspring. From this I infer that Lydia Fane is the daughter of the man in A-11.'

'It would explain, the guy's anxiety to see the picture, anyway,' Pulp Martin decided. 'Can't think of any other. As a work of art it stank.'

'And since we have no proof that Douglas Farrington was the dead man's right name — and 'Lydia Fane' is probably a stage name anyway — we've no clue that way,' Morgan remarked. 'I'll get in touch with the Sunrise Film Corporation and see what can be found out about this girl. A few words with her should give us a short cut to the killer, eh, Mr. Lincross?'

'Yes . . . indeed.' He started from a preoccupation. 'I was just thinking — what about the weapon which killed the man? Or aren't you interested in finding it, Inspector?'

'One thing at a time, sir. I'm moving as fast as I can. If there is a weapon it will be found. And so will the motive.'

'You know the motive, Inspector!' Fred Allerton burst out fiercely. 'Because I was afraid of that man talking to the police and causing me to lose my job! That's what you're thinking, isn't it?'

6

Despite the lateness of the hour when she returned to Roseway under its coating of frozen snow, Maria took time to bring her notes up to date — then she retired to bed feeling well pleased with herself.

The following morning she was in the midst of her normal college duties when to her surprise the Inspector himself arrived in his car, driving into the white quadrangle. In a moment or two he was entering the cosy study.

''Morning, Miss Black . . . ' He seated himself as she returned his greeting and nodded to a chair. 'I'm on my way to the cinema again to make a thorough examination of the place for signs of the weapon, and to check everybody's position at eight thirty-seven last Wednesday evening. Care to come along?'

Maria contemplated the notes on her desk, then she nodded her severe bun of hair.

'Yes, I think I can spare an hour, Inspector . . . But tell me, what of Lydia Fane? I thought — '

'That's in hand. I got into touch with the Sunrise this morning and it seems that Lydia Fane is at present in a cabaret show in London. It seems her real profession is that of a nightclub dancer — with acting as a sideline. I'll probably slip down to London this evening and have a word with her. She is to be found at the Blue Crystal Night Club in Regency Street.'

'Hmmm, I see. Well, the less delay the better, Inspector. Now, if you'll excuse me, I will just inform my Housemistress that I am going out.'

Miss Tanby was duly advised; then in fifteen minutes Maria and he were again in the now quite familiar foyer of the Langhorn Cinema, picking their way over the newly washed rubberoid squares towards Lincross's office.

Just outside the office door Bradshaw was busily folding up old streamer advertisements while Nancy Crane was dusting the rail of the Circle staircase.

She turned and came down as she saw Maria and the Inspector.

'Hello, Miss Black! Back again to look about you, eh?'

Maria did not reply. She was frowning at the streamer bills that Bradshaw was folding . . . Lydia Fane in 'Love on the Highway'. Lydia Fane in . . . Something! Something there sticking in the mind, but it insisted on remaining obdurate . . . Then the posters were rolled up in a bundle as Bradshaw picked them up to carry them out to the boiler room for use in the central-heating plant.

'Hello!' Nancy repeated timidly, as she stood waiting in her green overall and red bandeau.

'Oh, Nancy — How are you?' Maria's beaming smile restored the situation for the girl. 'Is Mr. Lincross about?'

'I'm afraid he isn't. But if you want him especially, I'll nip across to his house in Greystone Avenue for you.'

'Greystone Avenue?' Maria reflected.

'He lives there — number nine,' Morgan said. 'I've got his address down of course.'

'Yes, but — Mr. Martin said . . . '
Maria shrugged. 'Never mind. I don't think we really need him, do we, Inspector?'

'I shall when I want to search the place. Until he comes I can get my questioning done — '

Morgan paused as Pulp Martin came in through the swing doors. He raised a hand in greeting. This time he was without hat or overcoat, dressed in a suit of startling mustard shade.

'Hiya, Maria! You too, flatfoot. I saw you come in here from my hotel window so thought I'd be in on it. What's cookin' — ?'

Molly Ibbetson came out of the ordinary pay box, backwards and bent double as she ducked her head under the grille counter. Pulp contemplated the view with satisfaction, then he grinned as the girl straightened up.

'Hiya, Toots,' he greeted cheerfully. 'Feel like makin' a date sometime?'

Molly looked at the six-foot-two of mustard suit and shook her amazing waves and curls. They were so expressive she had no need to add 'no'.

'Oh, young lady . . . ' Morgan glanced at her as she minced across the foyer with a duster in her hand. 'I'd like a word with you.'

Molly stopped and waited, standing with her feet bowed inwards as though her shoes hurt.

'Can you tell me where you were at eight thirty-seven on Wednesday night?'

Molly turned her dark eyes upwards and thought. She was obviously a girl who lived from day-to-day and any uncommon strain on her memory upset her considerably. But at length her plump, pale face took on a glow.

'Yes, I remember! I was rubbing my chilblains!'

Morgan's huge eyebrows went up to the limit. 'You were — what?' he asked deliberately.

'Rubbing the chilblains on the sides of my feet,' Molly explained blandly. 'I get them awfully in this weather, standing there in that box with the draught blowing round my legs. I'd checked over the cash and was sitting on my stool with

144

my shoes off, rubbing my chilblains. I decided to get my other pair of shoes from the staff room before taking in the returns-sheet to Mr. Lincross.'

'And did you?'

'Oh, yes . . . ' Molly stopped abruptly as though she had thought of something. A curious expression passed over her uninteresting face, then she swallowed so hard that it was noticeable.

'That was all you did?' questioned Maria, noting the hesitation that had occurred.

'Yes . . . that was all.'

'At what time,' Morgan asked, tugging out his notebook, 'did you take the returns-sheet in to Mr. Lincross?'

'Oh, it would be about ten to nine.'

'All right, thanks. I hope,' Morgan added dryly, 'that your chilblains will soon be better.'

The girl smiled vaguely and continued onwards with her duster, again with that uncomfortable way of putting her feet down . . . Then Nancy Crane drifted forward slowly.

'If it's about me you're wanting to

know, Inspector, I was sat in the Circle all evening. Proving it wouldn't be as easy as it seems, of course, but it was so . . . Honest!'

'All right,' Morgan said, smiling at her earnestness. 'I'll take your word for it, miss — Oh, you! Mr. Bradshaw, isn't it?'

The doorman appeared through a side doorway and pushed up his cloth cap on his perspiring forehead. His face was bedewed from his efforts with the steam boiler.

'Aye, I'm Bradshaw. Want me?'

'Just a question. Can you tell me what you were doing at eight thirty-seven on Wednesday evening?'

'Why, I was . . . ' Bradshaw paused, his inflamed blue eyes suddenly sharp. 'Do I have to answer that?'

'You'd help me a lot if you would,' Morgan said.

'Well, I'm not goin' to! I've had about enough of you damned police about the place! Why don't you arrest young Allerton and get the thing done with?' —

'Why should I?'

'Because he was rowin' with the bloke

who got killed! I 'eard that myself — right up the 'Igh Street.'

'So did I, but it does not prove murder,' Maria said. 'I think you should answer the Inspector's question, Mr. Bradshaw.'

'Well, I'm not going to!' Bradshaw retorted. The doorman turned away impatiently and went through the foyer about his business.

'Shall I go make him open up?' Pulp asked.

'No, never mind . . . ' Morgan growled; then he looked across at Nancy Crane.

'Are the other girls about, miss? And the projection-room staff?'

'Yes, Inspector. You want them?'

'If you don't mind . . . '

Nancy went off on a search and after about five minutes had located everybody. They came into the foyer one by one, looking vaguely uncomfortable.

Mary Saunders, it seemed, had been seated in the advance booking office at 8.37 on the Wednesday evening, but had no means of proving the fact. The two other usherettes, Violet Thompson and

Sheila Brant, had been in the Stalls at their rightful posts at the time, just as Nancy Crane had been at hers.

Wearily Morgan dismissed them. His eyes settled finally on Fred Allerton, Dick Alcot, and Peter Canfield as they came down the Circle stairway.

Allerton he dismissed almost immediately since he already had a record of his movements, and instead concentrated on Alcot.

'You, I take it, were in charge of the projector?'

'I was,' Alcot assented calmly.

'Tell me, when Allerton left you did he tell you to put the sound up on the revolver shots?'

'Yes, he did. But that's only ordinary procedure. We'd done it at all the previous performances.'

'Then you must have rehearsed the film otherwise you could not have known there *were* any shots.'

'We rehearse every film,' Alcot explained. 'Fred makes out a cue sheet, which incorporates the changeover marks, special parts for editing, and so on. As for 'Love on the

Highway' we ran it through on the Monday morning.'

'I see . . . Now to something else. When somebody telephoned from below about the faulty hall speaker, did you hear what was *said* from below?'

'No. Fred answered the phone after it had buzzed, but I only heard him say he'd fix it up.'

'All right, Mr. Alcot. That's all for now, thanks.'

Alcot went off, and Morgan looked at the spotty-faced Peter Canfield. 'Now, young man. What were you doing at eight thirty-seven?'

'Sticking trailers together,' he growled. 'I hardly left the winding-room all evening. I remember Fred dashing past the doorway on his way to mend that hall horn.'

'That all?' Morgan raised an eyebrow.

'I'm sure of it, sir.'

'All right, son; return to your job.' Morgan closed his notebook.

Canfield went off whistling. Maria's eyes followed him. Then she glanced at the Inspector.

'Altogether, Inspector, we have only the doorman unaccounted for, unless of course Mr. Lincross had doubtful movements at that time. We shan't know until you ask him.'

'Alcot said the telephone *buzzed* up there and Allerton answered it,' Morgan reflected. 'That means the call was genuine enough — unless he somehow fixed it so that it would buzz of its own accord. Being a skilled electrical engineer he might even have done that.'

'Or squared somebody to telephone him,' Pulp suggested. 'Maybe that doorman guy since he won't say where he was.'

'He has refused information as to movements at eight thirty-seven,' Maria pointed out. 'The call was made some time *before* that. Two of the girls swear that nobody went near the phone all evening, and knowing young girls as I do, they wouldn't concoct such a story if it were not true. In these circumstances they would break down and confess . . . I imagine, Inspector, that we are left with only two conclusions: either, as you have suggested, Mr. Allerton made the instrument buzz of its own accord by some electrical device; or else the telephone wire was intercepted somewhere in the building and the person who called used a third hook-up telephone.'

'Well, we can soon settle that point by studying the telephone's circuit diagram,' Morgan decided. 'There should be one in the box itself. Let's have a look.'

He led the way into the Stalls, Maria and Pulp following. Morgan opened the telephone's front casing. On the back of this casing was a miniature blueprint of the complete circuit. Inside the box itself were the connector-wires, buzzer contact nipple, and the two flat two-volt batteries in their clips.

'Pole to point A; single screw contact; two main leads . . . ' Morgan muttered as he sorted the details out in his mind.

'Yes,' Maria said. 'It *could* be done! Baring the two main wires at some part of the building and fitting a third instrument like this would make it possible to send an impulse along the buzzer wire to the projection-room only. There would be no signal down here. Allerton would answer and then the person would speak from wherever he — or she — might be. Allerton may well have been speaking the truth, Inspector.'

Morgan frowned. It was clear that he did not relish discarding preconceived notions.

'Oh, good morning, Miss Black — And to you, Inspector. So sorry I was out.'

Lincross had appeared in the doorway of the Stalls, and came down the steps. Morgan shut the telephone box as Lincross nodded to Pulp rather perfunctorily.

'Examining the telephone, Inspector?'

'I am, sir. Purely routine. And I'd like a word with you, if you don't mind.'

'With pleasure. Come along into the office: it's a little warmer there.'

Inside the office Lincross drew up a chair for Maria, and then stood beside his desk expectantly.

'Where were you, Mr. Lincross, at eight thirty-seven on Wednesday evening?'

'Why, I was down in the boiler-room — yes, that's right!' He looked at Morgan in earnest confirmation of his words. 'I thought that the building was getting chilly — you remember how bitterly cold it was before the snow came — but I couldn't find Bradshaw at that moment. He did not seem to be at the front, where he usually is, so I presumed he was somewhere in the building on one of his inspection tours. You police are keen on things being right ... So I went down and shovelled coke on the boiler fire. It was nearly out.'

'I see ... Pretty dirty job for the owner-manager, sir.'

'Oh, not so very. Coke isn't so filthy as coal. It was a hot job, though.' Lincross smiled suddenly. 'I think I can prove what I have said, too. If you ask Fred Allerton he will tell you that when he came in to report his speaker repair I must have looked unusually warm for such a cold night.'

'Thanks; I'll check on that,' Morgan nodded. 'Not that I doubt your statement — but it's routine.'

'Of course ... ' Lincross's eyes strayed across to where Maria was sitting. She was regarding him levelly. When pupils at Roseway College saw that look on her clear-cut features they felt their knees go out of business.

'Mr. Lincross,' she said presently; 'it may interest you to know that Mr. Bradshaw refuses to say where he was at eight thirty-seven.'

'He does, eh? Well, he's a bit of a temperamental sort of chap. I have to handle him with kid gloves while the labour shortage continues. I'll try to find out, tactfully, what he was up to — but I'll wager it wasn't anything serious . . . Incidentally, Inspector, what did you find out about Lydia Fane?'

'Nothing yet: I'm dealing with that tonight. At the moment I am more interested in making a search of this building from top to bottom in an effort to find the murder weapon — and if possible, a third service telephone.'

'A third telephone?' Lincross hesitated and his face underwent a subtle change of expression. 'But why a third telephone?'

'Because it is my belief that one was used to summon Mr. Allerton from the projection-room,' Morgan replied stolidly. 'It might be somewhere in the building.'

'I suppose it might,' Lincross assented. 'Well, by all means have a look round, Inspector. You can manage it before the matinée, I suppose?'

'I think so. Maybe you'd come round with us, in case any little points need explaining.'

'With pleasure.'

Lincross followed behind Morgan as he walked towards the Circle staircase, gazing about him as he ascended. Halfway up, where the stairs took a sharp left-hand turn, was that adamant door marked STAFF ROOM ONLY — PRIVATE. Morgan surveyed it, then turned.

'What's in here exactly?' he asked. 'I've been intending to ask you.'

Lincross turned the door handle and switched on the electric light in the room beyond.

'Just the little department where the girls hang their hats and coats and do their bits of titivating. It's a rest-room, really — conforming with police regulations.'

'Hmmm . . . ' Morgan said, and looked at the coats and scarves on the pegs of the right-hand wall. Underneath them was a lone ottoman-like affair covered with green baize. On the wall facing it film star portraits had been pinned up with no attempt at neatness. Beside them was a mirror from the back of which the silver was departing.

It was only a small room with a tiny ventilator on the top of the wall containing the clothes' pegs. The ceiling was level and plastered, but in the centre of it was a square of stained boarding set into a wooden frame.

'What's that?' Morgan asked, looking up at it.

'Manhole. It leads to the water-tanks.'

'And to the roof?'

'Yes you can get to the roof this way,' Lincross admitted. 'But it means climbing a rather rickety old ladder up to the planks and beams in the false roof — that is the open space between the roof proper and the cinema ceiling. It's far simpler, and safer, to go into the roof by the proper ladder back-stage.'

'The fact remains,' Maria remarked, 'that this is a second way into the roof. I think a thorough examination is called for, Inspector.'

'I was thinking that,' Morgan said; and by reaching to the limit of his height he pushed the board on one side, gripped the edges of the wooden frame and muscled himself up. After some wheezing and effort, during which time his legs threshed wildly near Lincross's semi-bald head, he heaved out of sight. Then his face appeared in the opening.

'Get a torch, will you, please?'

'Right here,' Pulp Martin said, tugging one from his pocket. 'I like to be prepared. An' I don't see what stops me comin' with you.'

'Search thoroughly, Mr. Martin,' Maria instructed, as he drew himself up through the opening with consummate ease, then saw Morgan flashing the torch a little way ahead of him.

Up here they were in the midst of a cavern-like space between walls, and surrounded by galvanised iron water-tanks and copper cisterns furred over

157

with green mould. Dust and cobwebs abounded.

It required some skill to walk along the single plank set across the beams that led to the ancient ladder leading to the heights. Up there everything was totally dark. Morgan gazed above for a while, then gripping the torch firmly he began to climb.

In three minutes, Pulp coming behind him, they both emerged through a tiny trapdoor left permanently open on to a broad emptiness with the slated roof of the cinema building well above their heads.

It was icy cold. The torch beam lost itself in distance, but within its immediate range planks criss-crossed each other across the upper part of the cinema ceiling beams.

At intervals there were winches and strong chains, supporting the massively heavy electroliers depending over the auditorium.

Then, in the near foreground, there were wide, galvanised iron tubes — two of them — their bottom mouths fixed over two ornamental grilles. Actually the grilles were the two small air vents that supplemented the giant wall-to-wall ventilator.

The two galvanised iron tubes, forming a gigantic X, had a heavy box-like affair where they joined in the centre. In fact the box was as big as a hall wardrobe with a door across it.

'Fan house, I take it,' Morgan commented. 'We might take a look.'

They walked uncertainly across the planks and Morgan opened the box door. It was roomy inside and a strong draught blew down through it from the roof openings. In the exact centre of the boxed-in area reposed a large electric motor with a central shaft upon which were four blades, motionless at the moment.

'Looks like a master-fan,' Morgan murmured. 'There'll be others scattered about the building, I suppose.'

He peered as far as he could up the two slanting exit funnels, then down the inlet funnels where they came up from the cinema roof. Wind ruffled his hair. He withdrew and closed the door again sharply.

'I never saw less sign of a telephone or a murder weapon,' he growled.

'Yeah, copper, you're right,' Pulp commiserated; then he pointed behind them. 'Say, ain't that the ventilator grating which goes right over the Circle? We must ha' overlooked what it was when we crossed it.'

They moved back together and stood looking down through an interlacing of wood on to the Circle below. The cleaners' lamp illuminated it fairly clearly. The foreshortened figure of Nancy Crane was visible cleaning out ashtrays.

'You know,' Morgan mused, 'it would be a darned sight easier to shoot a man in A-11 from this angle than it would be to do it from behind that screen. Not much of a range — twenty-five feet at the most. There's A-11 below. See?'

They both looked down at it, then Morgan took a firm hold of the torch again, walked across the wide grating, and so back to the starting point of the ladder by the trapdoor.

'I think,' he said, as Pulp came behind him, 'the telephone wires to the projection-room ought to be here somewhere, since the projection-room is at the back of the Circle. Let's see what we've got . . . '

His search was ended almost immediately. The two wires in question, fitted in two separate metal conduits, were screwed into the wall behind the ladder. Morgan began to descend the ladder slowly, the beam of his torch on the two conduits — then when he finally reached the bottom of the ladder he gave a sudden little whoop of joy.

'Look here! Bare wire — !'

Pulp joined him. The torch beam was playing on the two conduits, but both of them had been sawn away for about an inch of their length, leaving insulated wire visible. But even this insulation had been scraped away for about a quarter of an inch and had left the warm glow of new copper.

'This settles one point anyway!' Morgan exulted. 'A third telephone must have been used and connected to these wires. Who-ever phoned Allerton did it from here

. . . But where did the phone go afterwards? Might be anywhere about here, and in all this muck and dust . . . '

'Why 'anywhere'?' Pulp gripped the Inspector's arm. 'Guys chuck murder weapons in lakes and bogs and places — Why shouldn't we look in these water tanks?'

Morgan swung the torch beam round and stood up. Lifting the wooden cover off the first water tank he sent the bright beam clear to the bottom — but there was nothing there. But not so with the second tank. There was something, distorted by refraction — something with a wooden front, push-pull buttons, and a length of wire trailing . . .

'Okay,' Pulp said briefly. He whipped his coat off, rolled his shirtsleeve to the shoulder, then plunged his arm in the icy cold water. There was a dripping telephone in his hand when he withdrew it.

'Fine!' Morgan cried. 'The very thing! But no sign of a rifle or anything? That's got me worried . . . All right, let's get back below.'

They clambered down into the staff room again to find Maria and Lincross anxiously awaiting them.

'A telephone!' Lincross cried, when Pulp dropped down with the dripping instrument in his hand. 'Your guess was right then, Inspector! Where in the world was it?'

'In one of the water tanks . . . ' Morgan batted at his dusty clothes impatiently.

'And were the wires to the projection-room bared?' Maria asked sharply.

'They were. Somebody made contact with the projection-room from the space just above this dressing-room.'

Maria looked at the instrument as Pulp laid it down on the ottoman. 'So somebody managed to get a spare service telephone to perform that little trick. Have you any idea how it might have been done, Mr. Lincross?'

'Well, the phone is the property of the sound company who equipped the theatre, of course, but sometimes when a theatre fits new phones the old ones are not always removed. As a matter of fact . . . ' Lincross paused. 'Yes! I think I know where this has come from! We had the projection-room phone replaced six months ago and I believe Fred Allerton bought the phone up cheap for some kind of electrical experiment. He's always up to electrical dodges, you know. I — er — last saw this telephone on the workbench in the winding-room, several weeks ago. I remember the deep scratch down the front of it.'

Lincross looked as though he had said something distasteful to him. Morgan gave up dusting his clothes and cleared his throat.

'Allerton, eh!' he exclaimed. 'Get him down here!'

As Lincross went out Maria remarked, 'I take it, Inspector, there was no sign of the murder weapon? The rifle, or whatever it was that killed the man in A-11?'

'None whatever. I searched the fan-chamber and we had a good look round up there. We might look again — with an extension flex. Torchlight isn't too help-ful — '

'But we noticed one thing, Maria!' Pulp

164

interrupted. 'Lookin' through that big Circle grille on to A-11 we figured it would be much easier to bump a guy off from there than from the screen. Only about twenty-five feet . . . '

'True . . . ' Maria gave a regretful smile. 'But the slug entered the man's forehead, not the top of his skull . . . '

Presently Lincross returned with Fred Allerton. A haunted look hung about Allerton's face as he looked from the Inspector's grim eyes to the telephone on the ottoman.

'This yours, Mr. Allerton?' Morgan asked brusquely.

'Yes . . . ' Allerton seemed to make a great effort at self-control. 'I was wondering where it had gone . . . Good Lord, it's ruined — soaked! Where's it been?'

'In a water tank above this staff room . . . Only I suppose you wouldn't know how it got there?'

'Of course not!' Allerton looked round bewilderedly at the faces. 'How could I?'

'Exactly,' Maria murmured. 'Please don't get alarmed, Mr. Allerton. The

Inspector is merely anxious to prove that this is your property. You say that it is . . . All right. Now answer something else. After you had repaired the speaker on Wednesday night and called in to tell Mr. Lincross about it, what did you notice about him?'

Allerton hesitated and glanced at his employer uncertainly.

'You will not be victimised for anything you may say,' Morgan prompted. 'How did Mr. Lincross look? What was his appearance?'

'Well, he looked — as though he had been working hard,' Allerton answered bluntly. 'His face was red and his forehead was moist.'

'There you are, Inspector,' Lincross smiled. 'I told you I'd been busy with that infernal boiler . . . Which reminds me,' he said, loosening his coat, 'this place is getting too warm. I must tell Bradshaw to cut the heat down or I'll be having my matinée patrons complaining. Fred, you might put on the main fan and cool the air a little.'

'Yes, sir . . . ' Allerton looked at

Morgan. 'Can I go now?'

'All right,' Morgan assented, eyeing him — then he picked up the telephone. At length his eyes strayed to Maria.

'I was going to question him further Miss Black, but you stopped me. That sort of thing might go under the heading of obstruction, you know.'

'And it might not,' Maria answered calmly. 'After all, Inspector, can you not judge mental reactions? That young man is getting so worried by the accumulation of evidence against him that he is liable to run away or even commit suicide if we don't stop plaguing him. He is the intelligent, highly sensitive type, so do not alarm him too much . . . If he should be guilty we don't want to have to toothcomb the countryside for him — or perhaps drag the river Bollin for the body!'

'But this is his telephone!' Morgan insisted.

'I am quite aware of it. Perhaps you will explain how he telephoned himself?'

Morgan tightened his lips. 'He could have got somebody else to telephone him and then have thrown the phone in the tank when he was backstage. He could get up into the roof from there.'

'Somebody else . . . to telephone him . . . ' Maria muttered. 'I just wonder . . . '

Morgan waited for her to elaborate, but she seemed to be lost in speculations. Impatiently he seized the telephone and moved to the doorway.

'I think I'll take another look backstage,' he said. 'The rifle we want may be there somewhere.'

Maria, still pensive, followed him, and Lincross and Pulp came behind her. As they walked down the Circle stairway towards the foyer Fred Allerton suddenly came racing past them, jumping three stairs at a time. He dashed straight into Lincross's office and vanished from view.

'What the — ?' Lincross looked blank for a moment. Hurrying ahead he met Fred Allerton just as he came out of the office again.

'What the devil's the idea?'

Maria, Morgan, and Pulp waited

interestedly at the bottom of the staircase.

'Sorry, sir, but it was urgent!' Allerton panted 'I put the main fan on, as you told me, but it had not been going above a minute before the fuse blew in the fan-switch. If I hadn't have dashed down here quickly and cut the main power-switch the Corporation fuse would have gone and blown every light in the building. As it was it was getting mighty hot.'

'Oh . . . I see.' Lincross turned and began explaining. 'The main fuses are in my office — in a cupboard-like affair.'

'But why should the fuse blow in the fan-switch?' Maria asked sharply.

'Something must have jammed the fan,' Allerton answered. 'I'd better go up into the roof and take a look.'

'Then I'll go with you,' Morgan decided. 'Frankly, I don't trust anybody up there or backstage just at present.'

Allerton led the way through the Stalls doorway en route for backstage. Morgan followed behind him, still clutching the damp telephone. They disappeared from view as the doors swung upon them.

'I wonder if the Inspector upset the fan in any way while he was prowling about up there?' Lincross said.

'No, he didn't!' Pulp Martin declared firmly. 'I don't reckon to have no truck with flatfoots, but as coppers go Morgan ain't such a bad guy. He never touched the fan, see? All he did was climb in that inspection-chamber for a look around.'

Lincross shrugged; then motioned to his office. 'Perhaps you would care to sit down until the Inspector comes back, Miss Black?'

She nodded and settled herself presently into the usual chair. Lincross regarded her.

'Might I ask you a question, Miss Black?'

'By all means,' she assented. 'After all, I am not compelled to answer it.'

'No — of course not. Well, upstairs, Morgan suggested that Allerton might have had an accomplice to telephone him, and I noticed that when he said that you got a sudden idea. Would I seem inquisitive if I asked what it was?'

'I was just thinking, Mr. Lincross, that

Miss Molly Ibbetson — your ordinary booking cashier — might have been the accomplice.'

'Molly Ibbetson!' Lincross gave a distinct start. 'But why?'

'Well, of course, you are a little in the dark . . . ' Maria looked across the desk. 'Before you arrived this morning Miss Ibbetson was questioned as to her movements at eight thirty-seven last Wednesday evening — just as everybody else was questioned. She said that at eight thirty-seven she was — hmm! — applying a little massage to the chilblains on her feet.'

'Well?' Lincross could not keep the tenseness out of his voice.

'She decided to put on her other shoes for comfort before bringing in the — er — night's returns-sheet. But to get those shoes, Mr. Lincross, she must have gone into the staff room, since I do not suppose she would keep them in the pay box — '

'No, she wouldn't. I forbid such things.'

'Good! Then she went to the staff room. There was nothing to stop her standing on that ottoman and then climbing up into the false roof, from where she could have telephoned Allerton at his request. The whys and wherefores — how he could bribe her into such an action — I do not prctend to know.'

'But . . . ' Lincross thought hard. 'But, madam, that cannot be correct. At eight thirty-seven the shot was presumably fired. At that time Molly was in her box. Allerton was telephoned some time *before* eight thirty-seven.'

'We have no guarantee that Miss Ibbetson is telling the truth,' Maria said calmly. 'She may have gone for her shoes long before eight thirty-seven. I recall that she hesitated quite a lot when questioned.'

'Then I think we should question her again — ruthlessly!' Lincross declared.

'My dear sir, Inspector Morgan represents the police, not the late Gestapo,' Maria murmured. 'Miss Ibbetson has answered all questions to Morgan's satisfaction — I presume; therefore she cannot be questioned again until there is real reason for it.'

'But isn't this real reason?' Lincross cried. 'What was the girl up to?'

Maria said: 'At what time did she bring the returns-sheet in to you?'

'Oh — about ten to or five to nine.'

'So she said . . . Hmm. Most interesting. Tell me, do you know if she has any contact with Mr. Allerton outside the cinema? I mean is she his — er — girl friend?'

'I don't think so. I try not to interfere with the private lives of my employees, but as near as I can judge Miss Ibbetson is somewhat attached to young Peter Canfield, the rewind boy. Their time off coincides and I have seen them about the town together now and again. After all they are both sixteen, so it is quite understandable . . . As for Allerton, Miss Black, I thought you knew that he is engaged to Miss Crane?'

'I know,' Maria assented blandly. 'But then, some young men — and women too — are not satisfied with just one in tow!'

'Is all this leading anywhere?' Lincross asked bluntly.

'Sometimes one has to gather a lot of

oysters before finding the pearl . . . But tell me something, Mr. Lincross. Can one lock the staff room door on the inside? If Molly performed the actions I have suggested I imagine she would have wanted to make herself safe.'

'There is a bolt, but the key was lost long ago. The bolt locks on the inside, so — '

The door opened suddenly and Inspector Morgan came bustling in with Fred Allerton behind him.

'Miss Black, we've found it!' Morgan was positively triumphant. 'Look here!'

Holding it carefully by a finger at each end Morgan laid down an air-rifle on the desk. It was not new, but some effort had been made to remove the slight rustiness of the barrel's exterior. It had a dull sticky shine as though oil had been used for polishing. To it adhered a fine coating of dust.

'Do you mean that this was in the roof?' Lincross asked.

'More than that, sir — it was jammed across the blades of the fan! Whoever used this threw it up into one or other of the fan outlet flues. Then maybe my activities this morning dislodged it from its slanting position and the slight vibration from the fan-motor caused it to slide down. Or else a sudden down-draught of wind could have caused it. It's pretty strong up there this morning . . . Anyway, it's *the* weapon!'

'Hmm, a B.S.A.,' Maria murmured, peering at it. 'I take it, Inspector, that it will now be examined for fingerprints?'

'Yes. I'll take it down to the station and have an expert over from Lexham in no time. I should have left it where it was and had it photographed, but that just couldn't be, jamming the fan . . . '

Morgan turned to Allerton who was holding the old service telephone for him. 'Ever seen this rifle before, Mr. Allerton?'

'No! And I don't know how it got in the fan vent either! Do you think, if I had used it, that I'd be idiot enough to throw it up there where it might jam the fan?'

Morgan kept his thoughts to himself and took the telephone. 'You've never seen it before, sir, Mr. Lincross?'

'Afraid not, Inspector.'

'All right, I'll see what fingerprints and ballistics have to say about it . . . For now I have all I need here, but you'll be seeing me again. May I drop you at Roseway, Miss Black?'

Maria nodded thoughtfully, and got to her feet. Pulp Martin accompanied her as far as the Inspector's car. Morgan gently laid the rifle on its barrel end in the car back.

'Still want me to snoop around that hotel room of mine, Maria?' he questioned.

'Definitely, Mr. Martin — But I also have another task for you. Find out, by any means you care to adopt — and without exciting suspicion — when the various members of the cinema staff have their days off. I may have reason to wish to know later on.'

'Leave it to me, Maria. Be seeing you.'

Pulp slammed the car door after she had settled beside Morgan, who started up the engine and drove off down the High Street.

'I am thinking, Inspector, how much

work Mr. Allerton must have given himself to fix the loud-speaker backstage, climb up into the roof, shoot the man in A-11, unfasten the telephone, and throw the rifle in the fan-flue. Then return downstairs, all in the space of something like twelve minutes ... I'm convinced that it could not be done.'

'Don't forget that the fellow is agile, sure-footed, and knows that cinema like the back of his hand. I think he *could* have done it, though I admit his motive — just fear of the police — seems flimsy. But there may be other reasons, not yet revealed.'

'Other reasons would mean that Allerton prepared the whole thing a long way in advance. He could not have brought the air-rifle into the building during normal working hours without it being seen: and certainly he could not have ridden a bicycle with it if, say, he had it concealed down the leg of his trousers. Secondly, from what you tell me, the conduit pipes to the telephone wires have been sawn away, and presumably filed through their sawn length as well in order to get them free. That, at best, would be fifteen minutes' work and extremely noisy.'

'All right then, he planned it some way ahead,' Morgan said heavily.

'And yet the picture with the coinciding shots — 'Love on the Highway' — was not seen by Allerton until Monday morning! It also implies,' Maria added, 'that Allerton has a duplicate key — or else he broke into the building . . . the further we go, inspector, the deeper we get.'

'Then what's the answer?' Morgan asked impatiently.

'Find the real motive behind Allerton's action and dispense with all thoughts of the bicycle accident. Then maybe we will see what realty prompted him to murder . . . '

Morgan drew up outside the college gates and Maria alighted.

'You are going to see Lydia Fane tonight, Inspector?'

'Alone,' Morgan answered firmly. 'But I'll let you know how I get on — and I'll hand on the report on this rifle. Say, tomorrow morning.'

'Excellent,' Maria nodded. 'And, Inspector, just a final thought for you to consider . . . Since Molly Ibbetson had to change her shoes because of chilblains she had to go to the staff room, and the staff room leads to the roof. Recall the times, and ponder. I think you will find much of interest.'

Morgan's bushy eyebrows rose up, but Maria did not elaborate. She considered her watch.

'Dinner-time, Inspector,' she announced. 'I will see you tomorrow.'

She left him and went through the gateway into the quadrangle entering her study in pensive mood. Coming to her desk she picked up the telephone and rang the 'Golden Saddle'.

'Mr. Martin, please,' she requested, as the voice of Mrs. Janet Ainsworth responded.

Presently Pulp's voice came over the wire. 'Yeah? Who wants me?'

'Black Maria speaking, Mr. Martin. I have just been having second thoughts . . . I want you to keep an eye on the girl, Molly Ibbetson, night and day so to speak. Never let her out of your sight when she is not either at home or at her work. Watch her go back and forth, take a note of all she does, discover with whom she spends her spare time ... You understand?'

'She the plump dame with the dark fizgigs on her napper?'

'The girl with the wave and curl coiffure, yes. And don't forget to learn all you can about the staff's various days off.'

'A cinch, Maria. I'll keep a line on the dame until you tells me to quit.'

'Thanks,' Maria murmured, hanging up her hat and coat. She had a few minutes yet before dinner was due in the staff dining hall, so sitting at her desk she pulled forth her black record book and began to write swiftly:

A telephone (with which a call was made to Allerton) has been found; also a B.S.A. air-rifle with which the murder was presumably committed. Am awaiting expert opinion on this. At the moment I am intrigued by many thoughts — i.e., the dead man asked the whereabouts of two roads from the proprietress of the 'Golden Saddle' Hotel where he resided — Millington Terrace and Greystone Avenue. I know that Gerald Lincross, the owner-manager of the cinema, lives in Greystone Avenue, so did the dead man require something of him? Or is it coincidence, and the man in A-11 really wanted the avenue in order to contact somebody else? I must consider this point very carefully . . . And Millington Terrace? Who lives there, I wonder, that the man in A-11 should wish to ascertain its whereabouts?

At the moment my interest centres deeply on Molly Ibbetson. I cannot forget her hesitation when questioned; nor can I forget that she would have to visit the staff room if she wanted to change her shoes (because of chilblains).

The perfect crime cannot exist because of these little unexpected factors. Chilblains! Unexpected? Yet maybe the most vital occurrence in the whole problem!

The time is 12.50 p.m.

7

When Molly Ibbetson prepared to leave the cinema at noon that same morning she was singing to herself and tying a blue woollen scarf round her dark head with more care than usual. In critical silence Mary Saunders sat in a corner of the small ordinary booking office and watched Molly's antics before the tiny mirror on the wall.

'You've enough paint on your face to redecorate the cinema,' Mary decided finally.

'Improves me,' Molly replied. 'Besides, Peter likes it.'

'Can't think what you see in *him*. Why doesn't he do something about those spots?'

'I can't hardly ask him that, can I?' Molly objected. She turned from the mirror and surveyed the limited space of the booking office. 'Well, see you tomorrow morning. I suppose half a day is better than none at all. Fred and Dick don't even get that while labour's so short . . . Got to give it to Peter though: he's under eighteen.'

Molly bent double under the booking-plan shelf and emerged backwards into the foyer. Then she minced over to the swing doors and beyond them down the pseudo-marble steps. Peter Canfield was waiting for her in an overcoat too small for him, the cold wind ruffling his untidy fair hair.

'All set?' he inquired briefly. Molly nodded and took his arm possessively.

They stepped out into the powdery snow and began to walk along High Street, quite unaware of the powerful man in the green trilby hat and vulgarly checked overcoat who had emerged from the 'Golden Saddle' Hotel opposite.

'Any ideas for today?' Molly asked presently.

'I thought,' Peter said, with the air of a man of the world, 'that we might make a change for once. I've got a bit of money . . . '

'You have?' Molly looked at Peter in

pleased astonishment.

'Never mind how I got it: women don't need to know about those things. Anyway, I've decided to spend it — and I've made a plan.'

They halted at the corner of a side street where they would perforce have to go their separate ways home. Nearby, but within earshot, Pulp Martin stood in a doorway with his back to them, his eyes absently studying ironmongery.

'There's an indoor fair on over in Lexham,' Peter explained. 'It came a week ago for the Christmas season. I thought we might spend the afternoon there and perhaps pick up a few prizes. Then we could go to the Temple Café for tea — '

'Temple Café! But their charges are terrific!'

'I said I had money!' Peter snapped impatiently. 'We'll go there and finish up with some dancing at the Palace. We might have a few drinks, too. They think I'm twenty-one in that place,' he added, grinning. 'And with your figure you'll pass for the same age. Are you game?'

Molly reflected. Nobody at home

would concern themselves with what she did, anyway: as one of four girls nobody would have the time.

'All right,' she said finally, 'Be a chance to try out my new frock. I'll have to look my best for the Temple Café and the Palace ... I'll nip home for dinner, change, and meet you at — '

'At the bus stop in the Square at two o'clock,' Peter decided, quite the man of the moment.

They parted, and Pulp Martin turned from surveying saucepans.

'A fair, huh? Temple Café? Seem to remember that joint from the last time I was in these parts. Be tough going for a guy like me — 'specially the Temple Café.'

He pondered for a moment or two, then remembering instructions he followed Molly Ibbetson until she reached her home a mile and a half from the cinema — a journey which took her down numerous side alleys and past the rearing, deserted skeleton of an ancient mining site. Her home was sordidly ordinary, the windows gaudy with yellow net curtains.

She lived in a house that was one in a block of twenty, where there were no front gardens and where the younger members of the Ibbetson family amused themselves in the icy wind by playing on the pavement in inadequate clothes.

Pulp surveyed the squalid scene for a moment, and made a note of the girl's house number then went back to the cinema and lounged into the foyer to beam on Mary Saunders in the booking office. Ten minutes later he entered a telephone kiosk and rang Roseway College.

Maria Black had to desert her dinner to answer his call.

'Pulp here, Maria. I've had a yarn with that Mary Saunders dame — without givin' anythin' away — and as far as I can figure only those under eighteen are gettin' days off at present. Somethin' to do with labour shortage. Even the under-eighteens are only gettin' half days. I worked up to it by trying to make a date with the Saunders piece. I like her hips, see . . .'

'Shame on you, Mr. Martin,' Maria

half laughed. 'Thank you, anyway, for the information. I — '

'Hang on, Maria! I ain't finished yet. This dame Molly Ibbetson an' the Canfield kid have their half days off today. They're goin' to give themselves the works. First they're goin' to an indoor fair in Lexham, then to the Temple Café, then to the Palace for a hoof around and a few belly-looseners . . . '

'A few — what?'

'Drinks, Maria, drinks!'

'Did you say the Temple Café?' Maria demanded. 'That's a costly restaurant for two such young people as Molly and Peter.'

'That's what I figured — but I heard this Canfield kid say he'd got money. Can't be his wages, I don't suppose . . . Anyway, I've trailed Molly to her hangout — helluva dive, too, with kids lyin' around outside the front door. What do I do now? Keep on the track to the Temple Café, or what?'

'I am rather interested in this boy's sudden acquisition of money, Mr. Martin. It may not mean anything, but I cannot afford to let a single lead slip. Remember that we have the thought in mind that Allerton may have bribed somebody to telephone him . . . I think I had better handle this myself. Did you find out where they are meeting each other?'

'Sure — the bus stop in Langhorn Square at two.'

'Splendid! And while I take over this task, Mr. Martin, you might spend a little time in Millington Terrace trying to find out what kind of people live there. Remember that the man in A-11 asked the whereabouts of that spot. It may contain somebody, or something, important.'

'I'll do me best,' Pulp promised. 'Be seein' you.'

★　★　★

Meanwhile Fred Allerton and Nancy Crane were entering the little snack bar a hundred yards from the cinema. They sat down at a corner table and at a signal the one waitress — who knew them well — filled up two cups with steaming coffee.

'Inspector Morgan has got it firmly fixed in his bullet head that I killed the man in A-11,' Fred confided bitterly. 'I think the only thing holding him back from arresting me is that he can't decide the motive. That telephone they found this morning is mine, of course, though when I last saw it, it was in the winding-room . . . Then there's that nosy old Headmistress from Roseway! I wish I could understand how she ever came to be in on this, asking awkward questions and snooping round.'

Nancy's hand slid across the table towards his. 'Fred, I've never kept anything back from myself to you, now have I? So I might as well tell you, Miss Black is so busy because I asked her to be!'

Allerton lowered his cup to the saucer with a loud clink and stared at her.

'Now don't start letting your temper run away with you! I just had to do it, Fred . . . I could see you heading for a lot of trouble, and if anybody can get you out of what you're in, she can. She's a criminologist, remember. After all, why shouldn't she help?'

'*If* she's helping. Looks to me as though she's piling things thicker all the time. Fact remains she's no help to me and for two pins I'd get rid of her — if I could. The way she looks at you sometimes: she's got the coldest eyes I've ever seen!'

'She'll prove your innocence, Fred — I'm sure of it . . . And by the way, I want to ask you something. I saw Inspector Morgan leaving with that air-rifle this morning. Have you ever seen it before?'

'Never, until we found it jamming the fan.'

'I have,' Nancy said, reflecting. 'Be some time ago. It was in Atkinson's, the second-hand dealer's window. You know Atkinson's? Just near the cinema . . . ?'

8

Attired in her 'working outfit' — heavy costume, beret, and umbrella — Maria Black entered the bus shelter in Langhorn's main square at ten minutes to two that afternoon. To her satisfaction it was empty . . . Seating herself, she opened the daily newspaper that she had brought specially for the purpose of concealment and proceeded to watch events outside over the top of it.

Presently Peter Canfield appeared and took up his position at the bus stop. He was dressed to kill, in a square-shouldered fawn overcoat, light blue and well-pressed trousers showing beneath it. The unruly fair hair was plastered down mercilessly and the tan shoes betrayed newness. But for the spots on his face, Peter Canfield was quite presentable.

As Maria had guessed he would, he scorned the shelter, preferring to stand with manly fortitude in the freezing wind.

He lighted a cigarette in somewhat amateur fashion, shielding the match flame in his cupped hands; then he began a slow pacing up and down, never bothering to glance into the shelter at the middle-aged woman in a beret reading a newspaper

Ten minutes later Molly Ibbetson appeared, her hen-like walk and plump figure betraying her from far away. She too was dressed in her best, in a blue coat with a belt trying to determine her waistline, and a blue hat. When the absence of stockings became noticeable to Maria the reason for chilblains became automatically explained . . .

In another three minutes the bus arrived and Maria watched the two board it and hurry upstairs. She put away her newspaper, then contemplating the pavement so that she could not be recognised from above, she entered the bus's lower deck and settled herself in a rear seat, paper up before her eyes once again.

She booked right through to Lexham, the bus terminus, so she could break her journey anywhere along the route if need be. It was not necessary, however. Peter and Molly did not get off until the terminus, and then Maria had no need to conceal herself because of the other people who alighted too.

Breaking free of the dispersing crowd she saw her two quarries lounging ahead, arm-in-arm, along the pavement, glancing in the shop windows as they passed them. Lexham, a fairly busy town, had far more to offer than old-fashioned and semi-defunct Langhorn.

So the two progressed, Maria keeping her distance but never losing sight of them — until at last they stopped before a rather garish façade emblazoned with the words — INDOOR HOLIDAY FAIR, and having paid their admittance they disappeared through a highly ornamental doorway.

Maria waited for a moment or two, then she too paid and walked up a passage of plywood walls covered in silver paper.

She emerged suddenly into a huge indoor expanse that smelled of hot machinery, paraffin and petrol fumes, and something else. Just people, perhaps. There was a most abominable noise of grotesque canned music and a back and forth movement of men, women and children round the various stalls and mechanical attractions.

Maria surveyed it all distastefully, catching sight of Peter and Molly some distance ahead in the throng.

Jostled and shoved by eager and entirely unmannerly children — and adults, too, for that matter; shouted at by red-faced gentlemen waving wooden balls or darts; invited to take a turn on the hobby-horses or ferris-wheel, she followed steadily and with only a semblance of her usual poker-backed dignity in the wake of Peter and Molly.

She watched them take a turn on the ferris wheel; then they went across to the dodgems and spent two turns deliberately crashing their cars into one another. Maria sighed, and entirely inconspicuous in the crowd, waited. Once or twice she wondered if she ought to desert the job and find her four o'clock cup of tea.

She was thankful when the two sought

the dubious pleasures of the many sidestalls. Most of the time, taking advantage of the crowd, Maria was near enough to touch either one of them — and certainly well in earshot, but neither of them discussed anything particularly interesting.

With increasing weariness, her ears throbbing to the frightful din which passed for music, Maria drifted from stall to stall, watched young Peter reveal the power of his biceps by throwing wooden balls in Hell's Kitchen, or else observed the clumsiness of Molly as she tried to throw rubber rings over a short pillar and win a watch. Then, as they drew near to the rifle range where steel ducks passed in endless procession against a painted landscape, and a glittering ball bobbed perpetually on the top of a water fountain, Peter Canfield gave a sudden whoop of joy.

'Just my meat! Watch this, Molly! Hey, rifle please!'

''Elp yourself,' the attendant invited, who did not seem to like either his job or Peter Canfield.

Maria watched without much interest at first as the youth put the rifle to his shoulder and took aim. Then her brows went up and Molly clapped her hands excitedly as the first shot knocked down a steel duck with a vicious ping of slug on metal.

'Good shot, sir,' said the attendant, somewhat suspiciously. 'Take your pick of the stall.'

'Later,' Peter promised airily. 'I'm only just getting into my stride.'

His next shot smashed one of the many bottles at the back of the range, and his third exploded the air-filled ball on top of the fountain . . . By this time Molly's face was quite hot and shiny with excitement and Maria was feeling that her time had not been wasted. Her eyes narrowed as she watched Peter take up another rifle.

Altogether he had six more shots and every one struck home dead true to the target. Grinning, he began to scoop up his rewards from the stall — packets of cigarettes, a silly-looking doll with yellow hair and a feather skirt, and a small clock.

The two went on again, and Maria

began to trail them once more — and to her satisfaction their loaded condition decided them against further stall excursions and instead they headed for the exit. Maria emerged after them, thankful for the cold fresh wind and absence of ear-splitting noise.

Molly carrying the doll under her arm and Peter the clock under his, they walked down the main street and entered the Temple Café. Knowing its exact interior layout from previous visits Maria gave them a chance to get well settled before venturing in; and then it was with a handkerchief to her face.

She caught sight of them immediately at a far table by the left-hand wall. Each table was set between oak partitions about five feet high, which in their turn formed lofty shelves for stiff-looking dried palms.

Slowly, she made her way among the tables, apparently searching for one to suit her and at the same time keeping her back to the two young people. Knowing the ways of youth intimately she judged that they would never even notice an elderly lady in a beret and costume, and finally manoeuvred herself into the partition next to theirs and sat down thankfully.

Resting her head back against the hide backrest of the seat she waited for her order to be taken — but Molly and Peter came before her. Her eyes widened a trifle as she heard Peter's loud, authoritative voice.

'Fresh salmon, salad, tea, and bread and butter for two. And the best cakes you've got . . . '

Maria picked up the menu and computed the price Peter Canfield would have to pay for his extravagance. It was a high price — for a boy of sixteen.

'First-class marksman — plenty of money . . . Amazing for a youth in a humble position.' Maria ceased meditating as a waitress hovered beside her. She ordered tea and buttered scones, then leaned back and did her utmost to catch the conversation from the next partition. But since the conversation seemed to be made up of comments upon mutual acquaintances — comments disarmingly frank at times — her effort was wasted. So she ate her scones and kept listening.

But nothing of importance floated in her direction and at last it was clear the two intended to leave. Maria glanced at her watch, found it was just after five o'clock, and wondered where next she would have to prowl. At least it would be easier for her now the early winter night was closing in . . .

For an hour, huddled against the wind in shop doorways, she kept track of the two as they surveyed the shops before closing time . . . then towards six o'clock by the Town Hall they entered the open doorway of the Palace Dance Hall and walked through the softly lit foyer into the lighted expanse beyond.

Maria took her place in the queue, majestically oblivious to the half-amused glances cast towards her by the bright young things of the district.

In three minutes she was inside the hall, standing at the edge of the highly polished floor watching the few couples circling round as an orchestra very hot on the cymbals plugged the latest number.

A glance to either side revealed tables and basketwork chairs with ornamental plants in brass tubs here and there. To one of these Maria retired, thankful to rest her aching legs. Seated at ease she watched the couples intently.

It was a little while before Peter and Molly appeared from the direction of the cloakrooms, minus overcoats, doll, and clock. Then clinging to each other as if afraid they might fall down they began to dance uncertainly.

Maria ordered a mineral as an excuse for her chair and kept her eyes fixed on Molly's fleshy gyrations in a tight pink frock — but as time passed the distinctive colour, and that of Peter's blue suit, too, became lost in the varied hues of the ever-swelling number of dancers on the floor.

Maria reflected that Molly and Peter's capacity for punishment was considerable. Save for two short intervals when they retired to a distant table to sip minerals, they were dancing for nearly two hours. Then, to her alarm, they finally left the floor at the opposite side of the hall and vanished through a doorway plainly marked — BAR.

For a moment Maria was nonplussed. Intoxicants she never took — unless under doctor's orders — and the very smell of liquor nauseated her.

'No, Maria, there is a limit!' she told herself firmly. 'There is nothing more to learn . . . But at least you can wait and see that the girl gets home safely.'

So she relaxed and regarded the people about her — quite unaware of the fact that she had for once made a wrong decision. Had she followed the two into the smoky atmosphere of the bar and sat near their table she would have heard a most illuminating conversation — words loosened a little by the action of powerful cocktails.

'I got a secret!' Molly kept insisting, after her third drink. 'Very special! Secret . . . all my own.'

'Wh-what secret?' Peter Canfield looked at her rather hazily, and stuttered as he always did when he changed from minerals to a man's drink.

Molly did not answer, and sat back in

her chair with her chubby arm draped languidly over the back of it.

She winked at Peter provocatively and he reflected in a bemused kind of way that her big round face was remarkably fresh complexioned. It was not all paint, either. Molly was not exactly intoxicated, for she had the inner common sense to know when to stop. It was just that she felt unexpectedly happy, and when she felt this way an overwhelming urge to tell her innermost thoughts and inhibitions took possession of her.

'*What* secret?' Peter demanded again, suddenly cross.

'Something not even Smart-Aleck Inspector Morgan knows . . . '

Peter Canfield sat up sharply, then winced as his head swam a little. But much of the haze had been blasted out of him at the mention of Morgan. He leaned across the table intently.

'What about Inspector Morgan? What are you talking about?'

Molly bent forward so her face nearly touched his. Her voice was low; her breathing heavy.

'I know who killed that man in A-11 . . . '

It was ten o'clock when Peter and Molly finally reappeared to Maria's anxiously watching eyes. She noticed as they headed towards the cloakrooms that they walked steadily enough, so evidently they had been spending the time talking. A few minutes later when Molly reappeared Maria revised her opinion slightly. The girl was obviously confused, and her face — as she drew nearer through the throngs of dancers pouring off the floor — was unusually flushed.

Supporting herself against one of the pillars beside the dance floor, Molly buttoned up her overcoat with fumbling fingers. Out of one pocket protruded the head of the yellow-haired doll. Maria turned her back as Peter Canfield became visible. He walked smartly enough, either because he had not drunk very much or else because he was used to it. He looked bad-tempered.

'Why the hell you should say that and then refuse to say any more I just don't know!' he snapped, clutching Molly's right arm fiercely. In his free hand he carried the clock.

'Just have my secrets . . . Can't tell everything . . . '

Molly's voice faded into the general noise of the place as she and Peter made for the exit. Instantly Maria was on her feet, following them.

They were hurrying for the last Langhorn bus when she saw them under the street lamps — and with a sudden shock she realised it was the last bus for her, too. Making a sudden tremendous spurt and holding her umbrella on high to attract the driver she managed to board the vehicle just in time. A covert glance round assured her that, as on the inward journey, Molly and Peter had climbed to the upper deck.

With her lips tight she watched her own stop for Roseway go past in the darkness, meaning that she was due for a long trudge back home again. In fact she would not have given herself such a task except for two things — her decision to see Molly Ibbetson safely home — a matter doubly important now she was not entirely herself; and the remembrance of her few words about a secret, in the dance hall.

Maria's speculations cut short as the bus reached Langhorn Square. Peter and Molly got out, then she trailed them under the dim street lights. At the second light they stopped and stood talking. Maria could not hear the words, but some kind of argument was plainly in progress. Finally Peter Canfield's voice became quite audible.

'All right, if you tell me half a secret and then leave me flat I'm finished with you! You can see yourself home — !'

He turned away impatiently and vanished round the corner of the nearest side street. Molly looked after him rather forlornly for a moment, half started after him, then she swung suddenly and crossed the road in the direction of her own home.

'The manners of modern youth,' Maria murmured, her eyes narrowed. 'Just as well I decided to keep an eye on her.' She kept the girl's short, plump figure in sight easily enough as she ambled lazily along the deserted High Street.

Dragging her feet somewhat from tiredness, Maria followed on quietly, keeping well to the shadow of the shops until at last the girl turned the corner of the first street leading to the dimly lit maze of back alleys and cheap property where her own home was situated.

Maria's nerves felt a little less steady as she marched on through these gloomy regions, catching sight of Molly ever and again under the flicker of the half-blacked-out street lamps. The snow at least provided a certain amount of reflected light and made things not quite so abysmal as they would otherwise have been. And, too, it muffled footsteps, for which Maria was glad —

Then, suddenly, with overwhelming force, Maria felt something. It struck on to her skull through her beret, with such fiendish impact that the whole universe seemed to burst apart in front of her and she went reeling into a darkness which had neither form nor substance.

Molly, some yards ahead, did not hear anything. Her wits were too dulled for one thing and she was busy brooding over her tiff with Peter Canfield for another. She went down an entry and turned into a further street without bothering to look up. She knew from long familiarity exactly where she was going. Then, after a time, she became conscious of the fact that somebody was following behind her. Just here, in sections, the snow had blown away and footsteps on the pavement were audible.

The instinct of self-preservation started to dominate Molly, banishing everything else from her mind. Her pulses quickened and she hurried her pace. She had not very far to go to reach home — one more entry and a side street . . .

The footsteps behind her accelerated — and gradually became louder. Molly glanced back over her shoulder as she hurried on, but she could not see anybody. Caught alone here, she knew she wouldn't stand a chance.

Abruptly the cocktails still confusing her mind crystallised into false courage. She stopped dead, swung round, then shouted:

'Who's there? Who is it? What do you want?'

A dim figure darted out from the shadows by the wall. Molly had no chance to see the face of the person before she was seized by the throat. Struggling, she stumbled over backwards to the pavement and found herself pinned down, a well-muffled man's figure over her.

She yelled frantically, but was cut off abruptly as one hand released her throat and clamped over her mouth instead. She struggled desperately, using all her flabby strength — but against her attacker it was useless. She could feel his fingers crushing into her throat with such force that the air was being shut off from her lungs. Her head, already dizzy, began to spin diabolically and pulses drummed in her ears and behind her eyes . . .

Confusedly she thought she heard other footsteps, then the iron grip suddenly left her and her assailant went speeding away into the dark. She lay where she was, gulping for breath, her hat lost and her prize doll cracked irreparably under her weight.

The swift footsteps stopped beside her. Strong hands dragged her to her feet. She looked up at a dimly visible face under a green hat.

'You okay, kid?'

'Yes, I'm okay.' Molly breathed hard. 'But I mightn't have been! I — I think somebody tried to kill me!'

'You think right, sister,' Pulp Martin answered grimly. 'Better lead the way to your home. I'll see you there.'

He felt her shaking against him as he held on to her arm. She began to walk uncertainly, sniffing and throwing broken pottery out of her pocket.

'I lost my hat,' she said miserably. 'It took a week's wages to buy that . . . '

'Yeah? One second — '

Pulp Martin vanished into the dark and returned within a few minutes, a battered blue creation dimly visible in his hand.

'Here's your lid, sister . . . '

'You're a real good sort,' Molly said gratefully. 'You're Mr. Martin, aren't you? How did you happen to come so handily?'

'Chance ... I'm a guy who gets around. This your place?' He knew it was, but pretended ignorance.

Molly knocked on the door of her home, then the moment he heard footsteps inside in response to it Pulp turned and left her, sped back through the gloomy streets to where he had left Maria. She was standing against the wall — as she had been when he had departed in the wake of Molly Ibbetson — rubbing her bereted head painfully.

'Is she all right, Mr. Martin?' she asked anxiously.

'Only just ... ' Pulp came up in the gloom. 'Somebody was trying to choke the life out of her when I got there. He got clear away before I could do anything.'

Maria gave a little groan. 'Our murderous friend packs a decided — er — wallop, Mr. Martin! I have a first-class headache. I believe that blow might have killed me but for the thick paper padding I wear inside my beret. An old trick which I first heard of in a — hmm! — fourpenny Sexton Blake thriller ... Incidentally, I haven't thanked you for arriving so opportunely.'

'Nothing to it, Maria. I'd got nothin' to do this evening — so I figured after I'd finished giving Millington Avenue the cold prowl that I'd go back and watch Molly Ibbetson come home. Just like you told me. I saw her come into this street and I was shadowing her from the other side of the street when I heard a scuffle. Next thing I saw was you lying on your back on the sidewalk. Whoever done it was hidden in the shadows between the street lamps. So I hops over and picks you up . . . ' Pulp stopped and reflected. 'But what in hell's it all about?'

'I believe — and have believed for some time — that this girl Molly Ibbetson knows who killed the man in A-11 — and the killer also knows it, hence the effort to blot her out. Only tonight, under the influence of drink, I think she had half-told Peter Canfield the truth and was then afraid to commit herself any farther. So I gathered from drifts of conversation that referred to some secret . . . I happened to appear in the picture as well

211

so the killer tried to finish me.'

'That why you asked me to keep an eye on the Ibbetson kid?'

'Exactly. And I should go on doing it. That girl is very dangerous — to somebody.'

'Well, if she knows the killer what's to stop us asking her who it is and save all this monkeying around?'

'One thing — proof — which I am collecting by degrees. And the other reason is that faced with such a question, and in her normal sober senses, I believe Molly would deny everything. Deep in her heart she is afraid to tell what she knows for fear of what might happen for withholding vital evidence for so long. But surrounded by proof in every other direction she will become prime witness number one.'

'I get it.'

'I'm glad you do, Mr. Martin. Now, if you will accompany me back to Roseway I will attend to the matter of your expenses.'

Maria felt nearly too worn out and dazed by the blow she had received to find her way into Roseway when she arrived. She was thankful for Pulp's assistance. With all the care of a devoted son handling his mother he led her through the gate, unlocked the private side door as she gave him the key, and finally helped her into her study. She sat down at her desk heavily, removed her paper-packed beret and rubbed her head. Then she glanced at the clock. It was 11.40.

'Who done this, anyway?' Pulp demanded, clenching his fists. 'Just name the guy who slugged you and I'll mash his jaw!'

Maria smiled faintly. 'Frankly, Mr. Martin, I do not know who it was — for certain. And while I appreciate your offer, I think you may take comfort from the thought that reprisals will be exacted in due course.'

She turned aside to the safe, brought out her cash-box and handed over some money.

'Here you are, Mr. Martin — and thank you for being so very attentive. Tell me, did you discover anything in Millington Terrace?'

'Sorry, Maria — I couldn't find out nothin'. All I did find out was that young Canfield lives there — in one of the cheaper dives at the far end of the avenue. Not that I suppose it means anythin'.'

'It might,' Maria said; 'I just don't know. I am rather surprised at what I have discovered about young Canfield. He is obviously a youth who likes to think of himself as a man about town, who is not averse to strong drink and who is also a first-class marksman at a rifle range.'

Pulp's eyebrows rose. 'Say, don't that sort of make him significant?'

'Obviously — and even more so since he lives in one of the roads about which the man in A-11 inquired. But again, we may be up against the old bugbear of coincidence. I think I had better get all the addresses of the staff from Morgan and find out the different domiciles. There might be a clue that way, unless Morgan has something definite to relate tomorrow since he has seen Lydia Fane — as I presume he will have done by now.'

Maria covered her eyes with her hand

for a moment. Pulp stood looking at her anxiously. Then she looked up at him and smiled.

'I must rest now. Thank you for all you have done. Remain at the hotel until I have need of you again.'

Pulp took the dismissal calmly.

' 'Night, Maria. Sleep tight.'

9

Thanks to her resilient constitution Maria felt better the following morning. Beyond a lump on the back of her head and a slight headache, she was none the worse — but she was in a grim mood which made the inmates of Roseway, those few remaining over the vacation, waft away from her as she stalked the college's corridors.

She took prayers in the chapel with an icy regard for detail; then she retired to her study to find Inspector Morgan awaiting her. He got to his feet immediately.

'Good morning, Miss Black . . . I've some news which might interest you.'

She acknowledged his greeting with a nod and sat down at her desk. 'I take it that you have seen Lydia Fane, then?'

'Last night — and done more besides . . .' Morgan seated himself again and looked at Maria as though uncertain of her mood.

'Last night, Inspector, an attempt was made on my life and that of Molly

Ibbetson! Fortunately I have Mr. Martin on constant watch over the movements of Molly and that fact saved her and me . . . But it is not calculated to improve one's temper.'

'So he's watching Molly, is he?'

'I have told him to, yes. Does it signify?'

'Well, I was visited early this morning by Mr. Ibbetson, and he told me about his daughter having been attacked. It seems she arrived home in a bad state last night, chattering about somebody having attacked her. I've got my men looking into it, but if Martin's on the job constant supervision can be left to him.'

'I think you will find, Inspector, that the attack on Molly and myself is bound up in the case we are working on. In fact, but for lack of proof — which seals my lips — I think I could tell you now who made the attack, though I might not be entirely sure of the reason for it.'

'So the killer of the man in A-11 is spreading his activities, eh? Anyway, that apart, you'll be interested to know that the dead man's real name was Kenneth Harcourt. Fifteen years ago he was sentenced to death for the murder of one Malcolm Landon, head of a financial combine. The sentence was afterwards commuted to life imprisonment due to extenuating circumstances. Harcourt was released from Pentonville Prison on Saturday morning last — exactly a week ago today, and two days before he appeared in Langhorn here on the Monday evening. I've checked back on all this from the prison authorities.'

'And did Miss Fane volunteer all this information?'

'Not exactly. In fact, I had a hard job to get any information at all. She's a cool, sophisticated sort of girl who obviously knows her way about, but faced with photographs of Harcourt and then the facial and ear similarity she had to admit the dead man was her father.'

'I see. I take it she does not read newspapers?'

'She must do — but she would hardly realise who the man was from the paper reports — and no photograph of the dead man was published.'

'Did she seem distressed by the news?'

Maria asked, thinking.

'Deeply. But since she is an actress among other things I could not tell whether her emotion was genuine. Offhand, though, I would say that she got the shock of her life! Anyway, she told me that her father was convicted of murder when she was a child of five. Her mother died when she was twelve and an aunt took care of her. Apparently she's cut her own way through life. It was a hard job to get her to tell that much — and she certainly refused to say more. I tried to make her give a possible reason for her father going to Langhorn so quickly after his release from prison, but she wouldn't. She insisted instead that she wished to forget her father, and for that reason had changed her name to Fane so nothing could besmirch her.'

'I detect an inconsistency, Inspector. She was deeply distressed — so you say, by the death of her father, yet she insisted she wanted to forget all about him! Either she is not telling the truth or else you misinterpreted her emotions.'

'I don't pretend to be able to judge

women accurately, Miss Black. I doubt if any man can. But I did prove the murdered man's identity, and that's a big help.'

Maria nodded a courteous assent, though she seemed to be thinking of something else. Morgan looked at her doubtfully, then added:

'I traced back to Harcourt's activities before his imprisonment, and it seems that he was then a financier in a big way of business — quite an important personage. At the trial the evidence showed that he had murdered this other financier, Landon, by whose demise Harcourt profited considerably. It was, as I have said, certain unresolved facts which produced the commutation.'

'Most interesting . . . None of which explains what Harcourt was doing in Langhorn.'

'As I see it,' Morgan lowered his voice confidentially, 'a man released from a fifteen-year sentence would not dash to a quiet little spot like Langhorn without a very definite reason. The only reason I can think of is that somebody in this district is connected with his imprisonment. Maybe he wanted to contact that somebody — and probably he could not do it on the Sunday, or else the poor railway travelling on a Sunday held him up . . . '

'So?' Maria murmured, her eyes half closed.

'Well, I've made further inquiry at the 'Golden Saddle' and have discovered that Harcourt asked the proprietress the situation of both Millington Terrace and Greystone Avenue. But nobody likely to interest us lives in either of those avenues.'

'Mr. Lincross lives in Greystone Avenue, and young Peter Canfield in Millington Terrace,' Maria murmured.

'I know that, Miss Black — but neither of them fits the case . . . No, there's somebody else in one of those roads who might be able to clear this whole thing up. I'm going to work on that angle next.'

'And have you any idea yet as to why Harcourt destroyed every trace of his identity?'

'I can only think that he did not want to be known.'

Maria smiled. 'I can elaborate on that, Inspector. He perhaps intended to commit murder — a murder of revenge, if you like — and took good care to cover his tracks beforehand. But somebody guessed what he was going to do and so killed him first!'

'Yes — maybe that is a better theory than mine,' Morgan admitted grudgingly.

'Naturally, you will now drop the case against Allerton? He is only twenty-one years of age. If we assume that Harcourt was trying to avenge himself on somebody who brought about his imprisonment we cannot include Allerton. He would only be six years old at the time.'

'He may be a relative of the unknown whom Harcourt was seeking.' Morgan was reluctant to let his theory go. 'I'll get in touch with his parents.'

Maria smiled rather cynically and gently fingered the bruise on the back of her head.

'Anyway, it will work out!' Morgan said confidently. 'And now I come to the ballistics report on the air-rifle. And it explodes one or two of our own pet ideas, too. Listen to this — '

He spread the report out on the desk in front of him and began to read:

'A B.S.A. air-rifle, and one of the best in the world. It has a muzzle velocity of six hundred feet per second and fires, under normal conditions, a sixteen-grain pellet. In our case though, Miss Black, a slug of solid copper was used and the lands ingrained in the slug taken from the dead man's skull exactly match those in the rifle barrel. That fact was more or less established, anyway, but here is the proof. There are no fingerprints on the rifle — evidently wiped off . . . But ballistics point out that even at a velocity of six hundred feet a second the slug would be unlikely to penetrate a man's skull at forty-seven feet range, at least sufficiently for the slug to go right through into the brain. Then there would be the initial check to speed from the rubber screen. Again, the angle from the screen to Row A in the Circle is nine degrees incline. It would bring the counter-action of gravity into the problem . . . So apparently Harcourt was not shot from behind the screen.'

'If you recall, Inspector, I doubted that possibility from the first,' Maria remarked. 'Everything was against it, apart from these expert observations. The light of the projector would be bound to dazzle the firer of the rifle, and one face in a row of faces takes a good deal of hitting even with so good a rifle.'

Morgan rubbed his jaw in fierce exasperation. 'But it has to be right because the wound was in Harcourt's forehead, so it must have come from the front!'

Maria got to her feet and began to pace up and down slowly. Then at last she gave a rather mischievous smile.

'I believe that Harcourt was shot from above, through the big central ventilator grille which spans across Row A. I thought so from the first, and even more so when Mr. Martin mentioned that it would be easier to shoot a man from there than from the area of the screen. Think of the advantages, Inspector! The reflected light from the projector-beam would illuminate the subject clearly. There would be nothing to dazzle the firer of the rifle . . . '

'I thought of that myself when I was up in the roof,' Morgan pointed out. 'In fact, I mentioned it to Martin.'

'I know — but you didn't follow the idea up far enough. Then again the slug would travel with gravity, and the distance would only be about twenty-seven feet — '

'But it would be bound to hit in the top of Harcourt's skull!' Morgan insisted.

'I think that was the intention,' Maria replied slowly. 'But we have established — at least in theory — that Harcourt was perhaps looking for somebody upon whom to exact revenge. Such a person would be highly alert for any possible attack on himself. I think he heard the killer above him, or at least an unusual sound that caused him to glance up. At that identical moment the screen shots exploded, the air-rifle was fired, and Harcourt received the slug with devastating accuracy: nobody noticed what happened in the transient excitement. Then his head fell forward on to his chest

— or rather his chin did. Hence the slug entered his forehead as he looked up.'

'You've got it, Miss Black! That is it — the only theory which fits!'

'Thank you, Inspector,' Maria murmured, still pacing. 'And now to something else. I take it that Harcourt visited the cinema three times purely to see his daughter act?'

'I imagine so. Obviously he would keep in touch with her somehow — through friends, no doubt. But I am struck by the amazing coincidence that the Langhorn Cinema happened to be showing a film with Harcourt's daughter in it on the very day he came to the town for some other purpose. He could not have known what was on at the cinema.'

'Amazing coincidence is definitely right!' Maria murmured. 'Yet, in a way, perhaps it narrows our search — '

She turned sharply as the house-telephone rang. She listened to the voice of the college porter for a moment and then said briefly:

'Send her to my study, please.'

Morgan's eyebrows went up in inquiry

as Maria put the phone back.

'Nancy Crane. Now I wonder what that incoherent young lady can want?' Maria resumed her seat and she and Morgan both waited in silence until the girl was shown in to them.

She was dressed in her usual tweed overcoat and woollen pixie. When she caught sight of Inspector Morgan she gave a distinct start.

''Morning, young lady,' he greeted genially.

'Well — er — ' Nancy fiddled with her gloves. Then she made up her mind. 'It's as well perhaps that you're here, Inspector. You'll be as interested in what I'm going to say as Miss Black will be to hear it.'

'Sit down, my dear,' Maria invited, and Nancy perched herself on a chair edge.

'I — I thought you ought to know something, Miss Black — and you too, Inspector, if it's coming to that. I managed to wangle some time off this morning so I could specially come and tell you. It's about that rifle I saw you were carrying yesterday, Inspector.'

'What about it, miss?' Morgan said sharply.

'You were going out of the building, carrying it with you. I saw you.'

'I presume you mean carrying the rifle, not the building?' Maria asked gravely.

'Yes. I've seen it before — in Atkinson's, that junk store near the cinema.'

'When?' Maria asked quickly.

'About three weeks ago . . . '

'Listen to me, Miss Crane.' Morgan leaned towards her paternally. 'What you are saying may be very important — too important to permit of mistakes. How can you be sure it is the same rifle?'

'Rusty marks on the barrel, for one thing — then there's other things that your memory sort of gets an impression of. I look in that store window every day on my way to work. I'm looking for a cheap camera, as a matter of fact, so I can photograph Fred and — '

'Please, Nancy — keep to the point,' Maria murmured.

'Well, I remember seeing that rifle some time before it wasn't there any longer.'

'When did it disappear?' Maria prompted. 'Can you remember?'

'About a fortnight ago, I'd say,' Nancy replied, thinking. 'It first appeared three weeks ago. It was there about a week marked at three pounds; then inside that week it had gone . . . '

Nancy's voice trailed off. 'I — I don't want this to get me in a mess,' she said. 'But I did think you ought to know.'

'And very right too,' Maria confirmed. 'I think you can rest assured that you will not get into any — er — mess. In fact, if everybody were as observant and helpful as you seem to be there would be far less crime.'

'There's something else worrying me, Miss Black. About Fred. I don't know if the Inspector ought to listen — '

'I am sure the Inspector will respect your confidence, my dear,' Maria smiled. 'What about Mr. Allerton? I know how concerned you are for him.'

'Well, I'm getting frightened he might do something awful! He told me yesterday that he didn't like you poking your nose in, Miss Black, and that it would be better if — if you were out of the way.' Nancy coloured violently. 'I thought I'd warn you to be careful.'

'In case, in a misguided effort to try to stop my activities, he should attack me?' Maria inquired.

'Yes . . . In case of that.'

'Young lady, you've been very wise in telling me all this,' Maria said, getting up and going over to where the girl was seated. 'And if he starts to rant again just tell him that he is no more under suspicion than anybody else — that you are just as much suspect as he is. He just happens to have been unlucky in the amount of circumstantial evidence surrounding him. If he is innocent, he has nothing to fear. Am I not right, Inspector?'

'If he is innocent — yes,' he agreed, shrugging.

Nancy got to her feet and flashed a smile of gratitude. 'I'll remember that, Miss Black — and whatever more I learn, if I do, I'll come and tell you about, whatever it is.'

'Good!' Maria agreed. 'Then we'll leave

it at that.' She saw the girl out into the corridor, then she closed the door again and came back to her desk thoughtfully.

'Very observant girl,' Morgan said. 'To look at her and hear the cock-eyed way she talks you would think she hadn't two thoughts in her brain. But she's all there.'

'And the head of the usherettes,' Maria added. 'Appearances can be deceptive . . . However, Nancy Crane apart, what of the rifle? Marked at three pounds and it disappeared about a fortnight ago. What is your angle on that?'

'That a local inhabitant probably bought it.'

'Or else somebody at the cinema,' Maria said slowly. 'Nancy saw it on her way to work: others who are employed at the cinema would no doubt also see it, too . . . I think, Inspector, that an interview with the second-hand dealer is called for.'

'Just what I was thinking,' he replied, getting to his feet. 'You'll be coming, too?'

'I think not, Inspector. I am still the Principal of this college, and I cannot run about at will — besides Saturday morning is rather a busy one for me. But I would be glad to know how you get on. Maybe we can then exchange any further ideas.'

'All right. I'll let you know what happens, and thanks for your various suggestions.'

Maria merely smiled; then as Morgan reached the door she raised a hand and stayed him.

'Oh, Inspector — before you go. In that report on the rifle slug it said that the slug was pure copper, did it not?'

'That's right, Miss Black — pure solid copper. But since copper is a malleable metal anybody could have got hold of a piece and shaped it into a slug. Wouldn't even need to melt it at its usual twenty-three hundred Fahrenheit degrees . . . Well, I'll be on my way.'

Maria sat down at her desk as the Inspector went out and pondered. Inevitably her black book came out of its drawer and she commenced making notes: —

Molly Ibbetson ceases to interest me as a central figure in this case of the man in A-11, though I am reasonably sure that she knows — or thinks she knows — the identity of the killer of Kenneth Harcourt (A-11). To try to extract the information from her is feasible, of course, but in case she might jump the wrong way I shall hold my hand for the moment.

Have just learned through Nancy Crane that Fred Allerton has conceived a violent dislike for my activities. Could it have been he who attacked me last night? If so, why did he also attack Molly Ibbetson?

Only because — if he be guilty — he might be aware that she knows his secret.

Yet somehow I cannot reconcile facts with Allerton's apparent guilt — i.e., the dead man having been convicted fifteen years ago; the apparent impossibility of Allerton telephoning himself . . . and so on. I might just as well consider where the doorman was last Wednesday evening at 8.37 p.m., or why the manager took it upon himself to stoke up the coke boiler instead of waiting until the doorman could be found.

Kenneth Harcourt was released from jail last Saturday, a week today. He was once a celebrated financier, so would not his release date find its way into the daily Press? If so, the killer might have seen it, and having also seen the air-rifle in the second-hand dealer's window, decided to buy it, At least it is a lead if the air-rifle vanished after the newspaper announcement. (If any.) There has to be some clue as to how the killer knew Harcourt was coming out of prison.

Lastly, the copper slug: I am wondering if the sheathing of an arc-lamp carbon — which is pure copper — might not explain it, not because I am again suspecting Allerton but because I have discovered that Peter Canfield is an excellent shot with a rifle and lives in one of the avenues about which Harcourt inquired.

I doubt if Lydia Fane telling all she knows. I think I shall pay a flying visit to London to try to coax more information out of her. The Inspector's official manner may have frightened *her. A girl who loathes her father's name and yet is shocked to hear of his death is still, to my mind, a paradox.*

The time is 11.10 a.m.

★　★　★

The Saturday afternoon children's matinée was in progress at the Langhorn Cinema when the swing doors opened and closed again to admit Maria. She was in her camelhair coat and model hat again, umbrella on her arm. Yet there was an odd gleam in her wintry eyes and the grim look she had had early in the morning had not entirely left her face.

'Why, Molly — how are you . . . ?'

Maria paused beside the ordinary booking office and looked across the ticket shelf as Molly lolled upon it. She did not look at all happy. Make-up saved her face from being deathly pale, and there was a pained look in her dark eyes.

''Afternoon, Miss Black,' she responded listlessly. 'Want a ticket?'

'For a children's matinée!' Maria looked horror-stricken. 'I am seeking Mr.

Lincross, as a matter of fact. Is he in?'

'Not yet,' Molly sighed. 'He will be soon . . . '

Maria nodded, then: 'And what have you been doing with yourself, miss? You look utterly washed out.'

'Just a hangover. 'Sides, I was attacked on my way home last night. Didn't that chap, Mr. Martin, tell you?'

'Yes . . . ' Maria compressed her lips. 'A pretty dreadful experience for you. Now the police know about it though you should be all right.'

Molly looked as though she wondered about this, and sensing she might be steered into awkward conversation Maria turned aside towards the opposite corner of the foyer where Mary Saunders's advance booking office door was slightly open.

Maria pushed the door open wider with the ferrule of her umbrella and beamed in upon Mary as she sat with her legs crossed, absorbed in a thriller between bookings.

'I take it that you enjoy murders in and out of business hours?' Maria asked dryly.

Mary smiled as she laid the book aside. 'Saves me getting bored . . . ' She flexed her arms and stiffened her back as though awakening from sleep. 'Don't often see you about here in an afternoon, Miss Black. Something important happened about the dead man?'

'No — nothing like that. I am simply waiting for Mr. Lincross.'

'Always late for the children's matinée,' Mary said, making a face. 'And I don't blame him. Little jammy-mouthed horrors, all of them. Listen to the din — !'

Maria leaned her ear back from the doorway and just caught the roar of applause from the closed area in the cinema hall.

'That's the serial,' Mary explained. ' 'Brushwood Rides the Sage', or something equally horse-opera.'

Maria nodded, but said nothing. She remained standing just where she was, inside the doorway, studying the walls where the booking charts hung, then the stacks of tickets and inevitable photographs of film stars cut from weekly periodicals.

'Tell me something, Mary . . . ' Maria's voice was casual. 'When you get an advance booking, what happens?'

'Happens?'

'Suppose, for instance, that for the moment I take the place of the man who was shot in seat A-11. If I booked that seat for tonight, tomorrow night, and the night after what would happen?'

'Well, if the programme were running that long — which it isn't because we change it at the weekend — I'd mark your seat number off on these three charts.' Mary nodded to them hanging on the wall. 'Each chart is marked for each coming performance — then it goes in to Mr. Lincross so he can keep a check on the returns, after which it goes to Nancy Crane as the head usherette, so that she can direct the bookings, by means of reserved tickets, before each show.'

'Very interesting. One would never suspect such complication behind the scenes. And I presume that if I booked for the Stalls the same process would apply?'

'If you *could* book for the Stalls, yes.'

'If I could? What would there be to stop me?'

'Block booking,' Mary explained. 'That means that every seat downstairs for every performance is booked permanently by somebody who has the seat each matinée and each night performance. Those people pay by subscription. It would not operate in a big theatre with a continuous performance, but it does here because the local population has no other cinema to go to. We are always full downstairs at any show.'

'Ah! Which means that no outsider could book for the Stalls in any case?'

'Correct,' Mary agreed. 'Only for the Circle. You'll see a notice over the ordinary booking office there — Stalls Admission by Block Booking Only.'

'I shall seriously consider asking Mr. Lincross for shares in this gold mine of his,' Maria murmured. 'And thank you, Mary, for being so explicit.'

'No trouble,' the girl picked up her thriller again as Maria moved away.

'Now I just wonder what the old girl

wanted to know all that for?' she muttered.

Maria crossed the foyer, surveying the stills for coming features and the rack announcing the forthcoming attractions. From the hall came the occasional roar of excited children as, presumably, the hero dashed to the rescue . . .

Then at last the swing doors opened and shut as Lincross came in. 'Good afternoon, Miss Black . . . Awaiting me?'

'Just a little favour I have to ask you,' Maria said, nodding.

'With pleasure. Come into the office, will you? Sorry to be so late.'

Maria followed him inside. He drew up a chair for her and hurried out of his overcoat. 'Now, madam?'

'While I am aware, Mr. Lincross, that you regard my little efforts at criminology as nothing less than intrusion, I think I ought to tell you that I have no intention of giving up my own particular line of research . . . '

'Forgive me, but . . . ' Lincross's eyes were full of earnest denial. 'I merely regard your activities as — unusual,' he explained. 'Just the same, I want to get this grim business settled as much as anybody. It casts a decided cloud over my cinema.'

'In that case I think I can rely on your co-operation. I wonder if I might take a look round the projection-room? I have a theory . . . ' Maria coughed primly. 'I cannot detail it, but let us imagine that the air-rifle was not fired from the screen but through one of the ceiling ventilators. Let us also imagine that nobody went near it to pull the trigger. Let us assume instead that a string was attached to the trigger, the end of the string dropping down into the projection-room — since it is on a level with the false roof — through a minute hole . . . '

'I see! You mean that somebody in the projection-room could have fired the rifle! That's a very clever idea!'

Maria smiled gravely. The whole theory was actually the worst on-the-spot nonsense she had ever conceived . . . but if it served its purpose that was all that mattered.

Evidently it did for Lincross got up and

turned to the door. 'If you'll come this way, Miss Black . . . ?'

She followed him majestically towards the Circle staircase. Then as he unfastened the lower door leading up to the projection-room she gave him a meaning glance.

'I think I had better investigate alone,' she murmured. 'I can keep them occupied up in the projection-room so that they will not guess my real purpose in being there.'

Lincross opened the door, nodded his semi-bald head solemnly, then went off back down the stairs.

For a moment Maria stood looking about her — at the staff room door, just visible round the stair angle, then at the closed doors leading to the Circle. She nodded to herself, then went through the projection-room main doorway and began to mount the concrete steps towards the winding-room.

10

There was nobody present in the winding-room as Maria looked into it. The lights were full on, the re-winding equipment carried an empty spool, and the arc rectifier was whirring rhythmically — but this was all.

Maria climbed the remaining steps into the projection-room itself. Dick Alcot, who was taking care of the machine nearest the door, gave a start when he saw Maria come in somewhat laboriously.

'Good afternoon, Mr. Alcot . . . ' Maria drew herself erect and nodded to him.

Alcot had possession of himself immediately. 'Last person I expected to see up here,' he said; then raising his voice he called over the machine's noise and the chatter of the monitor-speaker. 'Hey — Fred! Here's Miss Black!'

Fred Allerton and Peter Canfield came out of the steel-walled slide room. They looked as though they had been caught playing truant — then Allerton grinned sheepishly as Maria's quick eye dropped to the ace of clubs in his hand.

'Just passing the time on,' he explained. 'These kids' matinées give you the pip.'

'Quite,' Maria smiled. 'I am sorry I disturbed you, young man: in fact I must apologise to all three of you. But I just wanted to have a look at the business end of pictures. Mr. Lincross was kind enough to extend his permission.'

'Oh!' Allerton looked rather non-plussed. Peter Canfield took the line of least resistance, dodged round Maria's forbidding figure, and hurried from the room. Alcot's pale eyes, full of inquiry, watched the proceedings over the top of the hot projector lamphouse.

'My desire for a survey is really connected with those amplified revolver shots in 'Love on the Highway',' Maria went on, thinking out her words as she gazed about her. 'When you put the sound up three stages — '

'Three faders,' Allerton corrected, being a stickler for technical accuracy.

'Faders, I beg your pardon. What did you do?'

Allerton turned and pointed to a square box about four inches high and five broad on the wall between the projectors. In the centre of the box was a knob controlling a pointer. At each side of the pointer's arc were numbers. At the moment the pointer was at '4' on the right-hand curve of figures.

'This machine Dick is running is working on Fader Four,' Allerton explained. 'Stepping it up three faders merely means putting the pointer up to seven. Thereby the sound is that much increased.'

'I see,' Maria said, rather absently. Her eyes had travelled above the fader control to a square steel-framed notice that read — IT IS STILL ESSENTIAL TO SAVE COPPER DRIPS AND CARBON STUB SHEATHING FOR SALVAGE. ARE *YOU* DOING IT?

Allerton followed her gaze. 'Are you wondering what that means?' he asked, inwardly surprised at her lack of interest in his fader exposition.

'I am merely wondering what 'copper drips' and 'carbon stub' implies, young man. This place is a mystery to me, you know.'

'Simple enough,' he said, and went across to a big tin standing in a corner of the room. From it he took a handful of short carbon lengths, about three inches long, and held them out in his palm.

'Stubs! As Chief it is my job to count them when they are put in this tin. When they get too short for the arc-jaws to hold them we put them by for salvage. The copper coating is useful for war potential. Pure copper, you see. As for drippings, they are the carbon and copper amalgam that falls from the electrodes when they're heated. Rather like — metallic bread-crumbs.'

'Ah, I see! Most instructive.'

Allerton tossed the stumps back into the tin and then went on to explain all the mysteries of the projection-room in detail. Maria took a polite and apparently keen interest in all he told her, more out of respect for his ready generosity than anything else for she had already gathered all she needed . . . She chose a moment when Allerton and Alcot's backs were turned to dive her hand into the waste tin, snatch up a carbon stub and hide it in her palm — then again she was the ready listener.

At last Allerton led her out of the projection-room and down into the winding department. His fund of knowledge seemed to have come to an end at last and he stood looking at her, his sombre dark eyes reflecting an inner doubt.

'I suppose you didn't really want to know all that,' he said, after he had dismissed Peter Canfield from the room. 'You really only wanted to know about the fader?'

'Actually, yes — but it was all very instructive.'

Allerton rubbed the back of his head. 'This is the first chance I have ever had to talk to you alone, Miss Black,' he said finally. 'And it has upset a lot of the ideas I'd conceived about you.'

'About my being nosy?' Maria suggested calmly; and he gave a start.

'Nan's been talking to you again!' he snapped.

'Yes, young man, she has — but she has only your interests at heart, believe me.'

'Did Nancy tell you about that air-rifle?' Allerton asked. 'She's seen it before — '

'Yes, so she said. It is being checked upon by the redoubtable Inspector . . . ' Maria considered Allerton's earnest face for a moment, then: 'If anybody were to take a number of carbon stubs from that tin you showed me, would you know about it?'

'Of course. I keep count of them for the salvage officer.'

Maria smiled at his surprised look and turned to the doorway.

'Just an idea that struck me,' she said vaguely. 'I get them at times . . . '

★ ★ ★

When Maria left the cinema — after having assured Lincross that she had learned all she needed — she went to the police station at the far end of High Street, and found Inspector Morgan in his office.

'I gave you a ring at Roseway, Miss Black,' he said, when she was seated. 'They told me you were out on business for the afternoon.'

'Yes, indeed. And here is the nature of the business.' Maria opened her hand over the desk and dropped the carbon stub upon it.

'What's this?'

'A carbon stub, Inspector — '

'Yes, I can see that. But what's it for?'

'Spectrograph analysis. If you send that stub to your ballistics department and have its outer copper sheath spectrum checked with that of the slug which killed Harcourt I think it will be found that the two spectra are identical.'

Morgan picked up the copper stub and tossed it in his palm. Then he gave a grim smile. 'I suspect, Miss Black, that you have stolen a march on me!'

Maria looked at him blandly. 'I am merely trying to help you and improve my own knowledge of criminology. While you were busy in one direction I was busy in another. There are times when official-dom tends to frighten a suspect, whereas

I, as a private individual, do not.'

Morgan merely grunted.

'I simply put two and two together,' Maria resumed. 'We decided this morning that somebody working at the cinema perhaps bought the rifle. Whence came the copper? You said it might be from anywhere, but on reflection I felt inclined to disagree. I recalled that if there is one place where copper abounds in these days of shortage it is in a projection-room. So, under an absurd pretext — but convincing enough to Mr. Lincross — I got into the projection-room and appropriated this stub. If it checks exactly with the copper analysis of the slug, then we know that the copper for the slug came from the projection-room — and we also know that it was almost certainly somebody on the cinema staff who committed the crime.'

'Well, it's a nice bit of reasoning,' Morgan admitted. 'We'll see what ballistics have to say about this. But I've got rather a cold douche to throw on this theory. It was not somebody from the cinema who bought the air-rifle!'

'Then who did?'

'A boy! A boy whom the store proprietor had never seen before. He came in about ten days ago — in an evening — handed over three pounds and bought the air-rifle . . . ' Morgan paused, then went on with a touch of sensation in his voice.

'But I have established that young Peter Canfield sold the air-rifle to the store dealer some time ago, for thirty shillings. Atkinson — that's the junk dealer — knows him well. It seems he often drops in to buy odds and ends, as youngsters will.'

'So that is how we stand!' Maria mused. 'Young Peter sold it: he is a crack shot; the slug was possibly made from projection-room copper; and an unknown boy buys the gun at three pounds. Friend of Canfield's? Maybe!'

Sudden interest had dawned on Morgan's beefy face. 'Did you say young Canfield is a crack shot?'

'Yes,' Maria replied absently. 'I followed him to Lexham Fair yesterday afternoon and he swept the board when it came to the rifle range.'

'This makes it look bad for young

Canfield — if the copper sheathing is the same as the slug.' Morgan said. 'Obviously Canfield got his shooting skill from practice with that B.S.A. rifle. Then it looks as though, having sold it, he got it back again through a young friend and . . . '

'Shot Kenneth Harcourt with it? Maybe!' Maria narrowed her eyes. 'Inspector, I have done all I can for the moment and must be on my way. The good Miss Tanby will be wondering where I have got to . . . Might I inquire your next move?'

'I'm going to young Canfield's home and find out all I can about him from his parents, then from he himself when he comes home from the afternoon show.'

Maria reflected. 'Then I'm afraid Miss Tanby will have to manage a while longer,' she decided. 'You see, Inspector, I have one or two pertinent questions to ask that young man myself. I hardly think his lavish spending yesterday can be accounted for by the selling of an air-rifle for thirty shillings — and some time ago at that.'

Maria rose, and then stood considering as Morgan reached for his hat.

'A moment, Inspector. It might be more to our advantage to catch young Canfield when he is at home — and that won't be for about an hour yet. Until then I think we might occupy ourselves in a more profitable way by visiting Lexham reference library and looking through the daily papers for about a week before Harcourt was released from prison — or at any rate in the issues immediately preceding the time when that air-rifle was bought from the second-hand store by that boy. The killer must have had some notification that Harcourt was due to leave prison, and as a once-famous financier I have little doubt but what his release date would find its way into the Press.'

'Well, we can look,' Morgan agreed. 'Let's be on our way.'

★ ★ ★

They were in Lexham reference library in twenty minutes, both of them studying the large bound files of the daily newspapers for a fortnight previous. It was not a job that Morgan entirely relished — but he remained doggedly at the search in the hope that something might come out of it.

Something did when Maria finally nudged his elbow and pointed to an inconspicuous corner of the *Daily Clarion*.

'Here we are, Inspector — five days before Harcourt was released from jail. Read it . . . '

Morgan did so:

'Kenneth Harcourt, known in the business world as 'Moneybags' Harcourt during the '30s, and who was sentenced to life imprisonment for the murder of Malcolm Landon, in 1934, by Mr. Justice Clayton, will become a free man next Saturday, having concluded a fifteen-year sentence. He has been a model prisoner and . . . '

'Et cetera, et cetera,' Morgan murmured, glancing up. 'Yes, this is all we need to know. How about the other papers? Do they check?'

They looked through the issues for the same day but only the *Daily*

Illustrated seemed to think the information was worth printing. Satisfied at Maria's nod, Morgan put the files back and then went out with her to the car again.

'Well, that worked, anyway,' he said in satisfaction.

'True. We know now that it was possible for the killer to be aware of Harcourt's release from jail five days before the release, which would obviously give ample time to make arrangements for killing him.'

'Yes — and the air-rifle was bought a fortnight ago, if Miss Crane is to be believed. That would make it before the newspaper announcement appeared.'

'Nancy said 'about' a fortnight, Inspector. There is not much difference between twelve and fourteen days. I think we may take it that it was bought almost immediately after that newspaper announcement.'

'In that case our next move is obvious. Langhorn has only one big newsagent who supplies all the people in the neighbourhood. From him we can discover who, locally, takes the *Daily Clarion* and *Daily Illustrated*, and from the addresses we are given we can decide which of them is most likely to interest us.'

Maria sat back in the leather seat and smiled contentedly. 'We are making good progress, Inspector.'

Neither of them spoke until Morgan drew up outside Naysmith's, the large newspaper agents in the town square.

'Maybe I can make this inquiry better than you, Miss Black,' Morgan said, climbing out.

Maria nodded and sat thinking her own thoughts for nearly ten minutes until Morgan came back.

'Nobody we are interested in takes the *Daily Illustrated*,' he said, 'but Allerton's family, Lincross, and Bradshaw, all take the *Daily Clarion*.'

'From which, Inspector, we are to infer — what?'

'Just nothing beyond the fact that all three of them had an equal chance of knowing that Harcourt was coming out of prison. But it doesn't help us to pin anything on them.'

'True ... ' Maria sat with her eyes

half-closed. 'In which case we can only move on to something more tangible — to Peter Canfield's home, for instance.'

Starting the car up again Morgan drove down the side streets into Millington Terrace and drew up finally before Number 24 . . . The Terrace itself had no right to such a claim for half of its length: it was a jumbled mass of cheap property — but farther away, perhaps half a mile or so, more enterprise had been shown and massive detached houses had been erected, seeming like palaces by comparison with their lowly neighbours.

At Morgan's knocking a heavy busted woman in a soiled blouse and grease-spotted brown skirt opened the door. She was still fairly young and the yellowness of her hair and shape of her features placed her instantly as Peter's mother.

'Mrs. Canfield?' Morgan questioned, and as the woman gave a dubious nod he added: 'I'd like a word with your son — Peter. Nothing serious.'

'All right.' Mrs. Canfield stood aside, still clearly alarmed by the official uniform. "'E's 'avin' his tea in the back kitchen.'

Maria followed the Inspector through a narrow hall into a back room. A big window, across which the curtains had not been drawn, gave on to a flagged yard powdered with snow vaguely visible in the dying grey of the short afternoon.

Peter Canfield sat in the midst of a confusion of crockery, soiled tablecloth, old magazines, schoolbooks, and a general miscellany of odds and ends. He was eating bread and jam and reading a folded magazine at the same time. Beside him at the table a blonde girl was chewing her pencil over a history book, while yet another blonde girl about two years younger was lying on her stomach on the battered sofa, her black-stockinged legs kicking lazily in the air and her eyes fixed on a novel with a most sinister cover.

'Excuse the mess,' Mrs. Canfield apologised. 'The kids won't be tidy no'ow. Our Margy always does 'er 'omework on a Saturday night, y'see.'

"'Tisn't homework, ma,' our Margy volunteered, glancing up. 'We broke up yesterday for Christmas, or have you forgotten? I'm just looking if King Charles really did — Oh!'

Margy — and her sister too — became conscious of Inspector Morgan and Maria simultaneously. Instantly they both jumped up and went hurrying from the room. Peter Canfield set down his bread and jam and frowned deeply.

'You'd like a chair, wouldn't you?' Mrs. Canfield suggested, 'You too, lady?

Morgan shook his head but Maria gave an imperturbable nod and settled rather uneasily on the bentwood pushed across towards her.

'I'd like a word with you, young man . . . ' Morgan looked down at Peter in a vague attempt at geniality. 'I believe you're a pretty good shot with an air-rifle . . . '

'Yes, I am,' Peter admitted, with a glance at his mother's worried face. 'But how did you know?'

'It's my business to find things out, son. Now, I want you to give me some information. You sold a B.S.A. air-rifle recently to Mr. Atkinson, who runs the secondhand store near the cinema — and you received thirty shillings for it. Right?'

Peter studied his plate. Then his mother suddenly exploded.

'Peter! You didn't! Not that lovely air-rifle your Uncle Ted sent you — ? An' never tellin' me a thing about it, neither!'

'The fact remains, Mrs. Canfield, that Peter here did just that,' Morgan said. 'You did sell that gun now, didn't you, Peter?'

'Yes, I did! I wanted some extra money. A fellow can't get far these days on my salary, and I've — I've got private matters to look after.'

'Girls?' Maria suggested dryly.

'Look,' Morgan said, edging stolidly into the conversation again. 'You sold that air-rifle — but did you know it had been bought by another boy for three pounds?'

'No, I didn't! I saw it on sale at three pounds in Atkinson's window for a while, and I realised that he'd welshed me — but there was nothing I could do about it. Then I noticed one morning that it had gone.'

'But you knew that an air-rifle had

killed that man in A-11 in the cinema?' Morgan asked sharply.

'Yes — Fred Allerton told me. But I never connected it with my own air-rifle. In fact I never thought about it again.'

'And you've absolutely no idea who bought it from Atkinson's?'

'None, sir. Honest!'

Maria leaned forward. 'Young man, there are a few questions I would like to ask you myself. You don't have to answer, but if you are anxious to see justice done and help the Inspector to find a murderer you will tell all you can . . . Now, do I understand that you gained your prowess at shooting with the air-rifle which you sold?'

'I should think he did, mum,' Peter's mother declared. ''Is Uncle Ted sent it to 'im. 'E found it in his lumber-room and except for a rusty barrel on the outside it were all right. Once he got it, Pete 'ere never stopped firing the thing from out of 'is bedroom window. It weren't safe for me or the rest of the kids to look outside. 'E used to shoot at bottles, 'e did, and — '

'Quite, Mrs. Canfield, quite,' Maria

interrupted, then she looked back at Peter. 'So you practised here, did you? Did you ever take the rifle to the cinema and practise there?'

'No, m'm, I didn't. Be no chance to practise there.'

'Then nobody knew that you possessed such a rifle?'

'Don't see how they could've,' Peter said, logically. Then he frowned. 'I can't see how you know I'm a good shot, m'm. Who told you?'

'Nobody. I was a personal witness of your activities at the firing range at Lexham fair yesterday afternoon.'

Peter opened his mouth and then shut it again.

'I do not pretend to know, young man, where you obtained the money for such a — hm! — blow-out, but I noticed you did not hold your hand . . . I think you had better explain.'

'I should think you 'ad!' his mother declared hotly. 'There's enough uses for money right 'ere with your sisters still at school and your pa still in the army, without you gallivantin'. What's all this about? Speak up sharp!'

'I don't know,' Peter answered sullenly.

'I think you do,' Maria decided. 'You told Molly Ibbetson that you had plenty of money. You went to Lexham fair, to the Temple Café, and finally to the Palace Dance Hall. You did far more than could be done on thirty shillings, if we assume for a moment that you retained the proceeds from the air-rifle that long — which I greatly doubt.'

'Peter,' Morgan said, 'where did you get the money to have such a good time?'

'A — a man gave me five pounds,' the youth said sheepishly.

There was something resembling a strangled gasp from Mrs. Canfield at the thought of losing five pounds.

'Men don't hand out five pounds to boys of your age without a very good reason,' Morgan said grimly. 'Who was this man?'

'I met him in Langhorn Square a week yesterday . . . ' Peter did not dare to look up as he confessed. 'I wasn't looking for him: I never even saw him before. He just stopped me and asked if I was the third operator from the Langhorn Cinema. I said that I was, and then he said that he was an inventor and wanted some carbon copper in a hurry for an experiment. Only cinemas can get it in these days, or else essential works. He asked me if I could get some.'

'Then?' Morgan demanded, after he and Maria had exchanged looks.

'I said I didn't see how I could get him any since all the carbons — unused and stumps — are in Fred's keeping. He keeps them locked up, you see. Mr. Lincross gets them in every six months, then hands them on to Fred who keeps a careful check on the number we use. So this chap asked me if I could get him some stumps. I said I couldn't do that either because Fred had got them all counted for salvage . . . Then he said he'd give me five quid for a dozen carbon stumps. Well, that is a lot of money to me and I knew it would be two more weeks before Fred counts the stumps again. I decided I'd get a dozen stumps and risk being able to replace them somehow later on.'

'Obviously, then, you did,' Maria said. 'And then what?'

'I met this chap the same place on Saturday night — week ago tonight that is — and he gave me five pounds in notes.'

'Which makes tracing them impossible,' Maria reflected. 'Did you recognise the man? His voice? Anything?'

'No. Never heard his voice before — and as I said I never saw him before, either.'

'What did he look like?' Morgan asked.

'He was about my height, pot-bellied, wearing a cap and a light mackintosh. He had a sort of Old Bill moustache.'

Morgan wrote swiftly in his notebook. 'Did he give a name?'

'Yes. He said he was Mr. Andrews and that he lived in Langhorn here. But how he knew all about me, I don't know. Of course I didn't ask the girls if they'd seen such a man in case I gave myself away.'

'Did you get a clear look at his face?' Morgan questioned.

'No, sir. We weren't near a street lamp and that peaked cap sort of hid his features. I only remember that his face didn't seem to match his stomach. Men with fat stomachs usually have double chins, but he hadn't.'

Morgan closed his notebook and considered. 'Well, young man, I think that's all we need to ask you for now. But I'd advise you to be wary of strangers in future!'

'I will!' Peter declared fervently; then suddenly he seemed to resolve a thought that had been troubling him. 'Look here, Inspector, I think you are going an awfully long way round to solve this murder. Why don't you just question Molly Ibbetson? She knows who killed that man in A-11. She told me as much.'

'She — what?' Morgan's eyes went wide and Maria compressed her lips in silent vexation.

'Right enough!' Peter insisted. 'I tried to make her tell me who it was, but she wouldn't. She'd *have* to tell you!'

'I'll have a word with her,' Morgan promised, setting his jaw. 'That's a most useful piece of information, my boy, and — '

'One more thing,' Maria interrupted. 'What time did you get home last night?'

''E was in 'ere at exactly arf-past ten!' Mrs. Canfield said bitterly. 'Too late for 'im — and I told 'im so!'

'Half-past ten?' Maria repeated. 'And you didn't go out again, Peter?'

'No,' Mrs. Canfield declared. 'That 'e didn't!'

★　★　★

Inspector Morgan had driven the car halfway back towards Roseway before he put his thoughts into words. 'It begins to look as though another party whom we hadn't reckoned with enters into this: a fat man with a walrus moustache. It's confoundedly annoying.'

Maria smiled. 'If I recall my textbooks correctly, Inspector, a criminal seeking to achieve safety will often resort to over-elaboration and create an *alter-ego*. I'm sure that the man with the Old Bill moustache was disguised. A little padding under the mackintosh would create the pot-belly — as Peter rather indelicately put it; and the Old Bill moustache could have been a piece of hearthrug clipped into the nose bone with bent wire. Such a disguise would never fool an adult, and even less an astute police inspector, but on a dark night it would very likely fool an inexperienced youth anxious to make a little money on the side.'

Morgan began to look relieved. 'You think that it was perhaps one of the cinema staff in disguise?'

'Since the staff had all left the cinema at that time — we presume — I think it is possible. We don't know that it was one of the cinema staff, but we are entitled to assume so.'

'Come to think of it,' Morgan said, 'Bradshaw wears a mackintosh and cap. I noticed that when I was called to the cinema just after the murder.'

'True,' Maria agreed, 'but we must remember that Peter described the man as about his own height — which is about five foot nine. Bradshaw is all of six feet. Of course, there is the ancient subterfuge of making oneself look smaller by giving at the knees — very simple in the darkness and with the knees hidden by a mackintosh — but even so I dislike such a theory. It's — amateur.'

'There's another point,' Morgan went on. 'Why on earth did he go to such fantastic lengths to get a few carbon stumps when he could have got them out of the projection-room for himself?'

'I can only assume — very roughly — that it was done to deflect guilt on to somebody else, to make Allerton, or Canfield, or even Alcot, look as though they were responsible. An inquiry might have brought the mysterious Mr. Andrews into the picture — *via* Peter, of course — and thereby all suspicion would switch to him: Andrews. Just the old, old tale, Inspector, of a guilty party laying red herrings. But we, fortunately, have been quick to grasp the truth.'

'Yes indeed!' Something like a glow emanated from Morgan.

'And, of course, we can now dispense with Peter as the possible attacker of either myself or Molly Ibbetson. We heard it said that he was in the house at ten-thirty, under the keen eye of his mother. I was attacked at about twenty to eleven, and Molly shortly afterwards. So it was *not* Peter who did that, and so he recedes from my interest as the possible killer of Kenneth Harcourt.'

'Um — yes,' Morgan admitted. 'And talking of Molly reminds me that I've got to have a serious talk with that young lady. She actually knows who the killer is — if Canfield is to be believed.'

'Molly may well be speaking the truth,' Maria said, 'but last night, when I presume she made the partial confession, she was somewhat under the influence of drink. I think, knowing girls as I do, that you will only frighten her out of the picture altogether if you question her. And if she really knows something that would be a pity.'

'Surely you don't suggest that I leave her untouched when she may have the answer to this whole business?'

'By no means — but this is not the time. Later on she may become the chief witness, and if she gets scared away — to the extent of running from home — it would be most disturbing.'

'Well, I'll think about it,' Morgan growled. 'I don't see why I should leave direct evidence uninvestigated . . . '

'Naturally, Inspector, we shall have to find out whom the boy was who bought that air-rifle.'

'Yes, I know that.' Morgan sounded irritable.

'That boy has to be found — and questioned,' Maria said imperturbably. 'I trust also that you noted the fact, Inspector, that the carbon stumps were asked for after the rifle had been purchased? The rifle was bought ten days ago, and the stumps a week ago tonight.'

'I noticed; and I'm wondering why the killer did not use the proper slugs. Any ideas?'

'It would perhaps have meant that the killer himself would have had to buy them — or else he would again have employed a boy to do it for him. Now, when you get too many young people doing odd things they discuss it in private and trouble ensues . . . '

'Too many cooks,' Morgan agreed.

'Exactly. So our friend used another method. He obtained the copper from the cinema through Peter, knowing full well that that boy would never talk in case he got into trouble with his chief. That is the reason why the proper slugs were not used. There are other probable reasons — to deflect guilt on to the operating staff, shortage of such slugs in these days; and also to make a really vicious missile of destruction our friend preferred to make his own instead of relying on the manufactured type which might not have been so deadly.'

Morgan drew the car up at the gates of Roseway. The expression on his bulldog face was halfway between annoyance and admiration.

'Your theories have helped a lot, Miss Black,' he said, as Maria climbed out into the powdered snow. 'Just the same I have my own ways of working, you know. I'm going to question that girl Molly and take a short cut to the truth.'

Maria shrugged. 'As you will, Inspector. I hope you will be successful ... Don't forget to let me know the result of that copper spectrum — and also don't forget that in order to save her own skin from the killer Molly Ibbetson may not tell the truth. And if she does not, you may arrest the wrong person!'

11

To her annoyance, the normal school tea hour was over when Maria arrived in her study. Instead she put on the electric kettle and sat down to think while the water heated.

After she had drunk two cups of tea there came a knock on the door and Miss Tanby edged in to discuss college business — and if truth be known — to find out if their had been any developments in Maria's investigation into the Langhorn Cinema murder case.

'I'm afraid I am getting infected, Miss Black,' she confessed. 'I see you bob in and out: I listen to your expositions on how and how not crimes are committed — One cannot see and hear such things without becoming — well, slightly interested. After all, you did say something about clearing up your mind by bouncing your ideas against somebody else . . . Out of Sherlock Holmes, was it not?'

Maria straightened up in her chair. 'Your interest is unexpected, but quite welcome, Miss Tanby! I would rather like to bounce a few more ideas . . . '

Maria brought her up to date on the salient developments. She was pleased when, asked for her opinion, Miss Tanby confirmed her own belief that Molly Ibbetson might run away rather than get herself implicated. She sat back with a little gesture of triumph.

'I am indebted, Miss Tanby. I had already reasoned matters out that way — but I am afraid the tireless Inspector Morgan is likely to — er — put his foot in it and frighten away clue-piece number one.'

'That would be unfortunate,' Tanby said, sighing.

'I will now ask you, Miss Tanby, to picture yourself as a cabaret star of about twenty years of age . . . '

'Sophisticated, worldly, beautiful?' Tanby asked sadly.

'All of those qualities . . . If you were such a person and were asked for details of your murdered father's life, how much would you tell? Once more to a police inspector.'

'That would depend upon the extent of my affection for my father. If I had loved him deeply I would tell as little as possible for fear of creating too much scandal. If I had hated him I would hardly care how much I revealed.'

'The girl in question did love her father dearly, as far as I can make out — but I think she withheld a lot of information, so the two points don't tally, from your point of view.'

'Then perhaps the Inspector was too — well, blunt,' Tanby suggested. 'Or perhaps the girl, being in the public eye, was afraid to say too much in case of tarnishing her own career.'

Maria smiled. 'You have not failed me after all, Miss Tanby! Precisely what I think — and I also think that if anybody can worm the truth out of her, I can. I have not been dealing with recalcitrant young ladies all this time for nothing.

'How true,' Tanby admitted.

'There is nothing else for it,' Maria decided, striking the desk with her palm.

'I must go to London — preferably this evening — and thrash things out with Lydia Fane. Since the college is now on holiday for the Christmas vacation I have no particular calls on my time . . . '

'London?' Tanby's eyebrows rose.

'Precisely — the Blue Crystal Night Club in Regency Street, to be exact. That is where this young lady performs. A few details from her might make it possible to hasten the bringing of the murderer to justice.'

'You will wish me to deputise here, then?'

'I am sure you will not mind,' Maria beamed. 'So, for the moment — '

Maria infused into her voice that celebrated 'Get out!' order that everybody in the college knew so well. It got Tanby to her feet and she moved towards the door; then she paused and looked back.

'In case of an emergency, Miss Black, what time may I expect you back?'

'It may be in the small hours when I return. However, I am sure no matter of compelling urgency will arise in the few hours I shall be absent.'

Tanby swallowed the heavy sarcasm without even blinking and then went out. The moment the door had closed Maria pulled out her record book from the desk and began writing:

I feel confident that I can now rule out Peter Canfield as a possible culprit. My interest centres now in more or less degree upon Fred Allerton, Gerald Lincross, Bradshaw (doorman) and — albeit remotely — Nancy Crane. Of course it may be a fact that a girl with confused speech can still have an agile brain, but somehow I feel puzzled about her. Maybe it is only because I am so used to girls looking innocent when they are really up to something that gives me this impression.

I consider it imperative that I visit Lydia Fane this very night. Point: Just where was Bradshaw at 8.37 on the fatal night? The time is 5.35 p.m.

Maria put the book away and switched on the house-phone to the domestic regions.

'Send refreshment up to my study immediately, please,' she requested briefly. 'And prepare a few sandwiches. I have to go away on business.'

'Yes, Miss Black — right away.'

★   ★   ★

Gerald Lincross was not in the best of tempers. Arriving half an hour before his customary time for the evening performance he caught the staff on the hop — except Mary Saunders who always stayed in to tea in any case. But apart from Nancy Crane no other member of the staff had yet arrived.

In a few minutes Nancy found herself summoned to Lincross's office, and she knew from his petulant lips that something was definitely wrong.

'Where's Miss Ibbetson?' he snapped.

'Not got here yet, sir — but then she doesn't often until it's later than this. It's only quarter-past six. Nobody gets here much before quarter to seven.'

'Except you,' Lincross pointed out.

'My parents went out, sir, and I'd

nothing to stay at home for. That's my only reason.'

Lincross grunted and scowled at the booking plan on the desk before him.

'Miss Ibbetson can't be thinking what she's doing today. This booking sheet is all wrong — and for tonight, the Saturday performance, at that! She took on an hour's booking from Miss Saunders this morning — just to relieve her — and now I don't know where we are! I'd intended mentioning it this afternoon but it slipped my mind.'

Nancy Crane stood in silence. When Lincross was on the rampage she knew the value of keeping her tongue still.

'This may upset tonight's bookings if I don't get it corrected quickly,' Lincross said.

'Should I go to Molly's house and tell her to hurry up quick?' Nancy suggested.

'No — never mind. On second thoughts I'll make this an opportunity to discover at what time my staff *does* arrive in an evening. When Miss Ibbetson comes send her to me right away, and unless you've anything important until then don't bother me. I've got to try to sort out these bookings.'

'Yes, sir,' Nancy whispered, closing the door softly as she retreated. She went back up the stairs to the staff room to finish the rouge application to her cheeks.

* * *

Molly Ibbetson struggled puffingly into her coat. Sucking the remains of her recently finished tea lodged in her back teeth, she wound a scarf round her rich black hair, pulled open the front door, then stepped out into the gloomy, ill-lighted street.

Her thoughts, never very swift anyway, were not on the night's work ahead of her — she was wondering if Peter Canfield was worth going out with again, or whether she ought to go after bigger fish. She had great faith in her sex appeal, and if sex appeal were assessed per ounce of avoirdupois she had every justification.

Then her experience of the previous night returned to her mind sharply and banished all other thoughts. This change

281

in outlook came when she had to traverse the dark alleyways leading to the branch road that in turn connected with Langhorn High Street.

In spite of herself she walked with less emphasis, nearly on her toes, keeping her heels from clicking too sharply on the pavement. And as she walked she glanced about her. There was nothing unusual in sight — only the dim glimmer of street lamps, the dull rectangles of curtained windows, the icy stars overhead.

Gently, hardly making a sound, she progressed — then just as she was thinking that she had worried needlessly there was a sudden rush of feet behind her, so swift indeed that she had no time to turn round before a hand crushing brutally across her lips obliterated the scream she tried to utter.

Immediately she struggled, with all the power of her heavy body, but that hand did not budge. Another hand came round and clutched her throat. Despite all her efforts she had not the power to break free. Her assailant was muscular, lithe, and apparently knew exactly what he was doing.

Gradually, her heels scraping on the pavement, Molly found herself dragged into one of the entries, along it, and out on to a piece of wasteland powdered in frozen snow. It was in fact a dump, where her sisters often played despite the warning notices regarding disused mine shafts.

It was the thought of the old disused workings that set Molly fighting again. Her hands came up and seized the wrists of the man holding her, but she could make no impression on him. She dug in her nails, kicked, writhed, and still he did not let go, though he gasped a little.

Then, suddenly, she was whirled round and shoved in the back with terrific power. Stumbling helplessly over loose clinkers and half-rotted boarding she went tottering forward. A stone, or some heavy object, smote her with blinding force across the top of the head. With lights flashing before her eyes and her ears singing she caught stupidly at a thin wire that twirled and sagged between two posts.

In front of her, yawning black under the night sky, was a cavernous space darker than the night itself. Desperate hope that her faintness would pass off seized her. She dragged herself to a standstill, her vision blurred. Then out of the gloom a fist struck her with resounding impact under the jaw. Her battered senses reeled completely . . .

She toppled over the low, ineffectual guard wire between the two posts and had a remembrance of falling — clutching at emptiness, dropping down, down, down, in a fall that seemed as though it would never end . . .

The man above stood motionless, panting, waiting — until from a far depth came a remote echoing splash, and then silence. He relaxed slowly, pulled out a handkerchief and mopped his face. Presently he took a small torch from his pocket, and masking all but the slenderest glimmer of light he inspected the ground about him. It was too clinkery and patched with frozen snow to betray many footmarks, but just the same he went about the task of obliterating his own tracks all the way back to the solid paving of the alleyway where no traces could show in any case. When he got thus far he buttoned up his overcoat tightly, glanced about him, then began to walk swiftly away . . .

* * *

In the Langhorn Cinema Nancy Crane waited in growing anxiety for Molly Ibbetson to arrive. She did not like the thought of one of her workmates piling up trouble for herself. All the girls had arrived by now — it was quarter to seven — but not Molly Ibbetson.

Then the swing doors opened again and Nancy watched eagerly. But it was only Alcot and Peter Canfield coming in together. Alcot looked at Nancy in dispassionate interest as he saw her anxiously watching the doors.

'Something the matter, sweetheart?' he asked.

'I'm waiting for Molly. The boss wants her and he's not in his best mood . . . '

'Show me when he is!' Alcot said dryly;

then as he resumed his climb up the Circle staircase he looked back. 'Fred come in yet?'

'Not yet. He's late.'

Nancy turned back to her survey of the foyer, glancing anxiously at the manager's door with the light glowing underneath it and his shadow occasionally crossing it as he moved about. She had looked at that light and the shadow several times in the past half-hour and pictured the storm building up for Molly —

Then the door suddenly whisked open and Lincross came out, in his dress suit now, immaculate to the fingertips. Nancy noticed that his face was a trifle pinker than usual as though he had an extra close shave. She presumed it came from suppressed temper.

'Miss Ibbetson come yet?' he asked briefly.

'No, Mr. Lincross, I'm afraid she hasn't. I — '

'Then take this plan and watch for double bookings,' Lincross said, reaching inside to his office desk and handing over a big, square booking chart. 'If you get any mix-ups let me know and I'll try to straighten them out . . . I just wonder what I pay that confounded girl for?' he finished.

Nancy took the plan and hurried through the doorway into the Stalls to attend to her duties. Lincross pulled his black jacket tighter to the small of his back, jerked his stiff shirt cuffs, then stood gazing at the entrance doors malignantly. They opened at that moment and Bradshaw came hurrying in wearing mackintosh and cap, somewhat out of breath. He slowed down as he saw Lincross's blue eyes fixed on him.

'A bit late, sir — sorry,' he apologised. 'Clock at home must be wrong.'

'It isn't wrong here,' Lincross answered, glancing up at the electric chronometer on the foyer wall. 'It is exactly ten to seven, and you are late. Hurry up and get out on the job.'

'Right away, sir,' Bradshaw agreed, and wheezing slightly in the chest he hurried up the staircase to his own particular department.

Lincross began to pace the foyer slowly, regarding the faces of his patrons dimly visible through the glass doors as they waited for admission — then he went over to the advance booking office door and looked in on Mary Saunders.

'Miss Saunders, you'd better take over the ordinary booking and take your advance booking later. Apparently Miss Ibbetson isn't coming this evening.'

'Yes, sir,' ginger-haired Mary agreed; and closing her office grille decisively she came out of the tiny area and hurried over to the ordinary pay-box.

Lincross watched her for a moment, then turned as the doors admitted Fred Allerton, carrying his bicycle on his shoulder, his face hot and somewhat angry.

'Sorry I'm late, sir,' he said, seeing Lincross's look.

'Apparently it is a habit common to my staff,' Lincross said bitterly. 'Your clock wrong, too?'

'No, sir — my lamp went wrong again. Rather than risk an accident I walked part of the way and it delayed me.'

Lincross said nothing, so assuming the explanation had been accepted Fred continued on his way through the foyer, dumped his machine, then went on upstairs.

In a moment or two Bradshaw reappeared and at a nod from Lincross he opened the doors wide and began his usual shouting of prices. Lincross stood for a while bowing with forced geniality, then he headed towards the Stalls, outside the entrance to which Nancy Crane was taking tickets

'Miss Crane, you might slip along to Miss Ibbetson's and find out if she's ill, will you? I have to know so that I can make my arrangements. If she is ill remind her to bring a doctor's certificate when she returns. I've just been thinking, she hasn't looked very well all day.'

Nancy hesitated. 'I'd rather not, sir.'

'Why not?' Lincross demanded

'I — er — Well, Molly told me this morning that last night somebody went for her — attacked her, I mean. What if I should be attacked as she was?'

'I'm glad you mentioned that!' Lincross looked surprised. 'She told me about it, too, and it may have some bearing on her non-appearance. I don't want you or anybody else to take needless risks, Miss Crane. Carry on with your tickets and I'll have Bradshaw go a bit later on.'

Nancy heaved a sigh of relief. 'Thanks, sir.'

Lincross turned away thoughtfully and took up his usual position in the foyer, dividing his attention between the busy Mary Saunders and the stream of patrons. Then he glanced round as a familiar ox-like figure came hurrying in.

'Why, good evening, Inspector!' Lincross looked surprised.

'I'm looking for Molly Ibbetson,' Morgan said bluntly. 'I've just come from her house and they told me she'd left for here more than half an hour ago.'

'She . . . what?' Lincross said wonderingly.

'Well, where is she?' Morgan demanded. 'I want to ask her something very important.'

'So do I,' Lincross replied. 'But she is not here, Inspector. I've been waiting for her since quarter-past six. Come along to the office, will you?'

Morgan followed him into the privacy and took the chair pushed towards him.

'Do you mean,' Lincross asked, frowning, 'that Molly has disappeared somehow between her home and here? Why it's only about a mile at the outside.'

'This has me worried!' Morgan growled. 'She left home all right — her mother and sisters all say so — and now you say that she hasn't turned up! So where has she gone?'

'What took you to her house? Or am I not supposed to ask?'

'Oh, you can ask,' Morgan snapped. 'I happen to know that she has valuable evidence in this murder case and I was going to question her . . . '

'Oh, I see . . . But I'm surprised. She hardly looks the type of girl to be valuable in any sense — between you and me, that is.'

'You said you had something important to ask her.' Morgan suddenly seemed to remember. 'What was it?'

'Just a matter of carelessness in her booking returns, that's all. Mine is purely cinema business: yours is definitely important. Just what are you going to do about it?'

'Offhand, I don't just know! You know, of course, that that girl was attacked last night, that her father called on me this morning and demanded some sort of action?'

'I knew of the attack because Molly told me about it herself — but I did not know of her father's visit to you. Rather puts you in a bad light, doesn't it? This happening?'

'Dammit, I can't be everywhere!' Morgan snapped. 'I've had two men looking the alleyway over today where she was attacked, but there seemed no legitimate reason for giving her police protection. It looks now though as if she may have been attacked again. Can't understand how that could happen with Martin watching her.'

'Martin? Oh — that American?'

'I understand Miss Black detailed him to watch Molly night and day; that's why I didn't supply police protection . . . Of course, the girl may have run away. Miss

Black warned me of that possibility.'

Lincross tightened his lips. 'Miss Black warned you, did she? I thought you acted on your own initiative, Inspector?'

'Confound it, sir, I do! But only a fool refuses to heed a wise suggestion. That girl had every reason to run away knowing what she did. She could not have known that I was coming to question her, of course, but she could have taken herself off before things got awkward for her.'

'Just what does she know?' Lincross asked deliberately.

'She knows who killed Harcourt, the man in A-11.'

'Why should that make her run away? Unless she did the killing herself she would surely prefer to state her information and feel safe?'

'Be hanged if I know!' Morgan got to his feet impatiently, stood glowering at the silent fan on top of the desk. 'How am I expected to understand the workings of a girl's mind? The only person who seems to know how they're likely to react is Miss Black. I think I ought to tell her about this . . . Mind if I use your 'phone?'

Lincross handed the instrument over. He lighted a cigarette and sat back to listen while Morgan got through to Roseway College.

'Miss Black, please,' he requested finally; then his expression changed. 'Away? Until very late? Well, ask her if she would please ring Inspector Morgan the moment she comes back, will you? It's most important.'

He put the telephone back. 'Gone away for the evening,' he said slowly. 'It must be something in connection with this case. She never deserts the trail for other business, as I well know.'

'I think,' Lincross said, 'that this matter of Molly Ibbetson is perhaps far more serious than it looks at first sight. You ought to search for her, Inspector.'

'I intend to,' he answered grimly. 'I'll search everywhere between here and her home to see what I can find. What is more, I'll see if Martin knows anything about this.'

Morgan left the cinema with the briskness of a man who has much to do.

Once outside he headed straight across the road to the 'Golden Saddle'.

'Mr. Martin in?' he asked Mrs. Ainsworth, as she stood behind the reception desk.

'Who wants him?' a voice asked from a corner, and Morgan turned to behold Pulp seated in an armchair near the staircase. He laid aside the evening paper, and ambled across.

'You seen Molly Ibbetson?' Morgan asked him in a low voice.

'Should I?' Pulp looked surprised. 'Maria told me to stay here until she asked fur me — '

'But I thought she told you to watch the Ibbetson girl night and day . . . ? She told me — '

'Sure she did, but I always follow her latest orders. Last time I saw her, very late last night after she and Molly had been attacked, she said I was to stick around here. So I have.'

'My God!' Morgan groaned, 'And I thought you were watching over her, otherwise I'd have had my own men do it — '

'What's wrong, anyway?' Pulp demanded.

'The girl's vanished this evening — somewhere between here and her home. You'd better help me look for her.'

'Okay. Wait while I grab my hat and coat.'

In three minutes they were outside the hotel. Crossing the road to the cinema again they began to walk in the direction Molly would have come.

'I suppose you've figured that the kid might ha' run away?' Pulp asked presently. 'If so, we're gettin' a draught up our pants for nothin'.'

'Miss Black can't be right every time! She said Molly might run away, but — '

They turned the corner into the side street where Molly — and Maria, too — had encountered their assailant the night before. The long, dimly lighted vista was deserted. Silently the two men walked along it, looking about them, then they digressed into the alleys that led circuitously to Molly's home. When they came within sight of it and beheld only an empty street once more Morgan came to a stop and sighed.

'Can't find anything here, Martin. The pavement doesn't give footprints away and what snow there is has frozen hard. Besides, it's too dark. We're just wasting time.'

'I reckon,' Pulp said slowly, 'we should figure it out as Maria would. She'd try and reckon what *else* the Ibbetson kid might have done, or where she might have gone. After all, there are them two other alleyways off the main street that we didn't even peep down. Can't leave any part of the area around here untouched . . . That's the way Black Maria would figure it.'

'All right, we'll look down the other alleys,' Morgan agreed.

They retraced and presently reached and explored the first side alley leading to gloomy backs of houses. It led into a plain cul-de-sac so they came back. At the end of the second alley, however, Pulp stopped and gazed over an irregular heaping of wasteland to the distant green lights of the railway track.

'What's around here?' he asked, recalling daylight memory. 'Seem to remember something about mine workings . . . '

'This is a waste dump, part of some old disused copper mines,' Morgan answered. Then his voice sharpened. 'Old mines! We might do worse!'

'Just what I was thinkin',' Pulp acknowledged. 'Maria would have checked out this space in double quick time — Where in heck is she, anyway?'

'She's in London — up to something,' Morgan growled

They walked across the cindery, snow-patched area, Morgan now flashing a torch beam at his feet. After a while he stopped.

'What do you make of this?' he asked, in an odd voice.

Together they looked down at a long, gouged trough in the cindery ground. As they moved forwards the trough was repeated at intervals, then it vanished and suddenly gave place to distinct heel-prints of a woman's shoes.

'A woman's been dragged around here,' Pulp said grimly. 'She stood up on her own pins just here, but up to here she must have been dragged and her shoes left the troughs — Hell's bells!' he finished, as he came up against the slack guard wire swinging from two lopsided posts in front of the first of the mines. 'If anybody went over this — !'

They stood looking at the shoe impressions in front of the guard wire, then at the black abyss of the mineshaft into which Morgan flashed his torch beam. It lost itself in the depths but the faint glimmer of water was reflected back.

'I've told this damned Council time and again to board this off!' Morgan swore. 'Children might be killed around here — '

'Perhaps the Ibbetson kid was,' Pulp said, his voice low. 'If she went over the top into this shaft nothin' could save her. We'd better look.'

He strode over the slack wire, Morgan following. After some searching they found the old, rusty iron ladder that led down into the depths. Plashing his torch on each rung below for safety, Morgan began to descend with Pulp immediately above him. They went down perhaps a hundred feet when the ladder ended and below there was a region of water-logged planks, caved-in underpinnings, and the stink of stagnation.

'Look!' Morgan whispered — and his torch beam became steady

In the circle of light there was a view of two fleshily curved legs, without stockings. A red skirt and mud-splashed overcoat were rucked up round the knees. At the waistline came oozy, evil-smelling water. Out of it, some distance from the legs, a hand projected upwards with limp fingers, looking as though it were isolated from the body.

'I guess,' Pulp said soberly, 'that we've found her . . . '

He measured his distance to the boarding below, then taking a chance he jumped. Part of the ancient platform caved in under the impact but the main part of it held. In another moment Morgan was beside him. Between them they groped down into the water amidst multifarious echoes and caught at a submerged head and shoulders.

Morgan let out a long whistle of breath as the dead, puffed face of Molly

Ibbetson appeared in the torchlight, a bluish mark on the left side of her jaw.

'Couldn't have stood a chance!' Pulp decided harshly. 'She's been battered on the napper and then punched under the jaw as well. Or else she got those two wallops with falling down here. Anyway she fell down here and by sheer bad luck landed with her head under water instead of her feet . . . '

'Dead,' Morgan groaned, releasing the girl's still pulse. 'My prize witness gone! Did you know that she knew the identity of Kenneth Harcourt's killer?'

'Yeah, sure — Maria told me. But there ain't nothin' this kid will tell no more, copper — and I've a strong feeling that Harcourt's killer knows just that!'

12

When Maria entered the Blue Crystal nightclub she felt entirely out of place. The tremendous ostentation of it irritated her. The gilded walls, the profusion of dried plants, the bright red plush of the chairs placed just so in various positions, the revealing curves of the girl in the short white jacket and maroon slacks, with 'Cloak Room' inscribed in yellow cord on her pillbox hat — It was a world apart so far as Maria was concerned, and unconsciously she distended her nostrils to emphasise her disfavour.

'Can I help you, madam?' the cloak-room girl asked politely, as Maria paused, holding her umbrella firmly and looking about her.

'I think you can, young lady — yes . . .' Maria tried to keep her gaze from those maroon slacks. 'Tell me, where do I go to speak to Miss Lydia Fane?'

'She's just finished her turn, madam.

You should be able to reach her in her dressing room. That is down that corridor there, marked 'Artistes Only'. Over on the right.'

Maria set off in the direction of the girl's pointing hand. At the far end of it the paradise of gilt and enamel vanished into whitewashed walls and gigantic black letters intimating that there was NO SMOKING. An elderly man sat beside a bare table reading an evening paper. As Maria approached he looked at her suspiciously over his glasses.

'Taken the wrong passage, haven't you, lady?' he inquired.

Maria stopped beside the table and fixed him with her cold blue eyes.

'I would have you understand, my man, that I have not done anything of the kind! Be good enough to advise Miss Fane that I wish to see her.'

'She isn't seeing anybody at present. She's another dance to do before long — '

'I would be obliged if you will tell her that a Miss Black, from Langhorn, wishes to see her. Should it happen that my name fails to convey an impression kindly add that I have important news from the cinema. I think that should suffice.'

The elderly man got up with a sigh and shuffled away down the chilly brick-walled passage. After about three minutes he returned, jerking his head behind him.

'All right, she'll see you. Second door on the right: got a star on it.'

'Thank you . . . '

Maria stalked past the table and followed directions implicitly. When she knocked on the second door a pleasant voice bade her enter. Inside the dressing room with its bright horseshoe of globes round the mirror she found the girl in oriental clothes, busy removing makeup from her face.

'Take a seat, won't you?' she invited, in a soft contralto. 'I shan't be a moment.'

Maria sat down and glanced round the room. A maid came out of an adjoining chamber, laid down some clothes, then silently withdrew again and closed the connecting door . . . The girl before the mirror rubbed her face vigorously with cream, wiped it off again with a towel, then turned round.

'You'll be Miss Black?' she smiled, and rose with extended hand. 'You want to see me, I believe.'

'I am speaking to Miss Fane?' Maria asked.

'If it means anything — you are.'

Maria decided that she liked the girl's frank pleasantry. Not that there was any doubt of her identity. She had recorded perfectly in the film 'Love on the Highway'. She was rather taller than Maria had imagined, with heavy shoulders for a woman of twenty. Her face had something of the dogged quality that had characterised her father, but here it was redeemed from heaviness by smallness of features. The wealth of blonde hair and clear grey eyes brought her very close to beauty.

'I'm not quite sure how I should commence this interview,' Maria said slowly, as the girl seated herself again. 'It is about your — late father . . . '

'If it helps any,' Lydia Fane said, 'your name is not unfamiliar to me. When Inspector Morgan came to see me he mentioned you quite a few times. I gathered that you were the one who discovered my resemblance to my late father.'

'True,' Maria conceded. 'And — since your time is limited and I have a train to catch — I think I had better say exactly why I have come here. It is because I do not think you told Inspector Morgan all you really know regarding your father's death. Am I right?'

Lydia Fane smiled slightly and turned to the mirror. She combed her shimmering tresses for a moment or two, then her mouth set firmly. She looked at Maria through the mirror.

'No, I didn't tell Inspector Morgan everything,' she admitted. 'Instead of putting me at my ease he threw one shock after another into my lap, confused me completely, and then hinted at trouble being in store for me if I did not as good as bare my soul to him.'

'And you resented it?' Maria gave one of her rare chuckles. 'How like good, solid Inspector Morgan. Dogged and persevering, but not gifted with either brilliance or great tact. To be truthful, I think our sex frightens him.'

The hardness went out of Lydia Fane's painted mouth and she smiled. She considered for a while as she fitted on a night-black wig. Abruptly she tossed down the comb she had been using and faced Maria directly.

'Just what do you want to know, Miss Black? And in any case of what use would information be to you? You are not with the police, are you?'

'I am a private investigator,' Maria answered. 'I believe, and I think I can make Inspector Morgan believe it too, that you have some vital information which can help us put the slayer of your father under arrest. You see, there must have been a reason for his sudden trip to Langhorn when he was released from prison. Have you any idea what that reason could have been?'

'Yes . . . ' A sombre look crept into Lydia Fane's face. 'He went to Langhorn to kill the man who sent him to prison fifteen years ago! But there was another reason. He also wanted to contact his best friend, who also lives in Langhorn. I didn't tell all this to Morgan because I did not feel too confident of his powers: had it been a Scotland Yard official I would have acted much differently. You'll realise I have to be careful how much I say because I'm in the public eye a good deal.'

'I understand,' Maria nodded. 'Can you give me the names of the deadly enemy and the best friend?'

'Unhappily, no . . . ' Lydia glanced at the travelling clock on the dressing table. 'I like you, Miss Black, and I feel I can trust you. Since I haven't much time I had better begin at the beginning . . . Father was sent to jail when I was five years of age. Everything pointed to him having committed murder, but throughout his imprisonment he swore that he had been wrongly convicted — and he also swore that he would kill the man who had sent him to jail once he was released. I presume that the man who engineered this miscarriage of justice had expected the death sentence to be carried out. When life-imprisonment was substituted

— fifteen years with good behaviour — the picture was changed. From time to time dad wrote letters to me, as I grew old enough to understand them, I mean — and explained the truth. I believed every word he wrote, and I always shall . . . '

'Then?' Maria prompted, as a sad look crept into the grey eyes.

'His best friend knows the identity of the man who had father framed; and I suppose he still does. At father's request he kept an eye on this individual through the years, tracing him everywhere he went and keeping father informed. Finally the man settled in Langhorn, and so did father's best friend — still watching, and waiting. Right to the day of dad's release he kept him informed, but he never told me the names of the two men involved . . . All he asked me to do was fight my own battles. I have done that, pretty well ever since mother died when I was twelve years old. At dad's request again I changed my name from Margaret Harcourt to Lydia Fane, so my professional career would not be tarnished by anything dad might do, or had done. That is — or was — the measure of his love for me, to protect me from scandal . . . '

'Didn't you try to dissuade him from this ruthless idea of vengeance?' Maria asked, puzzling. 'You are an intelligent, sensitive girl, hardly the type to condone an intent to murder.'

'I tried everything!' Lydia insisted. 'But dad was determined. I begged of him, by letter of course, to come to see me when he came out of prison. I felt that if only I could get him to myself for a few minutes I'd be able to talk him into taking a legal vengeance and thereby get recompense from the State for all he had suffered — But it was useless. He said he would be sure to come to see me the moment he had completed important business. There was simply nothing I could do, I was tied to the film studio on the day he came out — last Saturday — and I just couldn't get away . . . The next thing I knew, to my horror, was of his murder. And the way Inspector Morgan told it to me! So brazenly, so calmly!'

The girl's hands had clenched tightly

while she had been speaking. Now she relaxed and gave a bitter smile.

'That's all I know,' she shrugged. 'I shall never cease to revile myself for not letting everything go hang and going to the jail last Saturday. Of course he had forbidden me to do so in case the publicity hounds got to know of it and tied two and two together.'

'Your father had served his sentence, Miss Fane. I cannot see that the publicity would have mattered.'

'Probably it wouldn't have,' the girl admitted moodily. 'I simply obeyed orders. I never visited dad when he was in prison: he simply would not hear of it. We wrote to each other instead, and I used to send him news-clippings and photographs of myself showing how I was progressing as a professional dancer and spare-time actress. He always used to encourage me . . .'

Lydia stopped, brushing her long eyelashes with the back of her hand.

'I'd rather not talk about the subject any more . . . Besides, I haven't the time. I only hope for one thing now — that

Inspector Morgan finds the murderer!'

'He will be found, my dear, never fear . . . ' Maria got to her feet. 'Much that you have told me, Miss Fane, verifies my own preconceived notions. But the pity of it all is that you don't know the names of either enemy or friend. There will have to be a way round that . . . Now I really must not detain you any more.'

She held out her hand and the girl clasped it firmly.

★   ★   ★

To Maria's surprise, when her train got into Langhorn station towards one o'clock on the Sunday morning, Inspector Morgan's official car was waiting outside the station exit. He climbed out the moment he caught sight of her.

'Glad you're back, Miss Black. I've just got to see you, late or otherwise. They told me you had gone up to London on business so I decided to catch you coming home.'

'I find your attentiveness most refreshing, Inspector,' Maria beamed as they settled into their seats. 'However, it must be something other than my company which prompts you?'

'There's ghastly trouble, Miss Black. Molly Ibbetson . . . is dead!'

'Dead!' Maria echoed blankly. 'When? How?'

'She either fell down a mine shaft near her home, or else she was thrown down. Either suicide or murder. I suspect the latter — very strongly.'

'But this is appalling! Poor, poor Molly! But — Tell me about it, Inspector. Every detail!'

'All right. I'll drive you to the college meanwhile.'

He talked all the time he drove and had come to the end of his story by the time the college gateway had been reached.

'Well, Miss Black, there it is!'

'And it is murder!' she declared harshly. 'That unhappy girl had to be silenced — but it should never, *never* have been allowed to happen! She was utterly alone — unprotected! Where was Mr. Martin, did you say? In the hotel? Why on earth wasn't he watching Molly, as I had instructed? I told him to never lose sight of her between her home and the cinema. You know that yourself because you withdrew police protection to let Martin take over. Now the very thing I was afraid of has happened!'

'I don't think you can blame Martin,' Morgan said. 'He seemed to think he had to stay put — Maybe a misunderstanding.'

'And it cost a girl's life and a star witness!' Maria snapped. 'Mr. Martin has been grievously at fault — and I shall not forget to tell him so . . . '

With an effort she calmed. 'Late though it is, Inspector, there is more I must hear. Have you questioned anybody?'

'Practically everybody. I had a most busy evening. Only two people were absent from the cinema staff about the time of the girl's death — Allerton and Bradshaw. Allerton said that his lamp had failed him and that he had had to walk. Bradshaw merely said that his clock at home was slow.'

'And the others?' Maria questioned.

'Their alibis are all sound enough; in fact they can all vouch for each other. The girls, barring Molly of course, were in the cinema preparing for the evening performance. Alcot and Canfield had gone up to the projection-room. Lincross was in his office and had been there since six-fifteen.'

Maria looked as though she had sunk into completely gloomy despair. She stared into the dark windscreen.

'Are we sure about Lincross?' she muttered. 'Was he in his office, or did he just say he was?'

'He was there all right. I have it from Nancy Crane. She saw his shadow under the door several times, the office light being on of course. He was correcting a booking plan, or something.'

'What are we up against, Inspector? In my own mind I had the whole thing cut and dried — and now we run into this! It has torn the bottom out of my whole conception.'

'And mine ... ' Morgan went on slowly, 'I am beginning to think about young Allerton again. We are not compelled to believe his bike lamp story, are we? Then there's the doorman. *Anybody's* clock could be slow. Allerton and Bradshaw are two who need checking carefully. But I'm rather sorry Lincross has such a perfect alibi. I've had my suspicions about him once or twice. Seems kind of downy, don't you think? But a man can't be in his office and committing a murder a mile away at the same time, now can he?'

'I am going to sleep on this, Inspector. If you will call on me tomorrow morning — Sunday notwithstanding — we'll discuss again. Or I should say *this* morning. If you have the spectra of that carbon copper, all the better.'

'I ought to have: I asked for the report to be sent over the phone immediately it is known . . . But doesn't it seem we have to start all over again? This new murder has bowled us out.'

'In solving the first murder correctly we automatically have the answer to the second one,' Maria said, climbing out into the night. 'You bring that spectra and I'll tell you how much I learned tonight from Lydia Fane.'

Maria dimly saw Morgan's mouth frame the girl's first name in amazement — then she closed the car door upon him decisively. She had the night porter let her in and then she went straight into the college by the private entrance, and so to her study.

On her desk was a neatly written request to ring Inspector Morgan. She tore it up, and from force of habit plugged in the electric kettle. Then she took off her hat and coat and she turned absent-mindedly to the trivial task of brewing a pot of tea.

While she drank she resumed her cogitations. At the end of her concentration she set down her empty cup.

Unfastening her desk drawer she laid her record book before her, brooding over previous entries.

'Yes, indeed — where was the doorman at eight thirty-seven? Even more interesting, what was he up to last night at about six-thirty?'

Picking up her pen she began writing, pausing to reflect, then writing again:

Dramatic development has occurred in the death of star witness Molly Ibbetson. In my opinion definitely murder. Possible culprits? As far as timing is concerned, the finger points to Allerton or Bradshaw. Have decided to find out more about Bradshaw . . . When I see Mr. Martin I shall censure him severely for relaxing his vigilance over Molly.

Have seen Lydia Fane. Like her. Intelligent girl with a flourishing career. Her father had two men he wanted to see in Langhorn — a great friend and a very dangerous enemy. One of them appears to live in Millington Terrace and the other in Greystone Avenue. I know Lincross lives in Greystone Avenue, but I do not know whether he is the friend or the mortal enemy. I might be better able to judge when I know the qualities of the missing person in Millington Terrace. I must find whom it was Harcourt sought here. Now that Molly is dead it makes it imperative to have every scrap of evidence before making an arrest. I am still gravely disturbed by the various alibis of the people who might have been connected with Molly's death.

Passing thought: There was something wrong with those posters Bradshaw was folding up last Friday morning. What was it? It may be vital . . .

The time is 2.20 a.m

★   ★   ★

It was half-past ten in the hush of the Sunday morning when Inspector Morgan put in an appearance in Maria's study.

'Well, Inspector, how do we find things this morning?'

'No worse — no better. I've got the mineshaft cordoned off and two men on guard. I've also examined the spot thoroughly by daylight. There are signs of a second set of tracks having been obliterated. Obviously there were two people, though why Molly's killer should have wiped out his own tracks, yet not hers, I don't quite understand. Unless it was to throw guilt on somebody else and to make it obvious that Molly *had* been murdered. Before she was thrown in the mineshaft she was hit on the head and jaw, according to doctor's report. The attacker made as certain as could be that she could not survive to tell the tale.'

'Obviously murder,' Maria said bitterly. 'Since it happened before you questioned her she had no reason to commit suicide. As to the obliterated tracks while Molly's remain, your guess of deflecting the blame is probably right. The point now is: what are you going to do about it?'

'I'm thinking of calling in Scotland Yard,' Morgan said gloomily.

Maria got to her feet and started slowly pacing of the carpet, watch-chain laced in and out of her fingers.

'As I see it, Inspector, there is nothing you can do about Molly's murder until we have finished with the tragedy of Harcourt. One will explain the other. And I don't think we need Scotland Yard now we have got this far. We only need the report on that carbon spectra, an interview with the boy who bought the air-rifle, and — er — an inspiration in regard to the posters for 'Love on the Highway'.'

'Posters?' Morgan repeated vaguely. 'What have they got to do with it?'

'A great deal, I think. But because of an extraordinary dull-wittedness I just can't seem to think what it is about them that worries me. It is something running contrary to all normal posters. Maybe I will write to the renters and see if I can resolve my troubles that way.'

'Well, that's your business,' Morgan said. 'As to the carbon analysis and the buyer of the air-rifle I've good results. First, I got the report on the carbon, over the phone this morning. The spectrograph analysis proves the copper is identical in the carbon to that used in the slug . . . though it doesn't prove anything more than the fact that somebody in disguise bought stumps from Peter Canfield — somebody who might — or might not — have been a member of the cinema staff.'

'True . . . ' Maria frowned and still went on pacing. 'I still wonder if perhaps the person we want was in the audience after all!'

'But we decided to rule that out because the shot came from the front — or above, as we found later.'

'I know, but somebody might have been a regular patron who knew the staff room and its manhole to the roof. That somebody could have done the deed and hidden the weapon after the murder. That somebody could have broken in at night and fixed the telephone. Lastly, that somebody could afterwards have left the cinema as an ordinary patron — even before the end of the show with such an uninteresting film being shown.'

'And have you any idea who this unknown patron might be?'

'I have. The unidentified missing factor in Millington Terrace!'

'I see . . . ' Morgan pondered. 'We haven't made any progress in that direction yet, have we?'

'No, and it is high time we did! He is either a friend of the dead man, or a deadly enemy. If we can prove which we know automatically where Lincross stands.'

'Where Lincross stands? I don't quite follow.'

Maria smiled faintly. 'Forgive me, Inspector, I've yet to mention my conversation with Miss Fane last night . . . '

She recounted it in detail while Morgan listened in rather injured silence. But at last he nodded in understanding.

'I can't see why the girl couldn't have told me all that she told you. Anyway, this makes the Millington Terrace person an essential unit in the whole. If he is the friend then Lincross is the man Harcourt wanted to kill.'

'Exactly so, but that does not prove — assuming Lincross to be the enemy — that *Lincross* killed *Harcourt*! It might have been the friend himself who did it to save Harcourt from really committing murder. Friends have done that much sometimes, especially when pretty sure of getting away with it. You will find relevant data to that fact in any criminal file.'

'These two-way possibilities seem endless, Miss Black! Yet I agree, they have to be considered . . . All right, let's suppose Millington Terrace is the enemy and Lincross the friend? How does that look? Why hasn't Lincross ever admitted his friendship for the dead man? He said he had never seen him before in his life.'

'If nobody knew you were the friend of an ex-convict — and ex-murderer indeed for all the world knows to the contrary — and if you were in a public position in the town, would you admit that he was your best friend if he were murdered on your very premises?'

Morgan considered. 'Put that way, perhaps I wouldn't. As a cinema manager and owner it mightn't be such good policy.'

'Exactly; and if you were his enemy you certainly would not admit it.' Maria ceased her pacing and shrugged. 'We are left with the unalterable necessity of combing out Millington Terrace before we can move farther. I trust you will take the matter in hand.'

'Definitely,' he nodded. 'Now, as regards the buying of that rifle . . . I've had a talk with Atkinson and it seems that

he would know the boy if he saw him
— so I had rather a good idea. The
schools have broken up for Christmas, of
course. If Lincross could be persuaded to
run a special children's matinée tomorrow — Monday — on the lines of his
Saturday stuff, it would bring the boys
and girls from miles around. If, then, we
could have Atkinson concealed somewhere, where he could still study every
face that came to the pay box, he might
get a glimpse of the lad in question. The
rest would be easy.'

'A splendid scheme, Inspector. And
have you put the idea to Mr. Lincross?'

'Not yet; I'm on my way now. If he's
not at the cinema, I'll go on to his home.
Care to come along with me?'

'I think I will, yes. I have little to tie me
here today in any case. And I'd rather like
a word with Nancy Crane . . . And I must
see Mr. Martin, too!'

13

Lincross was in his office when Maria and Inspector Morgan looked in upon him. He got up immediately from the desk where he had been busy sorting the stills for the next week's feature.

'Good morning, Miss Black — Inspector. Won't you sit down?'

Maria did so, but Morgan remained standing. Lincross resumed his desk chair

'I suppose,' he said, 'you want to know all about Molly Ibbetson? It's a terrible, shocking business! She wasn't exactly what one could call a bright girl, but she — '

'The murder of Miss Ibbetson is in hand, sir,' Morgan interrupted heavily. 'I'm here for — '

'Then she *was* murdered?' Lincross asked abruptly.

'There's no doubt of it. She was a girl who knew too much. Now, as to the reason for my visit: I've seen the second-hand dealer about that air-rifle, sir. He thinks he might be able to identify the boy if you will co-operate with us.'

'What do you want me to do?'

Morgan told him.

'I see. A special matinée tomorrow, for children only? Well, I don't see why not. I'll get the renters to send me some cowboy stuff for tomorrow morning. Patrons will not mind since we never have a matinée on Mondays in any case.'

'Good!' Morgan exclaimed. 'Now, is there somewhere Atkinson can go where he can see, and yet not be seen?'

'Why, yes,' Lincross replied. 'We have a sweet-stall near the downstairs entrance. We've not used it during the war. It has glass sides piled up with empty toffee tins. Our friend could stand in there and watch the children coming in.'

'Right!' Morgan rubbed his hands. 'Then we'll do that — eh, Miss Black?'

She nodded, but said nothing — so Morgan went on talking. While he did so Maria moved her gaze gradually to different parts of the office — to the filing cabinets by the wall, to the small table in the corner, to the bottom of the door, to the typewriter perched precariously on the broad ledge atop the roll-top desk, to the electric fan next to it with its paper streamers hanging limply on the outer cagework. Then she looked at the electric light, extinguished at present, overhead. Only a slight tightening of her jaw expressed the quality of her thoughts . . .

From the electric light her gaze moved on to the broad sash window with its frosted glass . . . She became aware that Lincross and Morgan had both finished their conversation and were looking at her.

'Are the details complete now, Inspector?' she inquired calmly.

'Everything . . . Didn't you hear me?'

'I am afraid I was wool-gathering.' she apologised, rising. 'Forgive me, Inspector. Incidentally, Mr. Lincross, I would like a word with Miss Crane if she is about. Just a little personal matter.'

'I'll call her,' he said, and opened the office door.

Maria and Morgan followed him out into the foyer and after a while the girl came down the Circle staircase quickly.

'Oh, hello, Miss Black! You want me?'

'Just a word, my dear. It won't take a moment.'

Maria looked at Lincross and he returned into his office, then she glanced at Morgan and sent him ambling towards the swing doors with a gruff clearing of his throat.

Nancy waited, her blue eyes wide and her fingers playing with a duster.

'I want to know about Mr. Lincross last evening, Nancy. Are you sure that he was in his office between six-fifteen and quarter to seven?'

'Definitely sure.'

'But how can you be so certain? As I understand it he went into his office and left instructions for Molly to be sent in to him when she arrived. You did not see him then for — how long?'

'About half an hour; but he was in there. I saw his shadow under the door every now and then, as he walked about, probably from desk to filing cabinet. Or else he was changing his clothes. He does, you know — every night. But I think it was the filing cabinet because I heard him rustle the papers.'

Maria's eyes sharpened. 'You *did*? When exactly?'

'About half-past six. I thought I'd better tell him it was time I had the booking plan; then I got scared because he was in such an awful temper last night. He might have said something nasty to me if I had told him his business so I didn't bother asking. But I did almost, and it was when I was outside his door that I heard him rustling the papers.'

'Hmmm . . . And does he usually come as early as six-fifteen?'

'Never done it before. He's usually here for quarter to seven. Just as it happened.'

Maria gave a little sigh then patted the girl's arm. 'Well, Nancy, thank you. You are a very observant girl.'

'Glad to hear you think so, Miss Black. Anything else?'

'No, that is all. And not a word to anybody, mind!'

Nancy nodded seriously and hurried off again to her duties. Maria wandered across to where Morgan was waiting.

'Anything wrong?' he inquired.

'I have just been exploding a theory, Inspector; or in other words making sure of Lincross's alibi in case he is the enemy side of the picture. However, Nancy saw his shadow and heard him rustling his papers in the office during that fatal half hour, so I'm afraid we're back with the Millington TerracE problem again.'

'Looks like it,' Morgan admitted — but he could see something was still sticking in Maria's mind. 'What about Martin? Do you wish to see him?'

'Oh, yes, of course! I . . . '

Maria paused as she caught sight of Fred Allerton approaching down the foyer. She made a gesture to the Inspector.

'To save time, Inspector, would you mind finding Mr. Martin in the hotel across the road? I've something to ask Mr. Allerton.'

Morgan nodded and went out. Allerton, dressed in a boiler suit and carrying an armature in his hand, nodded a greeting as he came towards Maria. A sullen, doubting look was on his grease-smeared face.

'Busy, Mr. Allerton?' Maria inquired, smiling.

'Always am on a Sunday morning. Only chance I get to check our equipment. I'm taking this round to the garage for a clean up . . . '

'Before you go, have you time for just a word?'

'Well — all right. What's the trouble?'

'I believe Mr. Lincross saw you talking to Harcourt — the man in A-11 — last Wednesday evening?'

'He did. Harcourt was just leaving by the private doorway to the projection-room when Mr. Lincross came up the Circle staircase from the foyer. I just couldn't avoid being seen.'

'Now tell me — and think carefully. What expressions were on the faces of both men when they saw each other?'

'Well, it's hard to say,' Allerton answered finally. 'I do not remember any expressions particularly — not on the part of Harcourt, anyway. He just looked at Mr. Lincross steadily as though he were trying to imagine who he was, then he went off into the Circle with a slight shrug of his shoulders. I remember that bit distinctly, just as though he felt he had perhaps been on private property and that there was nothing he could do to excuse himself. As for Mr. Lincross he registered a sort of faint surprise, then he became angry with me.'

'I see,' Maria nodded. 'Most explicit, Mr. Allerton. You have an excellent memory.'

Allerton gave her a brief, doubting glance then with a nod he went on his way through the swing doors. As Maria caught sight of Pulp and Inspector Morgan emerging from the 'Golden Saddle' opposite she hurried outside as well and climbed into Morgan's car. In a moment or two both men had joined her.

'Want me, Maria?' Pulp pulled off his green trilby and looked rather sheepish.

'I intend, Mr. Martin, to censure you severely!' Maria retorted, regarding him stonily. 'Do you realise that Molly Ibbetson was murdered because you relaxed your vigilance?'

'Yeah, I figgered you'd say that,' he said, his big red face deeply serious. 'I told that to the flatfoot here when we found the body. Go on — give it me proper, in the kisser. I can take it. But I ain't sayin' as I deserve it. I figured you wanted me to stick around the hotel case I was wanted urgent. You said just that . . . See?'

He tugged a notebook from his pocket and jabbed a red finger at a scrawled passage. It read: *Remain at the hotel until I have need of you again.*

'Them was your last words to me, Maria,' Pulp declared. 'On the level! I always jots down your last instructions and sticks to 'em. You know I ain't the sort of guy to let a kid like that Molly take the rap otherwise. I figured you wanted things left like that, so I did it.'

Maria rubbed her forehead. 'Yes — yes, I did say just that. I remember now. Truth to tell, I was so confused and dazed after being attacked, I wasn't thinking clearly . . . We are both to blame,' she decided. 'In future always follow an order until I specifically cancel it. Or else ask me what you are to do.'

Pulp looked relieved. 'No hard feelings then, Maria?'

'No,' Maria sighed. 'But it is still a thousand pities ... Now there is something else you must do, and you must do it thoroughly and without undue ostentation.'

'Huh?'

'I mean you must work without giving your purpose away. I want you to cultivate the acquaintance of Bradshaw, the doorman, and find out by gentle persuasion where he was at eight thirty-seven on Wednesday evening and also where he was between six-fifteen and six forty-five yesterday evening. He refuses to speak in regard to the former time; and in regard to the latter he has asserted that his clock at home was slow. You think you can do that?'

'I'll get it out of him, Maria,' Pulp promised. 'He looks to me as though he might do a spot of tipplin' on the quiet. In fact I've seen him dodgin' into the 'Golden Saddle' vault once or twice, come to think of it. I'll find out all you want, even if I have to souse him.'

'Good,' Maria nodded. 'The moment you learn something let me know — or else Inspector Morgan.'

'Be you or nothin'. I don't have no truck with flatfoots.'

Pulp climbed out of the car again, then crossed the road to the hotel. Maria turned to meet Morgan's questioning eyes.

'Good idea that, Miss Black,' he commented. 'Martin's just the man to tackle Bradshaw. It'll save the police showing their hand too much. I'll be glad to know just what he was doing.'

'I am pretty certain what he was doing, but I insist on verification . . . Now if you will drive me back to Roseway I have one or two matters to attend to.'

★ ★ ★

There was still an hour to go before dinner when Maria got back to the desk in her study. She noted the fact with satisfaction, took off her hat and coat, then sat at her desk resolutely.

In a moment or two she had her portable typewriter before her and was busy tapping out a letter to the Sunrise Film Corporation on plain paper. At the end of it, however, she did not add her signature. Instead she folded it away and began a second letter.

After the first line of it she paused and thought, then getting to her feet she went to an orderly pile of film magazines that she kept in a corner cupboard for the express purpose of the reviews they carried. Ten minutes' search brought her to the film review she wanted.

' 'Death Strikes Tomorrow',' she mused, studying the film expert's report. 'Yes, it should have been that one. Produced by Diamond Pictures, Diamond Studios, Ealing . . . Hmm!'

Returning to the desk she resumed her typing. Again she did not sign the letter, but she typed out the Diamond Studios address in the bottom left-hand corner. Then she relaxed and smiled to herself as she read the letter through. Finally she folded it up and laid it beside its fellow on the desk.

While she thought out her next move she prepared a cup of tea and drank it while she studied one of the innumerable books from her shelves — this time a fairly heavy leather-bound volume with the title 'Studio Make-Believe'. She traced her finger down the index until she came to a chapter headed 'Studio Artifice.'

'Splendid!' she murmured as she turned the pages quickly. 'I do believe you have played what Mr. Martin calls a 'hunch'.'

She drank the remainder of her tea and then looked closely at page 48. There was a section headed, 'The Creation of Firelight, Flickering Shadows, and Synthetic Fog.' She read the context carefully, making notes on her scratchpad.

Putting the volume back again in its precise place on the shelf she brought out her record book and commenced writing:-

This case is drawing to a close, but whether I am entitled to compliment myself on my deductions is hard to say.

This much I feel sure of — that Fred Allerton is a victim of circumstances and did not murder Kenneth Harcourt.

Facts to be resolved now include: the actions of Bradshaw and his possible motives for murder; interview (if possible) with the boy who bought the air-rifle; the identity of the unknown factor in Millington Terrace; and lastly — the posters. I must try to comprehend what was wrong with them. I shall — given time.

A lot of my preconceived notions were upset last night by the death of Molly Ibbetson and the perfect alibis of apparent suspects. Now I am left marvelling at the subtle ingenuity of it all.

Regret that today is Sunday and no moves can be made until tomorrow afternoon at a special matinée.

The time is 12.10 p.m.

Maria closed the book, locked away the two draft letters in her drawer, then tidied her severe hair-style before the mirror, preparatory to going in to dinner.

* ★ ★ ★

Pulp Martin stood a few yards from the 'Golden Saddle' Hotel, concealed by a doorway, but watching the comings and goings of the cinema staff across the street.

At twelve o'clock he saw the two usherettes, Violet Thompson and Sheila Brant, hurry off together — then Alcot and Peter Canfield also departed. Later came Nancy Crane and Fred Allerton, arm-in-arm and deep in conversation . . . then Bradshaw in his mackintosh and cap. Without looking to either right or left he came straight across the road and went into the below-stairs department of the 'Golden Saddle' inscribed 'Vault'.

Pulp glanced back across the street as Gerald Lincross left the cinema with Mary Saunders a little ahead of him. She nodded a farewell to him and went tripping up the street. He locked the glass doors, shook them, then walked slowly down the steps. The place was shut until the following morning.

Pulp lounged round to the Vault

entrance. He finally tracked Bradshaw down seated at a corner table with a drink in front of him and his cap on the chair beside him.

'Hiya!' Pulp greeted, raising a hand cordially. 'Mind if I join you?' He sat down before Bradshaw could answer.

'You're Martin, aren't you?' Bradshaw asked. 'Sort of bottle-washer to that stiffnecked headmistress from Roseway College?'

'You got me right, pal,' Pulp agreed amiably, ordering a drink for himself. 'Have a cigarette — a Yank cigarette. It'll knock your teeth out if you inhale deep.'

Bradshaw took one and lighted it. 'What do you want? It ain't just the pleasure of my company, I'll bet!'

'Just that I like to talk to guys,' Pulp shrugged. 'I'm a sociable guy — but I can't sort of drift around in them circles where they're high up. You an' me sort of live in the same street, see?'

Bradshaw grinned doubtfully. 'You mean you think that I'm hignorant? Well I'm not! I went to school. If I don't talk as well as I should it's because I've forgotten 'ow. I've not 'ad much chance to brush up my knowledge for a hell of a time now. Being a doorman ain't so hot, y'know. Shoutin' yourself 'oarse, moppin' floors, beatin' kids around . . . I once thought of studyin' to be a hengineer.'

Pulp eyed his drink as it was set before him. 'Been dozin' around this dump all your life?' he asked.

'Last twenty year, anyway. I was born in Lexham, but I've never got no farther than Langhorn. Think I'll move on soon, though. Can't stick the boss . . . '

'Why not?' Pulp took a drink and waited.

' 'E's a slave-driver!' Bradshaw declared. 'Can't never 'ave no fun. A drink now an' again is my idea of fun, y'know — or a bit of a flirt with the girls. Nothin' serious — just a bit of friendliness like. 'E don't like that don't Mr. Backbreak Lincross. Standin' there grinnin' at people as they comes in and mutterin' things b'ind their backs. Not a Patch on my other boss — 'im who 'ad the Langhorn before Lincross.'

Pulp took a long draught from his glass and drew his hand over his mouth.

'Yeah? I sort of figgered that Lincross owned the joint — sort of built it up.'

'Not 'im! 'E bought it . . . '

Bradshaw relapsed into moody silence. Pulp ordered him another drink and the works seemed to be oiled again somewhat.

'Yes, 'e bought it,' Bradshaw resumed. 'That there cinema, believe it or not, 'as been built twenty years. I remember when it were a silent cinema with a single piano. Then they put hin the talkies. Garvin — 'e was the other owner — sold it ten years ago to Lincross and 'e brought it hup to date. I've been doorman there now for nigh on twenty years. Ten for Garvin and ten for Lincross. It's the hell of a while! Wasted me youth . . . '

'Feller, you're in a rut!' Pulp said. 'I'm a guy who likes to get around . . . ' He reflected, then said absently, 'Sort of makes it tough on you havin' to dodge the big shot every time you want a drink. Suppose he found out?'

''E'd fire me! 'E's that sort! I say there's too much damned discipline in the place. But you know how it is when you're nearly passin' out for a drink? Well, I just sneaks across 'ere. Sometimes I manage one before the show and then eat a cachou so nobody notices . . . It's the devil of a life!'

'I can imagine,' Pulp sympathised. 'An' I'll bet you got the pins knocked from under you when you heard about that guy being bumped off in the Circle last Wednesday night, eh?'

'I got a surprise all right,' Bradshaw agreed, finishing his drink. Then, quite amiable now, he asked, 'You'll have one with me, eh?'

'Okay,' Pulp agreed, looking at his empty glass.

There was a pause while the replenishment took place.

'What surprises me,' Bradshaw resumed as drinks were brought, 'is that the police don't find hout who did it! In fact both murders.'

Pulp grinned faintly. 'They ain't been asleep, feller. Strictly off the record they think you done it!'

'Me?' Bradshaw sat bolt upright. 'What

the 'ell would *I* have to do with it?'

'I dunno, pal; I'm just warnin' you. I'm in pretty close touch with the racket, remember, and they figure it must ha' been you becos you can't explain what you was doin' at eight thirty-seven on Wednesday night. That puts you in bad, see? What makes it further bad for you is the murder of that usherette kid, Molly. The police don't fall for that yarn of yours about your clock being slow. I tell you, feller, you're in a pretty tough spot!'

Bradshaw took a quick drink and stared in front of him for a moment.

'I never thought they'd think that!' he breathed. 'But I'm still not goin' to tell 'em where I was because Lincross'll get to 'ear of it and then I'll be sacked for . . . '

'Boozin' while you should be on duty?' Pulp suggested candidly.

'Yes. I don't mind tellin' you. You're my sort — on my level, as you said. But you see how the boss would look at it? I slip out many an evenin' when things is quiet-like and 'ave a quick one in 'ere. Mrs. Ainsworth won't never let on, or let anybody else 'ere let on, because I gets her tickets sometimes. But that's all there was to it. On Wednesday night at eight thirty-seven I was in 'ere 'avin' a bitter . . . As for last night I 'ad one before the show an' met a fellow who 'andles some bets. It delayed me. I 'ad to tell Lincross my clock was slow. I never expected him to be in the damned place so hearly.'

Bradshaw had the expression of a man who is not sure if he has not committed an indiscretion. Then he looked at his watch.

'I've got to shift,' he decided. 'The wife'll kill me if I'm late for Sunday dinner. See you again . . . '

'So long,' Pulp acknowledged, and he sat thinking for a while after Bradshaw had hurried off. 'Maybe I ought to go into this detective racket at that! Better give Maria a tinkle and let her know what's cookin'.'

14

At a quarter to two the following afternoon — Monday — Morgan's car entered Roseway quadrangle and he was shown in to Maria to find her all ready for departure. She looked at his cheerful face and raised an eyebrow.

'I detect a change in mood, Inspector. You have discovered something?'

'I think so,' he answered guardedly. 'I've had two men combing Millington Terrace and just before I left headquarters one of them phoned in to say that he thinks he's found a lead. He'll ring me up later this afternoon — first to the cinema, and if I'm not there then to headquarters.'

'Excellent! That means that both of us have reason to feel pleased. For my part I am glad to say that Mr. Martin has proved himself still worthy of being my outside assistant. He phoned yesterday to state the real reason for Bradshaw's silence.'

'Well?' Morgan asked.

'He was — er — having a quick one, Inspector. I am of course quoting Mr. Martin's own expression.'

'That all?' Morgan gestured his disgust. 'Then that puts him right out of the running! Why on earth couldn't he have said so?'

'Because I understand it might have cost him his job if the truth had reached Lincross. In fact, behind the scenes, I gather Lincross is something of a stern disciplinarian . . . However, Mr. Martin managed to get at the truth. I have no doubt that witnesses will be able to prove Bradshaw's presence in the vault at the time mentioned. In other words, we can cross out Bradshaw — and Allerton.'

'Which leaves us with the unknown in Millington Terrace, and — remotely but still perhaps possible — Lincross and Alcot. Yes, Alcot. He's smooth, acid, an unpleasant piece of work, in fact. But it's Millington Terrace that holds my attention now.'

'As you say, Inspector . . . But, before we go there is something that needs your personal attention. I have here two letters I have drafted. I would suggest that you have them typed on your official stationery — which cannot be ignored — and sign them yourself.'

Morgan took the letters and read them through. Surprise knitted his brows. 'But how does it help us if we check the dates and times of 'Love on the Highway' and 'Death Strikes Tomorrow'?'

'I fancy you will discover how it helps us when we get the answers. Get them typed, signed, and mailed the moment you return to headquarters.'

'All right — though I'm a bit mystified.'

Morgan put the drafts in his wallet and then opened the study door, Maria following.

As they drew near to the Langhorn Cinema they gained an inkling of what was in store for them. A double queue of boys and girls had formed outside the glass doors — a struggling, arguing, fighting column of half-sized humanity.

Morgan drew the car to a halt. Youthful eyes watched him in awed wonder as he helped Maria out on to the pavement.

The arguments ceased and the surging throng fell back as Bradshaw opened the glass swing doors slightly to let Maria and he into the foyer.

Lincross was present, talking to a short, tubby man with black hair flattened down on a round skull. He looked up with sharp, expectant black eyes as the Inspector advanced towards him.

'This is Mr. Atkinson, the second-hand dealer,' Lincross said, and made introductions all round.

'Hope you'll be able to spot the boy we want, sir,' Morgan commented. 'Quite a lot depends on it.'

'If he is here to be spotted, I'll do it,' Atkinson said confidently.

Lincross led the party along the foyer to the sweet-booth near the Stalls entrance and unlocked the side door. Inside, despite Fred Allerton's bicycle, there was plenty of room. Lincross motioned Atkinson in Morgan took up his place beside him.

Maria retired to a plush chair near the base of the Circle staircase, Lincross hovering nearby. There they awaited

Atkinson's signal to catch the boy he recognized.

'Frankly,' she said, as Lincross signalled Bradshaw to open the doors and commence the onslaught, 'I don't understand why it should be necessary for Mr. Atkinson to conceal himself.'

'Only because the Inspector says so. Maybe he thinks the boy might shy away if he sees Atkinson and the local police chief together. After all, an air-rifle really needs a licence, you know.'

Maria nodded. 'Yes, maybe concealment is best after all . . . '

She broke off as the first children came rushing in, guided on their course by Bradshaw and then directed by a firm pointing of Lincross's hand towards the Stalls. Here Nancy Crane was standing ready for the tickets.

Slowly the stream of children thickened. Maria sat waiting, her umbrella before her in walking-stick fashion as though to act as a guard against Langhorn's urchin life.

Several minutes passed. Then suddenly Atkinson began waving his arms fiercely and Morgan was trying to scramble through the practically jammed doorway. Maria's eyes shifted to a youth of about fifteen, fairly well dressed in a blue overcoat. She looked back at Atkinson questioningly and he gave a firm nod.

Maria got to her feet and Lincross divided the crowd of youngsters by plunging forward. The youth in the blue overcoat gazed in surprise as Maria and Lincross suddenly appeared on either side of him.

'Just a word, my boy,' Maria said. 'Step aside, will you?'

'Over there . . . ' Lincross nodded towards his office.

'I've got my ticket!' the boy said desperately, as he found himself surrounded. 'I only want to see the picture . . . '

'So you shall, son, in a moment,' Morgan promised, adopting a paternal air. 'Just a question, that's all. Now — in here.'

The boy in front of them they all moved into Lincross's office and Atkinson shut the door.

'Do you know this gentleman?' Morgan asked, with a glance towards Atkinson.

'Yes,' the youth nodded. 'He runs the junk store down the street.'

'Right. What's your name, lad? Where do you live?'

'Eric Carter. I live at 16 Elizabeth Street.'

Morgan made a note. 'Now, recently you bought an air-rifle from Mr. Atkinson here. And it was not for yourself, either. Whom did you buy it for?'

'I — I don't know who he was. I never saw him before in my life. He was looking in the junk store one evening before it closed, just as I was going past. He stopped me and asked if I wanted to earn thirty bob. I said I didn't mind. Since he was willing to pay me all that money for buying the air-rifle in the window I went in and got it for him. I was going to ask him why he couldn't have got it himself — but he just gave me the money and then went off without a word, the rifle under his mackintosh.'

'And what did he look like?' Morgan questioned.

'Oh, not very tall. Maybe five feet eight or nine. He had a fat stomach, a black drooping moustache and was wearing a mackintosh and cap.'

'Hmmm . . . All right, son, you can go now and see your picture — but don't be too willing to do favours for strangers in future. It might get you into trouble. Off you go.'

Morgan shut the door after the boy hastened out and then glanced across at Maria.

'Same man again,' he said, shrugging.

'Same fellow?' Lincross repeated, surprised. 'Why, has he done something else?'

'He bought a dozen carbon stubs from young Peter Canfield for the sum of five pounds,' Morgan replied.

'He what?' Lincross's blue eyes seemed to glitter. 'Why, the young idiot! I'll give him his cards for this! I — '

'If you don't mind, Mr. Lincross, you'll do nothing of the sort,' Morgan interrupted. 'I promised him that he would not be victimised for telling the truth, and so far as he knows his confession is known only to me . . . and Miss Black.'

'Well, I don't like this sort of double-dealing going on behind my back!' Lincross declared acidly.

Morgan put his notebook away and turned to Atkinson. 'Thanks, Mr. Atkinson, you've been very helpful. I shan't need to keep you from your business any longer.'

'Always glad to help the police solve their problems . . . ' As Atkinson went out the telephone shrilled. Lincross picked the instrument up.

'Langhorn Cinema — Lincross speaking . . . Oh, yes, he's here . . . For you, Inspector,' he said, handing the phone over.

Morgan took it and listened. 'That's fine. Yes, I'll come right away.'

He put the instrument back and turned briskly. 'Important moves, Miss Black! I have to be on my way . . . '

'I take it you are referring to the information you expected would be telephoned by one of your men?'

Morgan nodded reluctantly and Maria rose to her feet.

'Then, having worked beside you this far I consider that I am entitled to know exactly what is transpiring. Remember, Inspector, I am still an important witness.'

'All right,' he sighed. 'Let's be on our way.'

'Does it really mean a big step forward to finishing this case?' Lincross asked, opening the door for them.

Morgan hesitated in the doorway. 'Official business, sir. I can't explain it to you now.'

When they were in the car again Maria turned a questioning eye. 'Well, Inspector, what did your sleuth find out about Millington Terrace?'

'My men traced things through the post office here. It seems that letters have been sent regularly to Kenneth Harcourt at Pentonville Prison by one Leslie Ackroyd, living at 142, Millington Terrace. He put his name on the top left-hand corner as the sender — as a good few people do. That is a stroke of luck for us. All we have to do now is go to 142 and see what connection he had with Harcourt.'

'Excellent,' Maria commented. 'We are fortunate to have a small rural post office which gets so inconsiderable mail that it has time to notice such things. I presume that prison address lent flavour to the breath of scandal.'

It took only seven minutes to reach 142, Millington Terrace, the opposite end to Peter Canfield's abode. Here the houses were solidly residential and well kept.

Morgan and Maria walked up the well-brushed front path beside a neat but wintry garden. The house itself was spotlessly kept.

A bell rang in the house as Morgan pressed the button, then presently the door was opened by a dark-haired woman in her early forties. Something very close to consternation crossed her lean face as she saw Inspector Morgan.

'I wish to speak to Mr. Leslie Ackroyd,' he said, 'I am Inspector Morgan of the Langhorn Police.'

'I'm afraid my husband isn't at home at the moment,' the woman replied quickly. She looked down the street nervously, then she stepped back into the hall and motioned inside. 'Would you mind stepping in for a moment? I am troubled with inquisitive neighbours . . . '

Morgan agreed — and Maria and he were ushered into a warm, well-furnished lounge. 'Do sit down,' Mrs. Ackroyd invited, drawing chairs towards the fire before seating herself on the chesterfield.

'This lady is Miss Black, the Principal of Roseway College,' Morgan introduced. 'She is a material — er — witness in the Langhorn Cinema murder case . . . '

Mrs. Ackroyd inclined her dark head in greeting towards Maria. 'I've read about the case and heard a good deal of local gossip. But I don't see why you should wish to see my husband.'

'It is a private matter, Mrs. Ackroyd,' Morgan said firmly. 'When will he be home?'

'Unfortunately I don't know. My husband is a traveller for a London firm of electrical equipment manufacturers. He covers all England for them. We have lived here for ten years, it being handy for London. Last Wednesday evening he left in his car for Keswick to see a client and I have not heard from him since.'

'When should he be back, Mrs. Ackroyd? You have some idea, surely?'

'He ought to have been back last night, but evidently business has delayed him . . . ' Mrs. Ackroyd gave a sad little smile. 'The wives of commercial travellers are notoriously grass-widows. Even last Wednesday night we only had a couple of hours together He came in hurriedly from Southampton, had just time to say hello and goodbye, so to speak, then he was off again.'

Morgan pondered. 'Tell me, Mrs. Ackroyd, about what time did he get in from Southampton — and set off again for Keswick?'

'It would be about five o'clock, leaving at half-past seven . . . '

'Why such urgency? It seems odd for a man to decide to drive to the Lake District in his car with such a long night journey ahead of him.'

'He breaks his journey at Leicester on the way. He said he wanted to get ahead of the snow. He felt sure — as we all were for that matter — that it was blowing up. I believe he had a contact to make in Leicester the following morning, then he would go on to Keswick from there.'

'To get ahead of the snow . . . ' Morgan repeated the words slowly, frowning. 'Well, do you know where we might telephone him in Keswick, or his address there?'

'Why, yes. You'll get him at the Highmount Hotel — Keswick four-two. He always stays there.'

Relief crossed Morgan's face as he wrote down the address and telephone number. Then he got to his feet.

'Inspector, what does this all mean?'

'Sorry, madam — private business. I cannot discuss it.'

'But as his wife, surely I have the right to know? You can't possibly be connecting him with that cinema murder!'

As Morgan remained silent, Maria spoke for the first time. 'Mrs. Ackroyd . . . Have you ever been visited by a heavily built man dressed in a grey overcoat and hat? A man with a very strong, dogged face, long nose, and powerful jaw?'

'Why, yes! He came last Monday evening — a week ago today — between half-past six and seven and asked if he could see my husband. I told him he was away in Southampton and did not know when he would be back. He refused to leave a name or anything. Actually,' Mrs. Ackroyd went on urgently, 'he rather frightened me when I saw him standing there. He was so big, so massive . . . '

'And did he call again?' Maria questioned.

'No, he didn't.' Mrs. Ackroyd frowned hard, then: 'Why, now I come to think of it he could have been the man who was murdered in the cinema! You, Miss Black, gave the self-same description as I read in the newspaper.'

'Yes, it was he,' Morgan acknowledged gruffly. 'His name was Kenneth Harcourt. Ever hear of it before?'

'No — never. I can't think what he could have wanted with my husband, or how he knew where he lived.'

'Possibly there is quite a lot you don't know,' Morgan commented. 'However, thanks for being frank. We'll get in touch with your husband over the telephone. Good afternoon . . . '

As he drove off towards his headquarters, Morgan glanced at Maria with grim satisfaction. 'Well, that seems like the last link, Miss Black! There couldn't be anything plainer than that!'

'Than what?' Maria asked impassively.

'Ackroyd was in Southampton when Harcourt was released — That could have been a gag. He could easily have been somewhere quite local. He went to the cinema Wednesday night when the show had started, instead of going immediately to Keswick as he had told his wife. He shot Harcourt and then set off for Keswick. Being a resident of this town for ten years he would know the cinema like a book.

'While he was supposed to be in Southampton he could have broken into the cinema   even as you yourself theorised at one point in this business — and prepared everything. He is the man who sent Harcourt to jail. Why otherwise should Harcourt try to find him as he did? Left quickly to avoid being overtaken by snow! I've heard a few alibis but that is the king of the lot.'

'Can you tell me,' Maria asked slowly, 'how Ackroyd knew that Harcourt was going to sit in A-11 in the Circle?'

'He'd find out somehow. A killer always does. We'll check up on Ackroyd in Keswick and if everything fits in as it should he's liable to find himself under arrest.'

'Might I ask how Ackroyd killed Molly Ibbetson if he was in Keswick?'

'He probably was not in Keswick at that time; maybe lurking about this immediate neighbourhood. He had provided a good alibi for his wife to trot out, anyway.'

'Come, come, Inspector!' Maria exclaimed irritably. 'We shall have to do better than this! We are practically sure that Molly died because she knew the killer's identity. She was murdered, we presume, by the killer because he knew her secret. How, then, did Ackroyd come to know that?'

Morgan drew up his car outside police headquarters and mused for a moment.

'Either somebody told him — and that might have been young Canfield who also knew the truth — or else Molly was murdered for a different reason altogether.'

'You have much in common with a bulldog, Inspector,' Maria commented, stepping out of the car. 'Maybe Keswick and a check on times and dates can help us.'

He followed her into headquarters and once in his office wasted no time in getting the Exchange. He waited impatiently, snapped 'All right!' then slammed the instrument back on its rest. 'The lines are down pretty nearly all over the Lake District! Heaviest snowfall for years! Blizzard! Blast!'

'How annoying . . . ' Maria loosened her coat. 'That means blocked roads — no chance of Ackroyd getting back; or he may even be marooned between here and Keswick if he had started for home. It would account for his wife not hearing from him if the railway is blocked too.'

'This is too much!' Morgan groaned. 'We've got to get at him somehow, Miss

Black — or at least find where he fits into the puzzle. We've no idea how long it will take to fix an emergency line.'

Maria reflected, then she reached forward to the telephone directory, found a number, and rang it.

' 'Golden Saddle' Hotel? Might I speak to Mr. Martin, please?'

After some delay Pulp's voice came over the wire.

'Mr. Martin? Black Maria speaking. I am at police headquarters. Come over here immediately; it is most important.'

'Okay, Maria. I'll be there in five minutes flat.'

He was — arriving in the Inspector's office somewhat breathless.

'What's the set-up?' he asked quickly. 'Headin' for the big showdown?'

'I think so, Mr. Martin,' Maria assented, nodding. 'Suppose, Inspector, that Mr. Martin tried to reach that hotel? Would you agree to that or do you prefer one of your own men to do it?'

'Broad as long,' he shrugged. 'It's not a question of an arrest just yet, anyway:

simply a statement of fact with dates and times.'

'Good!' Maria turned to Pulp. 'A vital personage in this whole puzzle seems to be snowbound in the Lake District — Keswick. We can't reach him by phone and there is probably heavy road blocking as well. Trains may be running by now, though. Since our friend has a car it is hardly likely that he'll use a train. His name is Leslie Ackroyd and he is a traveller for an electrical firm. At present he is staying at the Highmount Hotel, Keswick. You understand?'

Pulp, who had been jotting down notes on Morgan's scratchpad, nodded.

'I get it. You want me to play Father Christmas?'

'Find out *everything* you can about this man. Find out when he reached the hotel, his connection with Kenneth Harcourt . . . Do not leave a thing unturned.'

'Leave it to me. If the wires are up again when I get there I'll phone you. If not, I'll bring meself back . . . But s'pose he won't tell me nothin'? Where's my authority?'

'That,' Maria said pensively, 'is the point. This man may be the one we're looking for and it is essential that he gets no hint of the police being on his track. You have your own ways of getting information — witness Bradshaw. I leave it to your judgment. Here are your expenses — which I will see Inspector Morgan refunds later.'

'All right with me,' Morgan agreed, as Maria handed the money over from her handbag. Pulp took it along with the leaf from the scratchpad and put both in his wallet. He went out whistling 'Jingle Bells' strongly off-key.

'I think,' Maria said, 'that the best course has been taken . . . And now may I remind you to have those two draft letters typed and mailed right away?'

Morgan felt for his wallet. 'Of course! I'll see to it.'

Maria nodded and rose to her feet, took a firm hold of her umbrella.

'Would you care for me to drive you over to the college?'

'Thank you, no, Inspector. I shall call at a café for a cup of tea and then later I will take the bus . . . Incidentally, I've just thought of something interesting . . . Mr. Martin told me that Bradshaw gave the information that Lincross bought the Langhorn Cinema ten years ago. And Mrs. Ackroyd said that she and her husband have lived in that house for ten years. Remember? Well — good afternoon, Inspector . . . '

15

It was towards seven o'clock when Maria arrived back at Roseway, and the first thing she did was to make her record-book entries.

There is to my mind no longer any doubt of the killer's identity. Everything fits with the precision I like to see.

I consider again the following facts for debate before summing up: 1: The fact that the doorman said, when he saw Kenneth Harcourt enter the cinema on the fatal Wednesday evening, that he 'looked as though he wanted to shoot somebody'. 2: The electric fan on the roll-top desk in Lincross's office, and, 3: The fact that Harcourt sought out Ackroyd when he arrived in Langhorn. Very, very interesting points!

If a monument were to be erected

after this case I think it should be to poor Molly Ibbetson. Because she suffered from chilblains she literally sealed her own doom.

Re posters?
The time is 7.20 p.m.

Maria laid her pen aside, put the book away, then with characteristic discipline of mind she turned her attention to a few college details that she had so far been forced to neglect.

It was eleven o'clock when she finally retired. Hardly had she started to doze, however, before she suddenly sat bolt upright, her lace boudoir cap slightly awry.

'Of course! The posters! *That* was what was wrong with them! It said 'in' instead of 'with'. Hmm! Most extraordinary how flashes of inspiration come at the verge of sleep . . . The last link indeed!'

She relaxed again, smiled serenely to herself, then settled down for a night's solid rest.

The next day — Tuesday — Maria somewhat astonished her housemistress by behaving exactly as the Principal of a college should. In fact she made work for herself: anything to occupy her time She hardly knew how she got through the rest of the day, for patience was not one of her strongest virtues . . .

The next day, Wednesday, seemed an even more gruelling task, until it was relieved by the arrival of Inspector Morgan at six o'clock. He was shown into the study with a somewhat puzzled look on his face.

'I got replies to the letters, Miss Black,' he said, when she had motioned him to a chair. 'Here they are.' He laid the two letters on the desk and Maria studied them.

' 'Dear Sir, In reply to your letter — ' Yes! That is it — ! 1We beg to state that the film 'Love on the Highway' was ordered —' 'Hmm! Splendid! 'We are, yours faithfully — ' Maria's voice trailed off to herself as she read the second letter. Then finally she looked up with shining eyes.

'Perfect,' she declared.

'I don't quite fathom it,' Morgan said. 'One letter says that 'Death Strikes

Tomorrow' was cancelled; and the other says that 'Love on the Highway' was ordered. Well, what about it? Just ordinary business procedure.'

'The significance here lies in the fact that the film 'Death Strikes Tomorrow' was not cancelled by the renters themselves. And note the date of the cancellation — three days before Harcourt left jail.'

'Yes, but — '

'Excuse me,' Maria murmured, and lifted the telephone as it rang. 'Hello? Miss Black speaking . . . '

'A Mr. Martin calling from Keswick, Miss Black. Shall I put him through?'

'By all means!' Maria covered the mouthpiece for a moment. 'Martin,' she whispered; then sat back to listen.

Morgan could hear Pulp's voice squawking in the receiver but he could not make out what he was saying. A variety of expressions went over Maria's keen features.

'A most excellent job of work, Mr. Martin! I shall look forward to seeing you back in Langhorn as soon as you can manage it. Goodbye.'

She put the telephone down. A whimsical smile curved her lips.

'Inspector, the case is finished. We have the killer and the proof.'

'He found him then! Quick! Tell me — '

'I will — and a good deal else besides . . . '

Maria began talking, and for half an hour Morgan listened to her, putting a question ever and again. At one point he took the book entitled 'Studio Make-Believe' which she handed to him and studied it.

'This settles it, then,' he said grimly, when she had finished. 'I have work to do!'

'As the police official, that is your task,' Maria agreed. 'But I will accompany you to keep a check on the details we have exchanged. I'll have Miss Tanby take over meanwhile.'

Tanby did so, and within fifteen minutes Morgan had drawn up his car outside the police station. Into it he directed Sergeant Claythorne and a young constable by the name of Andrews. Then he started the car up again and drove steadily down the High Street until the Langhorn Cinema came within sight.

He drew up outside it.

So far only a few people had assembled for the evening performance, and beyond the glass-fronted doors in the foyer Bradshaw was just buttoning up his heavy greatcoat. Behind him in the distance Nancy Crane was studying a booking plan with Lincross.

Morgan's rapping on the door brought Bradshaw to open it. He stood aside in some surprise as the party entered, his red-rimmed eyes turning to Sergeant Claythorne and the constable.

'Why, good evening, Inspector, Miss Black.' Lincross came forward, shirt front gleaming. 'Quite a deputation this time, eh?'

'Quite, sir,' Morgan agreed heavily. 'Maybe we'd better discuss things in your office — privately.'

Lincross hesitated, then nodded. 'Come this way.'

When everybody was settled in the office it left very little room. Lincross sat at his desk with his mild blue eyes on the Inspector's face as he spoke.

'There are one or two points I'd like you to clear up, Mr. Lincross,' he said.

'With pleasure — though I can't see quite why you need these two other men to help you.' Lincross sat back, his hand fishing idly in one of the cubby-holes in his desk.

'We know now who murdered Kenneth Harcourt and Molly Ibbetson. We — '

Morgan broke off as Lincross twisted in his chair. His hand suddenly withdrew from the cubby-hole and was revealed holding a purple bottle from which the cork had been removed. He swept it up towards his lips but before it got there Maria's umbrella suddenly struck Lincross across the fingers with numbing force. The bottle was dashed aside and spewed its fuming contents over the papers on the desk. There was a brief confusion while incipient fire was batted out and acrid odour and fumes began to defile the air.

'You damned, interfering old bag!' Lincross screamed at Maria as he jumped to his feet. 'You infernal — ' Gone was all the suave civility, the bending to and fro like a mechanical doll . . .

'Sit down!' Morgan snapped, pushing Lincross back in his chair again. 'And keep quiet! Andrews, stand behind him!'

The young constable moved into position.

'I'm glad you played your final card badly, Mr. Lincross,' Maria commented, her cold eyes fixing him. 'I wondered what you would do when the last way out was closed. What surprises me is that you have not done it before now . . . Go on, Inspector. This is your province.'

'You knew, Mr. Lincross, when Harcourt came out of prison by an announcement in the daily paper. You knew, too, that he would seek you out with the avowed intention of killing you. So you laid a trap. You knew his daughter to be Lydia Fane, and — being in the cinema business — that she had recently completed a picture. Probably you saw it at a trade show and recalled three revolver shots in it . . . You then wrote to the renters of 'Death Strikes Tomorrow' and told them to cancel it. It was not cancelled by them, as you told us: we've made sure of that. You also wrote to the renters of 'Love on the Highway' and hired that film for the period you knew would probably coincide with Harcourt's arrival here. You reasoned that if Harcourt saw his daughter was in a picture, showing at a cinema owned by you, he would inevitably come inside . . .'

'How the devil could I know of his intentions?' Lincross snapped.

'That,' Maria remarked, 'is not a provable point, but it is open to inference. You are aware, I think, that one Leslie Ackroyd has always been a close friend of Kenneth Harcourt's. You would be aware of his residence in this district and that he had no doubt told Harcourt all about you. I deduce that from the fact that both you and Ackroyd have been in this town ten years. That man Ackroyd has kept track of you ever since Harcourt went to jail. You knew about Ackroyd, and you knew he would tell Harcourt that you could be found here.'

Lincross tightened his flat lips but he

did not say anything.

'Letters from the renters prove that you changed the films over,' Morgan went on. 'From Miss Saunders you could obtain the booking plans and would no doubt ask her who had booked the same seat in the Circle for three consecutive nights. She would not have the name, but she could have given you a description of Harcourt. We do know that your ruse worked and that Harcourt was seated in your theatre, ready for you to get him before he got you. That he decided to see his daughter in the film three times was a slice of good luck for you for it gave you time to prepare . . . '

'To add further to the bait,' Maria put in, 'you billed her on your posters as the star — which is utterly at variance with the laws of publicity. Those posters should not have read 'Lydia Fane in Love on the Highway' but 'Betty Joyce in Love on the Highway with Lydia Fane'. You did it solely to attract Harcourt's attention!'

'Whether you planned to kill him in the cinema or not I don't know,' Morgan resumed. 'You could not have known when — in disguise — you got that air-rifle and carbon stubs that Harcourt would decide to come three times. I suggest that you planned to get him here and then follow him when he left the cinema, so that you could be sure where he was staying. That he happened to choose the hotel opposite was just chance . . . When you knew he would be in the same seat for three nights, when you had time to observe how he always took his hat off, you decided on other methods. You had ample time to take Allerton's spare telephone and fix it during the night, ample chance to put the rifle up in the roof in readiness. On Tuesday night you surveyed the position and maybe did a mock rehearsal. On Wednesday you did the deed itself after sending a faked phone call through to Allerton . . .

'That faulty chain on the speaker you must have loosened yourself. That hole in the screen you no doubt made after the Wednesday night show when you knew it looked as though Harcourt had been shot from the front. This was again a piece of luck for you. Until then you had no doubt imagined Harcourt had been shot in the top of the head. Due to some slight sound you made he got the slug in the forehead . . .

'You got rid of the rifle and telephone, and when Allerton called in your office after you had finished your activities you explained away your heated condition by saying you had been shovelling coke. You knew Bradshaw had slipped out and made everything turn on that . . . '

'And I went through all those exploits in the roof without getting myself dirty?' Lincross asked dryly.

'I don't say that — the coke dust would be similar to the dirt up in the false roof. Anyway, there are such things as overalls. You'd have it worked out.'

'But,' Maria remarked, as Morgan stopped to reflect, 'you reckoned without the unknown quantity — Molly Ibbetson! She had chilblains and decided to change her shoes. Going to the staff room and found it bolted on the inside. Remember how I asked if there was a key? Since there was not — and yet a keyhole — she could obviously look through it. Presumably she did, and saw *you*! You would undoubtedly have had to put the light on to see what you were doing. She put two and two together, but being scared of her job and even more so of the police she only confessed her knowledge to Peter Canfield — and that only partially when under the influence of a few drinks. You *had* to eliminate her. For that reason I told you as much as I dared in the hope it would lure you into the open . . . Something went wrong and, instead of her being protected and you apprehended, she lost her life and you got away with it.'

Lincross glared across the desk. 'How could I kill Molly when I was in this very office all the time? Practically everybody on the staff could swear to it.'

'Since you had murdered Harcourt you obviously had no compunction about murdering Molly!' Morgan retorted. 'You have only one life to lose. And you were *not* in this office: you devised a trick. I'll let Miss Black explain that bit.'

'At the college, Mr. Lincross, I have a

book called 'Studio Make-Believe'. It is well known and widely distributed, and since you are in the film world your knowing of it would not be surprising. Do you recall the chapter in it which explains how shadows are sometimes created for studio work?'

Lincross remained sullenly silent.

'The book reveals how rags hanging on a stick are moved back and forth in front of an arc lamp to give — in the film — the impression of flickering firelight. It also shows how a rotating drum with paper ribbons upon it can keep passing a lamp at regular intervals and give the effect of moving shadows. This trick was done chiefly during a scene inside a taxi when the players are apparently being driven under street lamps . . . '

'You are a most observant reader, madam,' Lincross commented bitterly.

'I read to learn — not to amuse myself. And I'll tell you just what you did in here. You used the electric fan on this desk! It turns slowly on its universal base. If you place it on the extreme end of the desk here and switch it on, the papers in front of it are naturally projected by the wind force. As the fan slowly turns the streamers cross the light from the bulb overhead and cast their shadows along the bottom of the door. Nancy Crane, on the other side, thought the shadow was yours and that the paper rustling was executed by your own hands. You made reasonably sure that nobody would interrupt you during that half-hour by pretending to be in the vilest of tempers. You also made careful inquiry as to Molly's whereabouts and came half an hour ahead of her. Then you set off through this office window here, murdered Molly on her way here, and came back and changed into evening dress. Allerton and Bradshaw being late, it deflected suspicion to them. I assume that you had found that Martin had ceased to watch Molly.'

Lincross looked at the empty poison bottle and the ruinous mess on his desk, his face as colourless as white marble. 'I knew Martin had been watching Molly the day before, but I noticed that during Saturday he was in and out of the 'Golden Saddle' and not watching Molly at all. That is why I took that chance. All right — I admit the thing.'

'I suspected you from the moment I knew you did not like the police about your cinema,' Maria commented. 'It suggested some unpleasant drama in the background of your life. Then I recalled Allerton's statement of the expressions exchanged between you and Harcourt when you met. I also remembered how on the night you talked to me in the foyer you suddenly left me when Harcourt appeared in the crowd . . . '

'Would a signed confession do me any good, Inspector?' Lincross asked, looking up. 'I intend to plead that it was my life — or Harcourt's. He had sworn to kill me and it seemed policy to strike first.'

'And how will you excuse murdering Molly?' Morgan snapped.

Lincross shrugged. 'Washes me up, doesn't it? I gambled — and lost. I did get Harcourt into prison, yes — but it was not my doing alone. Later, when the financial world got a bit too hot for me, I bought this place and, as I thought, settled away from everybody. I even changed my name, legally, to Lincross. Then I realised Ackroyd was on my doorstep. Somehow he had kept track of me and would never let go. I wondered once or twice if I ought to wipe him out and decided it was too risky. Once I had killed Harcourt, though, I was determined to get Ackroyd because he could tell too much . . . '

'I was confused about Ackroyd,' Maria said. 'Then I realised that Harcourt would never go to see an enemy by paying a friendly visit. I knew then that you were the guilty party.'

Lincross got to his feet and stood waiting.

'I'll see Allerton and Miss Crane before we leave,' Morgan said. 'I shall simply tell them to carry on for the moment until it is decided how the cinema will be handled. We can't interfere with public business. So far as anybody knows you are simply coming with us to answer a few questions.'

'Thanks for the favour,' Lincross said cynically. 'And I'd have got away with it if I'd had only you to deal with, Morgan . . . '

Maria rose, her umbrella on her arm. She was smiling serenely to herself. Then Morgan spoke:

'Gerald Lincross, I must ask you to accompany me to Langhorn police station. There you will be formally charged with the murder of Kenneth Harcourt and Molly Ibbetson, and placed in custody to appear before the magistrates in Lexham a week from today . . .'

THE END

We do hope that you have enjoyed reading this large print book.

Did you know that all of our titles are available for purchase?

We publish a wide range of high quality large print books including:
Romances, Mysteries, Classics
General Fiction
Non Fiction and Westerns

Special interest titles available in large print are:
The Little Oxford Dictionary
Music Book, Song Book
Hymn Book, Service Book

Also available from us courtesy of Oxford University Press:
Young Readers' Dictionary
(large print edition)
Young Readers' Thesaurus
(large print edition)

For further information or a free brochure, please contact us at:
Ulverscroft Large Print Books Ltd.,
The Green, Bradgate Road, Anstey,
Leicester, LE7 7FU, England.
Tel: (00 44) **0116 236 4325**
Fax: (00 44) **0116 234 0205**

DR. MORELLE AND THE DOLL

Ernest Dudley

In a wild, bleak corner of the Kent Coast, a derelict harbour rots beneath the tides. There the Doll, a film-struck waif, and her lover, ex-film star Tod Hafferty, play their tragic, fated real-life roles. And sudden death strikes more than once — involving a local policeman . . . Then, as Dr. Morelle finds himself enmeshed in a net of sex and murder, Miss Frayle's anticipated quiet week-end results in her being involved in the climactic twist, which unmasks the real killer.

THE THIRTY-FIRST OF JUNE

John Russell Fearn

There were six people in millionaire Nick Clayton's limousine when it left a country house party to return to London: Clayton himself, and his girlfriend Bernice Forbes; Horace Dawlish, his imperturbable servant and driver; the unhappily married financier Harvey Brand and Lucy Brand; and the tragic socialite Betty Danvers. But neither the car, nor its six occupants, would ever arrive in London. Instead, just after midnight, the car travelled some thirty miles along the country road — and disappeared . . .

MAIMED

Lyn Jolley

Joanna Coles was driving her children to school, as she did every morning of term time. On this particular dreary December day, however, a decision was being made about her, a decision of which she knew nothing. Soon after Christmas, Joanna Coles would be a name known to millions. Her photograph would appear on the television and in every newspaper in the land. Unfortunately, Joanna would know nothing of her tragic fame . . .

BOOMERANG

Sydney J. Bounds

The happy camaraderie of the Porth-cove Studios holiday hotel is shattered by the arrival of the misanthropic George Bullard. He goes out of his way to annoy both staff and fellow artist guests. So when Bullard is found brutally murdered, everyone in the hotel comes under suspicion as having a motive to kill him. Then there is a second murder ... The police are baffled, and it falls to the unorthodox lady detective Miss Isabel Eaton to unmask the killer.

THE FROZEN LIMIT

John Russell Fearn

Defying the edict of the Medical Council, Dr. Robert Cranston, helped by Dr. Campbell, carries out an unauthorised medical experiment with a 'deep freeze' system of suspended animation. The volunteer is Claire Baxter, an attractive film stunt-girl. But when Claire undergoes deep freeze unconsciousness, the two doctors discover that they cannot restore the girl. She is barely alive. Despite every endeavour to revive the girl, nothing happens, and Cranston and Campbell find themselves charged with murder . . .